Teresa Solana has a deg
University of Barcelona, where she also studied
Classics. She has worked as a literary translator and
directed the Spanish National Translation Centre
in Tarazona. She has published many essays and
articles on translation and written several novels
she prefers to keep in her drawer.

The Sound of One Hand Killing is the third in the
Barcelona series featuring twin private detectives
Eduard Martínez and Borja "Pep" Masdéu. The
first, *A Not So Perfect Crime,* won the 2007 Brigada 21
Prize and was followed by the bestselling *A Shortcut
to Paradise.*

Also available from Bitter Lemon Press
by Teresa Solana:

A Not So Perfect Crime
A Shortcut to Paradise

THE SOUND
OF ONE HAND
KILLING

Teresa Solana

Translated from the Catalan by Peter Bush

BITTER LEMON PRESS
BITTER LEMON PRESS
LONDON

BITTER LEMON PRESS

First published in the United Kingdom in 2013 by
Bitter Lemon Press, 37 Arundel Gardens, London W11 2LW

www.bitterlemonpress.com

First published in Catalan as *L'hora zen* by
Edicions 62, Barcelona, 2011

Bitter Lemon Press gratefully acknowledges
the financial assistance of the Arts Council of England

The translation of this work was supported by
a grant from the Institut Ramon Llull

A CIP record for this book is available from the British Library
ISBN 978–1–904738–06–5

Typeset by Tetragon
Printed and bound by CPI Group (UK) Ltd, Croydon, CR0 4YY

For my cousin Margarita,
in memoriam

"You know the sound of two hands clapping; tell me, what is the sound of one hand?"

Zen Master Hakuin Ekaku

PART I

When the Agency told him his next posting would be to Barcelona, Brian was all smiles. He was ecstatic. Yippee! They were finally sending him to a European city, a city with a more than decent climate and nightlife. Not that he could complain – unlike most of his colleagues, he'd only taken nine years to secure a desirable operating base. His tour of duty in far-flung, exotic spots had started to drag.

First there'd been the four years he'd languished in Singapore, dripping with sweat in the humid heat of its streets and freezing his balls off in its bars and restaurants, not to mention the dire boredom he'd endured while rubbing shoulders with cohorts of business executives, doctors bingeing at lavish congresses and swarms of students of English. As he spoke French they'd then sent him to Dakar, and after that to Marrakesh where he'd been holed up three interminable years, suffering from the stifling heat in a dingy flat where the air conditioning broke down every other week. Nonetheless, his time in Marrakesh had been a big improvement, particularly after he'd got to know Charlotte, who had a smattering of Arabic and knew the bars and dives in the city where you could drink alcohol. However, that bitch had it taped and didn't live there the whole year; come June, when the city turned into an oven unfit for tourists, she headed back to California and said goodbye until October. Now he'd probably never see her again, not that it really bothered him. The news of his move to Barcelona had exceeded all expectations and amply compensated the need to bid a final farewell to Charlotte and their drunken nights of wild sex. Anyway, she'd made it clear from the start that she wasn't making any commitments and he'd done the same.

When he got to Barcelona, he was surprised to discover that most people spoke in a language that vaguely reminded him of Italian. Sure, everybody spoke Spanish as well, and most people were considerate and addressed him in that language when they detected his foreign accent, but a few insisted on using that other language he didn't understand and scolded him for not learning it. After making the effort to learn Spanish at the Cervantes Institute in Marrakesh, Brian had neither the time nor the inclination to start studying Catalan. Even so, within a few months he'd started to grasp enough of the local lingo not to have to ask them to repeat everything in Spanish, and in fact everyone spoke English in the circles in which he moved: he didn't need either Spanish or Catalan.

With its streets teeming with tourists, its beaches and endless bars, Barcelona was a different world, where he felt at home; and that was odd, because he hailed from Philadelphia. Obviously he was forced to pull his finger out in Barcelona: unlike Singapore, Dakar or Marrakesh, the city was a hive of activity, and his boss wasn't happy with second-hand information. In that sense, it was very different from his other postings, where secret agents knew each other and had everything well under control. Barcelona saw a constant turnover of personnel and it was difficult to tell the people you could trust from those who would try to get one past you at the first opportunity. Not that he was complaining. For the first time ever, life was beginning to look like what he'd imagined when, at the age of twenty-eight and armed with a degree in sociology, he'd decided to catch a flight to Langley and knock on the Agency's door. He'd finally made it to Europe, every secret agent's dream destination. All he needed now was the Aston Martin and a white tuxedo.

John's phone call both surprised and delighted Brian. He had no idea John was in Barcelona. When John said he'd come on routine business and suggested going for a beer or two – meaning a night on the tiles – Brian said yes straight away. John had offered to drive by and pick him up, and he'd readily agreed. He arrived punctually, and Brian reflected how highly unusual that was for him. He said he was dying of thirst, and Brian, though famed for his meanness, could be hospitable when he wanted and offered him a beer. He was in the kitchen opening the fridge and touching the bottles to find an ice-cold one when he heard John say, "I'm sorry, lad. Nothing personal."

Before he could turn round, he knew what was coming, not that he had a clue as to why. What the fuck had he done wrong? It would be futile to try to reason with John: orders are orders and John was a true professional.

"Did they tell you why?" he asked.

"You know they never do. It's easier this way. I'm very sorry."

The first shot hit its target between his eyes. The others to his chest were simply to finish the job off properly: it wouldn't have been the first time someone had survived a shot to the head and lived like a vegetable for the rest of their days. That had never been the case with John's assignments, but he would have regretted fouling up with his mate Brian. They may not have been the closest of friends, but they'd enjoyed their moments in Singapore.

13

What a pity, thought John as he left the flat, Brian couldn't show him Barcelona now and he'd have to put himself into the hands of city cab drivers if he wanted a drink and a quick romp between the sheets before heading off to the airport.

1

"Hey, you still in bed?" I yelled at Borja when he finally picked up the phone, sure he'd say that he was.

"Mmm…" came his sleepy reply.

"Get a move on or we'll be late. Remember we said twelve."

"Can't you go by yourself?" he growled. "I feel dead…"

"Jump to it," I insisted, trying to sound authoritarian. "I'll come to collect you in an hour's time, so get up and under that shower right away."

I imagined him struggling with his silk sheets and groping his way to the bathroom, like he did when he was a kid, and could only smile. It's Monday, and on Mondays, when there is no urgent business, Borja and I never go to the office. As far as we are concerned (or rather, as far as Borja is concerned), the week begins on Tuesday, at worst Monday night, if something pressing requires our immediate attention. My brother reckons that Mondays are good for nothing, except rest, which is why he spends Mondays loafing around, while I give a helping hand at home and do a shop.

However, we'd agreed to meet a client in the office at twelve, and that meant Borja had to forgo his Monday day of rest. He might like to grumble, but, as things stood, in the midst of an economic crisis that, in my case, was expressed in distressingly red digits at the bank and threatening calls from the late-payment department, we couldn't risk my brother's hedonistic habits losing us a customer.

I'd been up since a quarter to eight and hadn't stopped in all that time. Luckily, that week I was responsible for preparing the mid-morning snack and taking Arnau to school (I hate it when it's my turn to wake up the twins, make sure they don't spend three hours in the bathroom prettifying themselves or watch they don't hit the street dolled up in some fancy outfit or other), and, on my way back, I had to pop into the supermarket and stock up on packs of water and milk. Right then, I was doing the washing-up in the kitchen while Montse was in and out of the bedrooms, making beds and gathering up the dirty clothes before shooting off to work. Her Alternative Centre for Holistic Well-being was also suffering from the crisis, and that morning she and her partners had a meeting with their bank manager to try to negotiate a loan to avoid the closure of their source of livelihood.

"Don't raise your hopes. The banks haven't turned on the tap yet," I warned her.

"You and Borja better get some work, right?" she retaliated. And while she grabbed her bag and painted her lips red in front of the hallway mirror, she added with a deep sigh, "But this time, make sure you don't get yourselves into deep water!"

"Of course we won't!" I retorted in an offended tone. "I give you my word."

I kissed her on the cheek so as not to smudge her lipstick and wished her the best of luck, though I was sure the guys at the bank would act ruthlessly and refuse any help that wasn't accompanied by a lengthy list of draconian conditions in the purest *Merchant of Venice* fashion. While I was thinking about what we'd do to survive the crisis started by those very same institutions that were now sinking us, and deriving sad consolation from the fact that many were worse off than ourselves, I warmed up my second cup of coffee in the microwave and idled in front of the TV until it was time to go and meet my fraternal business partner.

In recent months I'd become hooked on the political debates on a channel called *Inter-Economy* that I watched now and then as if it were a weird kind of comedy show. The opinions and comments of the participants – representatives of an antediluvian Spain I'd thought extinct before I latched onto that channel – never ceased to shock me and bring tears of laughter to my eyes. They were like characters out of an Almodóvar film, though no caricature could ever emulate their chauvinist, homophobic attitudes, their xenophobia masquerading as paternalism, their grandiloquent language with fascist overtones, all orchestrated to express the nostalgia they felt for a Spain of surplices and death sentences, the good old days of Generalísimo Franco. Right then, they were dissecting a murderer with a taste for necrophilia (a wretched guy who didn't look totally with it) and establishing parallels with Judge Garzón, who they were also dubbing a necrophile because he'd given permission for mass graves of Republicans murdered during the civil war to be opened. The participants thought the analogy so witty they were splitting their sides. Text messages sent by viewers were no less bizarre. After a while, when I realized the pearls of wisdom dropping from the lips of that array of troglodytes in suits and ties no longer seemed funny and were putting me in a bad mood, I switched off the TV and got up from the sofa. As it was still early, I thought it would be sensible to go for a stroll before catching the bus and meeting my brother. The doctor had recommended that I should stretch my legs, and before lethargy won out I said goodbye to Joana (that is, my mother-in-law) and headed downstairs.

The moment I stepped out onto the pavement, I was pleasantly surprised to find that the sky had turned a sunny, postcard blue and that there was a warm breeze. The day that was cold and cloudy when I woke up had become one of those gloriously sunny mornings in Barcelona at the beginning of April, when at last you feel that spring is here not because some calendar has been saying so for a couple of weeks, but because the sun feels hot for the first time in months. Winter had been especially cold, and the prospect of switching off the central heating and giving the rickety state of our savings some respite helped restore my good spirits.

In fact, my good mood was also down to the great weekend we'd spent at home, which had been unusually quiet. The twins had disappeared to Begur, to a chalet belonging to a girlfriend's parents. My mother-in-law, who's been staying with us for months, ever since she gave in to the company that owned the flat where she lived on an ancient pepper-corn rent and that had been trying to evict her, had gone on a pensioners' outing to Andorra and hadn't come back until Sunday night. Borja, for his part, had taken Lola off for a weekend in Cadaqués (I don't know whether she was paying), and that spared us my sister-in-law's moans about my brother's comings and goings. Lola was smitten and Borja gave her a nibble, or rather, led her a "now I love you, now I don't" dance that meant Lola, a woman prone to violent ups and downs who loved making a drama out of everything, lived on a rollercoaster of emotions we were all forced to ride. The problem was straightforward enough: my brother continued to be the official lover of Merche, a rich, married lady of leisure, who played a central role in Borja's finances and, on the rebound, in ours.

When I reached Borja's flat, just before eleven, my brother was already showered, shaved and dressed. He welcomed me with a broad grin that underlined the fact that, although I'd dragged him out of bed on a sacrosanct Monday morning, he too was in an excellent frame of mind: no doubt the weekend with Lola had paid dividends. Nonetheless, he screwed up his nose when he saw I'd decided to dispense with the Armani tie and suit he'd forced me to buy for work purposes (he footed the bill).

"Hey, you ought to have smartened yourself up a bit!" he growled, suggesting he didn't think the new jeans, leather blouson and short-sleeved cotton shirt I'd selected were ideal apparel for welcoming a client. On the other hand, he was sporting one of his elegant spring jackets and a brand-new lilac tie.

"It's so hot, and the Armani suit makes me sweat," I countered. "Besides, writers aren't so fussy about these things," I added, making a reference to the profession of our latest customer.

"But *we* are, and don't you ever forget that. That's exactly the impression we want to give our customers, whatever their line of business: they should think they are dealing with serious, respectable professionals." And while he looked me up and down yet again, raising his left eyebrow in a sign of disapproval, he added, "Luckily they're designer jeans, and your blouson is almost new!..."

"Bah! I reckon you are the only one who notices these things."

Borja rolled his eyes and sighed loudly.

"Kid brother, will you never learn?"

As he'd been away the whole weekend, we'd not had an opportunity to discuss the peculiar call he'd received on Friday afternoon before leaving for Cadaqués. Borja had been at pains to say it was from a novelist by the name of Teresa Solana, without going into details, although after our unpleasant experience in that Hotel Ritz case I wasn't at all sure I was in favour of more dealings with the city's pen-pushers.

"God knows what she can want!" I snarled.

"Bah! I expect she will ask us to keep an eye on her husband in case he's having a bit on the side. That's what women are always worrying about. You just see, it will be a doddle," Borja said, seemingly quite sure of that. "A few hours spent trailing a guy, and money in the bank."

"It would be a good idea to come out of the meeting with a cheque," I had to admit. "I'm cleaned out."

"Well, in terms of money, I've got involved in an activity that will sort our problems for a good while. I'd not said anything because I wanted to give you a surprise."

"I hope it's nothing illegal."

"Of course not!" After musing for a few moments, he added, "Well, that is, not entirely, from what I've seen so far. But, anyway, I'm a mere go-between."

"So, I *should* start to get worried…"

"In no way." Borja put his jacket on, looked in the mirror and ran his hand through his hair. "Let's get going. I've not had any breakfast yet."

As it had been weeks since we'd had any clients and we'd hardly been to the office, we'd thought it would be a good idea to arrive well in advance, ventilate the space and spray some of our non-existent secretary's perfume around, as we always do before meeting someone. Our office, which is on Muntaner, near plaça Bonanova, is very close to Merche's flat on Balmes that has become Borja's pad, so we walked it. En route we stopped in a café and Borja stuffed his stomach while I had a quick coffee with a spot of milk.

"She must be a strange lady," I said, thinking aloud, referring to her profession. "Devoting her days to writing about murder…"

As I'd discovered from a Google search, Teresa Solana wrote noir novels, but neither Borja nor myself had read any. Mariona Castany, who acted as Borja's guardian angel in Barcelona high society, didn't know who she was either, so that meant she was neither rich nor a member of the most select circles in the city. Nevertheless, as business was bad and we were in no position to be snooty, we'd decided to give her a go and see if we couldn't lean on her for an advance. We expected that any assignment commissioned by Teresa Solana would be routine and wouldn't involve deaths or murders.

Borja paid and we lit our respective cigarettes as we walked to the office. Before we got there, we threw our fag ends into a gutter so as not to dirty the part of the pavement Paquita, our concierge, had to sweep and thus avoid hassle from her. As we went in through the lobby, Paquita simply looked at us disapprovingly as we wished her good day and walked to the old wooden lift that was very beautiful and entirely impractical because its motor broke down every other day. Fortunately – because our office is on the third floor, and, with the mezzanine and lobby floor, is actually on the fifth – it was working that morning.

"What the hell?" exclaimed Borja, coming out of the lift onto the landing and seeing our office door unlocked and ajar.

We immediately identified the problem: someone had forced the iffy lock we'd never got round to changing because we kept nothing of value in our office. The burglar, or burglars, had merely levered it open with an iron bar, probably over the weekend, when Paquita isn't around and the building is almost empty. Borja switched on the light in the tiny lobby and we went into the main room where all our suspicions were confirmed: they had broken in and burgled us, and it was obvious that the thief or thieves who had done the job were no disciples of Arsène Lupin, but had done it more in Terminator or Rambo style.

"Shit!…" growled Borja, clicking his tongue. "Why did they have to do it today!…"

The intruders hadn't simply rifled through the drawers of the desk belonging to our non-existent secretary and thrown around the empty files that littered the shelves, they'd also gutted the sofa and armchairs and wrenched the mahogany doors of our fake respective offices off the wall.

"I suppose they must have lost it completely when they saw we had nothing of value…" I said with a sigh, realizing we couldn't ring the *mossos* and initiate an investigation.

Borja surveyed the scene and shook his head.

"What a disaster! It will cost us a fortune to put this lot right!"

"And in the meantime, Mrs Solana will be here any minute," I said, looking at my watch.

"We have to think of something."

"We can't see her here. An office that is supposed to pride itself on confidentiality, but that thieves can break into so easily, is hardly good publicity in our line of business," I argued.

"Quite right. Besides, she'd see the doors are fake and that there's only wall behind them." He shook his head again. "Pity about the doors. They cost a fortune."

"But you never paid for them!" I protested. I knew the carpenter was still waiting to be paid for the two mahogany doors that simulated two luxury offices, the one belonging to the company's chief exec – that is, Borja – and his deputy – namely, yours truly.

"That's neither here nor there!" yelped Borja. "In any case, we'll have to find a different carpenter to make replacements."

"We should call Mrs Solana immediately and cancel our meeting on some pretext or other," I said, making a move as if to take my mobile from my pocket.

Borja gently took my arm and stopped me.

"We need this assignment," he retorted. "It'll be some time before I'm paid for that other business I mentioned. And, in the meantime, we need a cash injection. I'm as broke as you are."

"We can call her and arrange to meet somewhere else," I suggested. "We can say our office has been flooded."

"There's a slight problem. I left my mobile at home and don't have her number," he replied.

"We could go downstairs and wait for her in the street..."

"And then what? Take her to a bar and ask her to recount her life story surrounded by total strangers?"

"Well, you tell me..." I said, glancing around our office. "There's nothing doing here."

"Don't you worry," Borja replied, grinning at me like a Cheshire cat. "I've just had a brilliant idea."

I fear my brother's bright ideas more than the plague, because they have a mysterious tendency to introduce chaos into our lives. I was about to tell him to forget it, which would have been the most sensible move in view of what happened later, but, instead of that, I simply listened to what he suggested.

"Our upstairs neighbour is away and I've got the keys to his flat," said Borja. "We can tell Mrs Solana we've had a burst pipe and that a friend let us have his flat for the meeting."

"You've got the keys to a neighbour's flat?" I asked, trying to hide my amazement.

"Yes, that's right, the American who lives in the flat upstairs..." responded Borja in his most matter-of-fact tone.

"You have the keys to the American's place?" I repeated, even more perplexed. "What was his name? Something Morgan, right?"

"Brian. Brian Morgan." And he added, as if the information was vital, "He's from Philadelphia."

"Oh!"

I had no idea my brother was on good terms with any neighbour on our staircase, let alone that he was so close he had the keys to his flat. All I knew about the said Brian was that he spent very little time in his flat; according to Paquita, who likes a good gossip, he was always off and about with his suitcases. He was younger than us, though I'd say he was nearer forty than thirty-five, spoke Spanish with a strong American accent and was as tall as Paul. That was all I remembered, because we had passed each other on the stairs a couple of times at most.

"So, I take it you're the best of friends," I said to prod him.

"No, not at all," responded Borja. "It was just that one day when you weren't around, he came down to the office and asked if I wouldn't mind keeping a duplicate of his keys in case there was an emergency."

"An emergency?"

"Well, as he is always on his travels and spends very little time in Barcelona…"

"And why did he ask you? I don't get it. It would have made more sense to give the keys to the concierge, wouldn't it?"

"I've no idea. The fact is I do have the keys to his flat and he's not around…" grunted my brother, looking at his watch impatiently and trying to change the subject.

"I hope this isn't another fine mess you're going to get us into."

"Of course not!" he rasped, as if I'd insulted him. "It was just a favour I did a neighbour."

"Pep, I know you only too well."

Although I couldn't imagine what murky machinations were lurking behind that set of keys, I assumed Borja *was* hiding something.

"Haven't I told you time and again not to call me Pep?" he grumbled. "One day you'll let it out in company!"

"I'm sorry."

Sometimes, when we are by ourselves, I forget to call him Borja and come out with Pep, which is, in fact, his real name. The pompous name of Borja Masdéu-Canals Sáez de Astorga that he decided to adopt when he came back to Barcelona, alongside the aristocratic ascendancy, he invented to help him hobnob with the upper classes of Barcelona as if he were one of them. We don't look like each other, although we are twins (Borja seems younger, perhaps because he still has all his hair), so nobody apart from Inspector Badia knows we are brothers. Not even Montse and Lola. We tell our clients we are business partners, and our entrepreneurial strategy has worked well so far.

"Come on, we're running out of time," he said, looking at his watch again. "Let's go up to the American's flat and make sure it's fit for our visitor."

And he walked out of the office and sped upstairs without giving me the right of reply.

2

Unlike our office, which just about has a small lobby, a room where we see clients and a tiny, definitely bijou toilet, our neighbour's flat was state-of-the-art. The dining room was some twenty square metres and, according to Borja, the flat had a couple of bedrooms, a bathroom, a second toilet, a kitchen and a laundry room that looked over an inner courtyard. Brian had certainly rented it furnished, because, although the furniture was brand new and quite expensive, the final effect was far too impersonal: everything was just so and matching, and nothing was out of place. In fact, the flat was so tidy it didn't look as if anyone lived there, but Borja and I immediately noticed a strange smell in the air that was coming from the kitchen.

"I expect it's because the flat has been shut up for so long," I suggested. "Your friend must have forgotten to put the rubbish out the last time he was here."

"Phew!" Borja wrinkled his nose, his sense of smell being much more developed than mine, perhaps to make up for his colour blindness. "There's rotten meat somewhere. We can't see anyone here with this stench. It's awful."

"Perhaps if we shut the kitchen door and open the windows to make a draught…"

"We must do something. Why don't you go down and get Mariajo's bottle of perfume. We can use it as an air freshener.

In the meantime, I'll put the rubbish in the laundry room and open all the windows."

"I'll be right back," I said, rushing downstairs.

Mariajo, our secretary, doesn't exist, even though my brother and I have got into the habit of talking about her as if she were real flesh and blood. Borja thinks we need to give our customers the impression we employ a high-class company secretary, not just a series of temps. When we see clients in the office, we say Mariajo is out on an errand for us, while the classic fragrance of *L'Air du Temps*, a small pot of red nail varnish from Chanel that's always on her desk and a Loewe scarf draped over the back of her chair create the illusion of a beautiful crème-de-la-crème secretary who, according to Borja, lends a touch of distinction – what he calls "glamour" – to our company.

I struggled to track down the bottle of perfume among the debris. It had lodged itself under a sofa in one corner of the room, but was fortunately intact. I left the door so it looked shut and not as if it had been broken into and hurried back to the American's flat. I had to ring the bell twice, and when Borja finally opened the door I could see from the look on his face that something was wrong.

"What's the matter?" I asked.

Borja was as white as a sheet.

"I feel a bit queasy…"

"Have you got pains in your chest? Are you finding it difficult to breathe?" I gripped his arm firmly to make sure he didn't collapse on the floor, if he fainted, and split his head open. "I'll ring for an ambulance."

I imagined a worst-case scenario and had diagnosed cardiac arrest. My mind dizzily reviewed the packet of cigarettes he smokes a day, the gin and tonics we sometimes drank at Harry's, Mariona's dry martinis and all the crap he eats because he hates cooking. I naturally also thought of the effort and physical wear and tear involved in satisfying two women who are no longer young innocents and know what they want.

"No, nothing like that," he said, as if he'd read my thoughts. "The truth is… Excuse me, I'm going to be sick…" and he rushed to the toilet.

Luckily, he got there in time to avoid vomiting the croissant and coffee he'd eaten for breakfast in the middle of the hallway. I helped him to wash his face with cold water, and the second I saw the colour coming back to his cheeks, I calmed down.

"I need a brandy. Let's go into the lounge. It's got a minibar," he whispered.

"A doctor is what you need," I replied. "We ought to go to a hospital."

"I'm fine." His voice was still shaky. "It was the scare. I'll tell you later."

"The scare? What scare?"

"There's no time for that now. Did you find the perfume?"

"Yes."

"Spray it around the flat. And then go down and wait for Mrs Solana. But don't go into the kitchen," he whined as he gulped down his cognac.

"Why not?"

"I'll tell you later."

"What's in the kitchen?" I insisted, heading down the passage, not giving it a second thought, determined to find out what had upset him so.

"Eduard, please, don't go in…"

"But, what on —"

I should have listened to him. As soon as I opened the door, I too started retching and puking. There was no sack full of rotting organic waste, as I'd imagined, but the corpse of a man crawling with insects and beginning to stink in the middle of a pool of congealed blood. I shut the door, leaving my vomit behind me, and tottered queasily back to the lounge.

"Pep, on the kitchen floor there's a…" I didn't finish my sentence. My legs were giving way and I had to sit down.

"I did tell you not to go in. Here, have a shot," he said, pouring me one.

"But there's a corpse in there!" I shouted.

"My hunch is that he's been there for a good long time."

"Is it your American friend?"

"I think so, although I didn't get a proper look at his face."

"His face was covered in blood and insects…" I responded, still shaking.

"I know. I think he was shot in the head."

"We must tell the police immediately. The best thing would be to ring the *mossos*," I suggested.

"Wait, take it easy," said Borja, recovering his sangfroid. "Remember that Mrs Solana is about to arrive any moment now."

"And you want me to sit back and relax?"

"I mean we should just wait a bit before we inform the police. First we must speak to her."

"But you're not intending to talk to her here, are you?" I shouted. "With this stench and that corpse covered in creepy-crawlies in the kitchen! Not to mention that this must be the scene of the crime!"

"Here's our plan of action. I'll spray Mariajo's perfume around the flat while you go down and wait for her in the street," he said, getting up from the sofa and ignoring my protests.

"Borja, I don't think it's a good idea…"

"You just do what you're told," he said, looking at his watch. "We don't have much time."

My stomach was still churning and I didn't feel strong enough to argue with him, although I couldn't help thinking through the consequences of using the scene of a crime as a place to welcome a client who, to boot, was a writer of crime fiction. I didn't want to imagine what might happen if the police found out, but, on the other hand, I supposed that by virtue of her profession Teresa Solana must be used to visiting morgues and, thus, only too familiar with the reek of death stinking out the flat. Despite Mariajo's perfume I was afraid she'd soon realize that there was a corpse decomposing in the room next door, and for a moment I was tempted to turn round and tell Borja this was complete madness. At the end of the day, it wasn't such a blow to lose a client, I told myself, and then I recalled that our company wasn't enjoying its best moment and that Montse's business was also looking shaky, thought how it wouldn't be the first time Borja and I had managed to survive a dodgy situation and decided to put on a brave face.

Fortunately, Teresa Solana arrived a quarter of an hour late. While I was waiting for her in the street, I had time to smoke a cigarette and get over my scare. Borja was right: it seemed our neighbour (if it really was him) had been shot dead. The puddle of congealed blood around him indicated he had hardly died from natural causes, and that meant the police would begin an investigation and we'd have to answer a pile of questions, like what we were doing in the flat and why Borja possessed duplicate keys.

Over the weekend I'd done a Google search on Teresa Solana, as I do with all our clients, and I had seen the odd photo of her online, so I recognized her the moment I saw a woman with short dark hair walking quickly towards me and anxiously glancing at her watch. The way she was dressed reminded me of Lola's showy style, and I assumed they must both frequent the same boutiques, far from that neighbourhood. Unlike Lola, however, Teresa wasn't wearing high heels but flat, red shoes. Nor was she heavily made up.

"Mrs Solana? I am Eduard Martínez, Mr Masdéu's partner," I cheerily greeted her when I saw her stop in front of the entrance to our building and scrutinize an address in a notebook.

"Pleased to meet you. I'm sorry I'm late," she said, looking sincerely repentant as she shook my hand. "I had a devil of a time finding a taxi…"

"Don't worry," I smiled. "We've had a hectic morning and that's why I came downstairs to welcome you."

"Are you leaving already? Good heavens, I am sorry…"

"No, not at all," I hastened to reassure her. "We've had a burst pipe and the office is flooded. We're waiting for the plumber."

"That's really unlucky!"

"You can say that again! If you don't mind, we'll have our meeting in the flat of a friend who's away on holiday and has let us borrow his flat. It's in this same building. My partner's up there already."

"That's fine."

"This way, please," I replied, opening the door and letting her go in first, like a true gentleman, as Borja had taught me.

We walked towards the lift and the concierge was quick to peer out of her cubbyhole and eye us suspiciously, as she did whenever strangers passed through her lobby. Although it was a stylish old building, most of the flats had been split up, and their owners had converted them into offices or flats for visiting executives, which meant there were few long-standing occupants, lots of strange faces and, according to Paquita, the occasional tart who went up on the sly to service an executive. As most of the offices were

31

usually empty, Borja and I suspected they were only used as fiscal addresses to receive correspondence and sidestep the claws of the Inland Revenue. As for our office, the owner was a friend of my brother's, who owed him a favour and let us have it for a ridiculously low rent. Although I'd asked Borja more than once what kind of favour was involved, I'd never got a straight answer.

When we reached the landing, I rang the bell and Borja quickly opened the door and welcomed Teresa Solana with one of his seductive smiles.

"Mrs Solana. I am so pleased to meet you at last," he gushed, shaking her hand. "I imagine my partner has told you about the little problem we have in our office this morning." Borja signalled to her to come in. "Don't you worry. This flat belongs to a friend who's away for the moment. We can talk here. I assure you everything will be as confidential here as it would have been in our office."

"Well, it's not as if I'm going to tell you any state secrets," she replied with a smile. "Although I expect you already know quite a few…"

"Yes, and will take them to the grave," my brother assured her in his best jocular tone as he looked her up and down.

The three of us walked down the passage to the lounge, with Borja leading the way. Although the windows were wide open and there was a through breeze, I still caught a whiff of the stench that was now blending with the smell of our vomit and Mariajo's sophisticated perfume.

"Would you mind closing the window?" asked Teresa Solana. "I know it's hot, but I've got a cold, or perhaps it's an allergy, I'm not sure. I've been sneezing the whole morning."

The truth is that the breeze was quite unpleasant and Borja rushed to shut the dining-room window. Quite unconsciously, my eyes turned to the kitchen and the swarm of flies that was flying over our heads. For the moment, Teresa Solana didn't seem to have noticed anything.

"I am really grateful you found the time to see me," she began. "As I told Mr Masdéu on the phone," she continued, staring at me, "I am off on my travels tomorrow and will be away for almost a month."

"Holidays or promotional tour?" I asked, trying to ingratiate myself.

"A bit of everything. I'll do a little tourism between talks," she replied.

"And while you are away, there's a little matter you'd like us to look into in Barcelona, I believe?" Borja prompted her.

"Yes. Last week a friend suggested I should contract your services," she confessed, crossing her legs. "Frankly, the idea would never have occurred to me."

"Well, be assured you *have* come to the right place," said Borja with a knowing smile, egging her on.

"First of all, you should tell me your rates," she sighed. "I don't have limitless funds, unfortunately."

"I am sure we can agree a fee, don't worry on that front," my brother replied, adopting the stance of a man without a financial care in the world. "Now do tell us what's on your mind. And do rest assured: discretion is the hallmark of our company. Not a word will leave our lips."

"Well, there's nothing really top secret..." responded Teresa Solana, rather taken aback.

"You take your time. We know it's not easy to explain whatever it might be to complete strangers. Might I enquire which friend of ours recommended us?"

"Inspector Badia, of course. You do know him, don't you? We were shooting the breeze and he mentioned you, and said you could definitely help."

Borja and I froze there and then. The last thing we could have imagined was Inspector Jaume Badia personally advising that writer of thrillers to have recourse to our services, a woman who didn't at all look as if she was familiar with Barcelona's criminal underworld. The Inspector knows perfectly well that we aren't professional detectives and are unlicensed, and is too clever by half to think our kind of endeavours are at all legal.

"The Inspector is right," Borja reacted after a short pause. "There are certain matters where it's best to keep the police at arm's length."

"You'll perhaps think what I'm after is rather strange. I mean, I don't know if it is the kind of work you normally undertake," said Teresa Solana, who, despite her apparently naive, innocuous manner, was making a mental note of everything around her, us included.

"I can vouch that my partner and I are extremely versatile and have tackled projects of all shapes and sizes," Borja was quick to reassure her yet again.

"In any case, I want you to feel it is your kind of —"

"Absolutely. Besides, I think I know what we're talking about," Borja winked, sprawling, his arm round the back of his chair.

"Really?"

"It might be preferable to let Mrs Solana explain herself," I interjected, trying to stop my brother from putting his foot in it. However, Borja adopted the pose of the experienced detective who is rather ragged at the edges and slouched even more in his chair.

"You want us to keep an eye on your husband. I assume that's what this is about?" Borja glanced at the wedding ring Teresa Solana was wearing on the ring finger of her left hand.

"My husband? Why should I want you… Ah, I see now!" She burst out laughing. "No, it's not that. I don't think I've made myself clear. It is a professional, not a personal matter."

"Oh!" was all Borja could manage by way of response.

"Excuse me," Teresa Solana asked, looking at the ashtray on the coffee table out of the corner of her eye. "May I smoke?"

"Well, of course!" said Borja, quickly extracting a packet of cigarettes from his pocket and offering her one. That's a piece of luck, I thought; the smell of tobacco will help hide the stink from the kitchen.

"The fact is I am writing a novel about alternative therapies," she continued, still amused by my brother's wild assumption.

"What kind of therapies exactly?"

"Particularly ones based on homeopathy and Bach flower remedies," she replied. "But also any that promise to bring happiness or cure illnesses via yoga, meditation or feng shui... I've visited centres to see the kind of services they offer, but would like to set some of my chapters in the higher reaches of the city. That is, north of the Diagonal. I envisage it as an exclusive, luxury alternative centre. And that's where you come in."

"Where we come in?" echoed Borja, who was still rather shamefaced.

"When I told Inspector Badia about the project I was working on, he told me that you, Mr Masdéu, have excellent contacts in the upper side of the city."

"That's true enough," purred Borja.

"I need you to find me a centre that's in fashion, north of the Diagonal, and go there for, say, a couple of weeks and then tell me all about it: how it works, the services they offer, the treatments, the kind of people that go there... I thought you might enrol on a short course and use that as an excuse to talk to clientele and staff. Then report back to me, naturally."

"But wouldn't it be better if you did that yourself?" I asked.

"I mean, if you need the information to write a novel, you ought to have it first-hand."

I saw Borja give me one of his looks that killed. And I shut up.

"My problem is I'm going on my travels today and will be out of Barcelona for almost a month. And when I get back, I've got to go into hiding and write a couple of keynote lectures. I really don't have time to do my own fieldwork. And my publisher wants to bring the book out in October…"

"I understand."

"On the other hand, I have to say, I don't feel at ease in such places," she continued, smiling rather nervously.

I smiled too, and nodded vigorously. I perfectly understood what she meant because I have the same problem: the rich put me on edge and I never know how to behave.

"Well then? Will you give me a hand?"

"Of course. My partner and I are highly adaptable. Aren't we, Eduard?"

Teresa Solana started smiling again and looked much more relaxed, and she said we should organize ourselves as we thought fit, that she had full confidence in our *modus operandi*. She had started her novel, she confessed, but needed that information to give the story a touch of realism. After we'd agreed our fee, she signed us a cheque that Borja quickly pocketed. She stayed a while and told us how she was angling her novel, until she looked at her watch at a quarter to two and leapt up from the sofa, looking alarmed.

"You must excuse me, but my plane leaves at five and I've still got to pack," she said. And then she wrinkled her nose and asked, "Can you smell something peculiar?"

"It's the burst pipes," explained Borja, deadpan. "The stink comes from the courtyard."

"Yes, that's what it must be. Good, I'll give you a ring as soon as I'm back in town. Good luck."

"Don't worry. Eduard, my partner, and I will find you material to write a first-rate novel." And, as if he'd had a kind of premonition, he kissed her hand in his gallant style and added, "No need for *any* worries on that front."

3

When Teresa Solana had disappeared, Borja loosened the knot of his tie and opened the window. He then took the bottle of brandy and a couple of glasses from the cocktail bar.

"If you ask me, Pep, I don't think this is the time to get plastered," I said, putting my hand over my glass to stop him filling it. "I'd like to remind you we are in the flat of an American who is prostrate on the floor of his kitchen, apparently murdered. And right now our fingerprints are everywhere."

"I don't want to get plastered," he replied. "I just want us to calm down and think through what we should do."

"Phone the police, I imagine? What else *can* we do?"

"And what will we tell them? That we came up here to water the plants and found a dead man in the kitchen? That, as our office had been burgled (an office we've never signed a rental contract for), we took advantage of the fact we had the keys in order to see a client there – even though there was a corpse in the kitchen that we suspect to be Brian – because we didn't want her to see inside our office that's more like the stage-set for a comic opera?"

"Well, if you put it like that…"

"They will question us about our company and our client. And when we tell them she writes crime fiction…"

"I suppose the plot will thicken."

"Besides, when Teresa Solana finds out, I don't think she will be at all amused to know we saw her in a flat where a guy had been shot in the head. She'll think it some kind of macabre joke, or worse, will be furious. And she told us she was a friend of the Inspector, don't you forget that."

"You know, for someone who writes thrillers, Teresa Solana wasn't what you'd call very perceptive. I don't reckon she noticed a thing."

"She said she had a cold," said Borja, shrugging his shoulders. "I expect her nose was bunged up."

"Well, I can still smell the stink."

"So can I. And we've used up all our perfume," grumbled my brother, holding the bottle up against the light to check that it was empty.

Borja was right. We had to find a way out of that mess without being implicated. I let him pour out shots of brandy that we drank in silence, aware that Brian Morgan was not going to go away and that we had to think up something so the police would have no reason to link us to his death. While I sipped my brandy, I saw how clean and tidy our neighbour's flat was, compared to the chaos in our office. You'd never have dreamt someone had broken in or done him in. Brian Morgan's death bore the mark of an execution, and the mere thought made me shudder. I told Borja what my fears were and asked him yet again why he kept a set of keys to the flat of a man who'd been shot in the head and murdered.

"I've told you already," he insisted in a tone of voice that suggested I was being paranoid. "One day when you weren't around he came down to our office and gave them to me…"

"Hey, come on… You don't expect me to swallow that, do you?"

"I swear it's the truth. He said he was always travelling and wanted a neighbour to have a duplicate set of keys in case he lost his or there was some kind of problem, like burst pipes or a gas leak. He also said he didn't trust the concierge, and that I seemed the ideal kind of person."

"Fuck, the guy holed in one there!" I retorted sarcastically.

"I thought he seemed plausible and I agreed to take the keys. Obviously, after what's happened…"

"Do you have any idea what he did? His line of business?"

"I think he worked as an executive for an American company. Something to do with electrical components…"

"Do you know the name of the company?"

"I don't remember."

"But, Pep, what if he was a crook? Or belonged to a gang of criminals?" I suddenly blurted out.

"Hey, don't be stupid! I'm sure there must be a straight-forward explanation. Besides, Brian was a handsome guy and the women must have been after him. It's probably a crime of passion, you just see."

All of a sudden my brother jumped up from the sofa as if he'd remembered something very important.

"I'll be back in a minute. I must check something…" he said, rushing into the corridor.

Borja went into the spare bedroom and straight to the wardrobe. He opened one of the doors and took out a small package hidden behind a pile of sheets. He picked it up gingerly with both hands, unwrapped it and put the contents on the bed.

"My lucky morning!" he shouted, looking visibly relieved. "I'm what you call a lucky man!"

I'm no expert in antiques or works of art, but you didn't need to be to realize that it was a very old sculpture, like the ones you see in museums. The piece, only a few centimetres high, was an anthropomorphic representation, perhaps of some deity, with an animal head and human body. I noticed that its hind legs were missing.

"What the hell is that?" I asked.

"An antique."

"I can see that much. I don't understand how you knew it was in the wardrobe."

"That's easy. I put it there."

"You did?"

"I thought it was a good hiding place. As I had the keys to the flat…"

"You mean Brian didn't know you'd hidden it in one of his wardrobes?"

"Of course he didn't! That was the whole point. Nobody should know."

I took a deep breath and shook my head. I understood nothing.

"Wait a minute, Borja," I said a few seconds later. "What if they killed him because of this sculpture? If it's an antique, it must be worth a packet…"

"Nah, it's too small! You can fit it in the palm of your hand… And, besides, I told you Brian knew nothing about it. Whoever killed him didn't even turn his flat over, that much is obvious." And he then added, sounding convinced, "It's altogether a highly unfortunate coincidence."

"When did you hide it?"

"Last Monday, only a week ago. Do you remember that I went to Provence with Merche?"

"Yes, you told Lola it was a business trip, but kept to yourself the fact that Merche went with you…"

"Well, it *was* a business trip. As I had to go to Arles to pick up this sculpture, I decided to take Merche with me. She's been quite irritable recently. We went in her Audi. Though she doesn't know anything about the statue either."

"So, now you are trafficking in antiques!" I said, with a deep sigh.

"Well, if you put it that way…"

"You tell me how else I should put it…"

"I'm really doing someone a favour. Three weeks ago I had a call from that antique dealer in Amsterdam that I sold some of your mother-in-law's paintings to."

"Passing them off as fake Mirs, I presume…"

"He offered me an easy, well-paid assignment: I had to go to Arles, collect this sculpture, bring it to Barcelona, keep it here for a few days and hand it over to a person who would get in touch by phone. And that was it."

"And you couldn't think of anything better than to hide it in the American's flat?"

"Well, as I was helping him out by holding on to a set of keys to his flat and he —"

"He was an accomplice, but didn't know it!"

"Something of the sort," he concurred, looking at the floor.

We stayed silent for a while, Borja with his head down and yours truly at a loss for words. Although I knew that when my brother was really broke he acted as a middle-man for a smuggler of designer mobiles and shades in the Barceloneta, I suspected this small statue belonged to a rather more perilous category of shenanigans.

"Very well then, what do we do now? I hope you get one of your bright ideas before a neighbour notices the stench and tips off the *mossos*…" I rasped.

"The first thing we need to do is to clean everything and remove all traces of our fingerprints. Let's look in the laundry room and see what cleaning materials there are."

Luckily we found everything we needed. Borja slipped an apron and rubber gloves on and asked me not to move or touch anything. He painstakingly wiped all the surfaces we'd touched with a cloth soaked in window-cleaning liquid and told me that it contained alcohol and was the best thing there was for removing fingerprints. Although chemistry had never been his strong point, I imagined he'd heard that in one of the police series he liked to watch. Then he grabbed the mop and bucket to make sure none of our vomit was still on the kitchen floor, and finally washed out the brandy glasses with soap and water, dried them and returned them to the cocktail bar along with the bottle. As soon as he'd finished, he returned his arsenal of cleaning items to the laundry room and left everything exactly as he'd found it.

"We can go now," he said, using one of his cotton handkerchiefs to open the flat door.

"Aren't you going to shut the door?" I asked when I saw he'd left it wide open.

"No, I also left the kitchen door open. That way, the stench will spread downstairs and the neighbours or concierge will ring the police."

"But, when the *mossos* walk up, because you can be sure they *will* come up the stairs, and not in the lift, they will see that our door has been broken into and will take a look at what's inside. Or rather, at what isn't."

"Blast, you're quite right! Change of plan."

Borja shut the door to Brian Morgan's flat, took out his mobile and rang a locksmith. While we were waiting for him to arrive, we gave our office a bit of a tidy. An hour and a half later, our door had a new lock and we had two hundred euros less in our pockets. Before we left the building, Borja went back to the American's flat and left the front door wide open.

"The concierge gets here at five," I said, glancing at my watch. "Do you think she'll go upstairs and have a look?"

"I'm sure she will. I bet you anything we'll have a visit from the cops this evening."

What with one thing and another, it was now four p.m. We still hadn't had any lunch. I suggested going to our place for a bite to eat.

"Joana will be the only person there at this time of day. She goes to collect Arnau from school at half past four, so we will have the place to ourselves."

"What about the twins?" asked Borja.

"They're into romance and spend every free moment with their girlfriends. I don't think we'll see any sign of them before eight."

We went off to get the Smart that was parked halfway between the office and Borja's flat and drove to our place. Fortunately, my mother-in-law wasn't around. I prepared chorizo rolls in the kitchen, and took a couple of beers from the fridge. As it's a small kitchen and only fits a tiny table, we chomped our rolls in the dining room. We had yoghurt for afters and, now that Borja had got over the fright provoked by his macabre discovery, he ate two, lemon and strawberry flavours, like when he was a kid.

After we'd finished, I boiled up some coffee in the kitchen. While we were savouring our coffees in the dining room, I opened the window so we could enjoy a clandestine smoke. Better if the twins didn't suspect somebody had smoked in our flat, or else Montse or I would have to endure one of their enlightening sermons on the drawbacks of nicotine-addicted parents.

"I wanted to ask you something," said Borja as he extinguished his cigarette.

"Fire away."

"I'd like you to keep the statue here," he said, taking it from his pocket and putting it on the table.

"Well, after what happened to the American..."

"I told you that it was pure coincidence. Brian's murder has nothing to do with this statue. The people who did him in weren't looking for anything. They didn't even search his flat."

"So why don't you hide it in *your* flat? That would seem the most sensible…"

"It will be safer here. You know how Merche and Lola like to turn my drawers inside out."

"Is it very valuable?" I asked.

"I don't know. I suppose so. They are paying me twenty thousand to do this job."

"Fucking hell!"

"Ten for you and ten for me. You know, it will only be for a few days, a fortnight at most."

"But it's got to be stolen goods. Or smuggled."

"Well, I couldn't give a monkey's," he replied, shrugging his shoulders. But the second he saw the little light of my moral scruples start to flicker, he added, "Look, it's only a small piece of stone. It's not drugs, or arms, or anything dicey like that. We're not hurting anyone."

"Hey, if it's stolen, I don't think the owner would agree…"

"Bah, you can be sure he's some rich guy who will have it insured and is going to collect the insurance payment, don't you worry. That is, supposing it is stolen. Perhaps all they're after is tax avoidance," he added, as if that didn't matter.

"And it's our taxes that pay for schools and hospitals, in case you didn't know," I retorted sarcastically.

"Look at it from another point of view: the twenty thousand euros they're paying me must be black money that's been kept for years in some safe. We'll put it back into circulation and help reactivate the country's economy."

"True enough," I was forced to admit.

"What's more, as we will have to spend the money, we will pay taxes to the state in the shape of VAT."

"When you put it like that…"

"So, there you are," he said, getting up. "Think where we can hide it so the girls don't find it."

We decided the best place to hide the statue would be the trunk in the double room where Montse keeps our thick winter wear. I think the twins and Arnau creep in there from time to time and rummage through the drawers – and perhaps my mother-in-law does, too, as she spends a lot of time by herself in the flat and has discovered the pleasures of poking your nose everywhere. That trunk only had cold-weather items, and I was sure nobody would pry there. I very carefully removed a stack of jerseys, wrapped the statue in one of my woolly jumpers and returned it to the bottom of the pile.

"It'll be safe enough there," I said.

"Thanks so much, kid."

"It's almost half past six," I said, looking at my watch. "Do you reckon the concierge will have rung the police?"

"We can drive by and take a look to see if the filth's cars are around," he said. But the second he saw the alarm on my face, he added, "Don't worry. We'll take the Smart. And we won't stop."

We saw a fire engine, an ambulance and a couple of patrol cars parked in front of the block that housed our office. The *mossos* had cordoned off the entrance to the building with tape and a crowd of onlookers had gathered round who didn't want to miss the spectacle of the male nurses carrying a corpse in a black sack to the ambulance. Paquita was standing next to the ambulance, replying to questions she was being asked by a plain-clothes policeman who was taking notes.

"Poor woman! She must have had the fright of her life!" I said. Deep down I felt guilty for preparing the terrain that meant she was the one to find poor Brian in his kitchen.

"I wouldn't be too upset if I were you. You can bet she's enjoying every minute."

"Hey, you know, coming across a stinking corpse is hardly fun. We've probably traumatized her for life."

"Traumatized her? For Christ's sake, this is Paquita!" rasped Borja. "Finding a murdered tenant in her building must be the best thing that has happened to her in years! This will allow her to queen it over the neighbourhood for weeks, and you just see how that rejuvenates her."

"If you say so…"

A depressed, angry Montse was waiting for me at home. She was angry because she'd been ringing me all morning, and, for a change, my mobile was flat. She was depressed because the bank manager had told her and her partners there was not a cat in hell's chance of getting a loan.

"Don't you worry, we've got a good job on," I said to cheer her up. "On top of that, Borja and I are dealing with a little matter that will save our bacon, if it turns out right." And I tried to sound convincing when I added, "I expect things will sort themselves out in the end."

4

The following morning we met up in the San Marcos, a café on the high street in Sarrià that we convert into a kind of second office in winter, because the central heating doesn't work in our own office and we freeze to death. After everything that had happened, we decided it would be best not to go to the office for a few days and thus avoid bumping into the *mossos*. That way, we'd not have to give explanations or answer any questions.

"Remember we know nothing and have never seen the inside of Brian's flat," said Borja, chewing on his Danish pastry.

"What do you mean?"

"From now on we forget this whole business and concentrate on the Teresa Solana investigation."

"Our next move being…"

"To ring Mariona. She will know which door we should be knocking on."

Mariona Castany was undoubtedly our shortest route to finding a centre to fit our client's needs, even though I felt it unlikely my brother's friend would be a fan of alternative therapies and esoteric medication. Mariona was more one for martinis, antidepressants and plastic surgeons – in that order, I think – although she didn't have much use for the last one. Unlike many of her friends, who looked like failed experiments performed by Dr Frankenstein's most inept apprentice, Mariona had yet to have recourse to Botox or silicone lips, even if everyone knew that her adolescent breasts were the fruit of the endeavours of the city's most prestigious plastic surgeon.

Borja phoned Mariona from the San Marcos to tell her we needed her help and suggest meeting up.

"Ah, this morning is rather difficult," she replied. "I'm just leaving the house. And this afternoon I have to visit a friend."

"Don't you worry," said Borja. "Whenever it suits you. You choose a day."

"My friend lives on Santaló. We could meet there today in the Gimlet for drinks before dinner."

"Eight o'clock, usual table?"

"Perfect. See you soon, dear."

"Goodbye, my lovely."

Mariona is one of the richest, most illustrious women in Barcelona. She is sixty-seven, the age our mother would be if she were still with us, though you would never have guessed. When Borja discovered she'd attended a school in Santander as a child, he immediately used the information to tell her she and his imaginary mother, a Sáez de Astorga, had studied together in the same boarding school and had even been friends. Mariona swallowed that and took Borja under her wing, or rather, the character he had invented for himself: the heir with aristocratic names who'd lost his inheritance because of foul play by the Revenue. I sometimes think Mariona must know the truth by now because she is nobody's fool, but I have the impression she finds his little game amusing and laps up all his extravagant tales. Borja, on the other hand, behaves towards her with the exquisite manners of a nephew out of a Victorian novel,

49

and Mariona, a widow with two daughters she can't stand and no nephew fawning on her, lets my brother benefit from all her contacts.

Borja announced he had business to see to (that is, Merche) and had to be off. I went home and, on the way, stopped at the supermarket to buy powder for the washing machine, which we'd run out of. When I reached our flat, my mother-in-law was in the kitchen, at the ready in her apron, but, as she'd not started cooking lunch, I told her not to bother because Montse and I would have lunch out. My wife and I were worried, because we'd received a letter from Arnau's school saying he was having "problems".

Gràcia is full of small restaurants that offer decent, cheap set lunches. Even so, the crisis meant that lots of people had renewed the tradition of going home for lunch or taking sandwiches to work, and most places were empty. The spectacle of empty tables and idle waiters was depressing, and in the end we chose a restaurant on Verdi that had a couple of customers and a spark of life. Even so, the waiters were on the slow side and we had to rush off without eating our puddings so as not to be late for our meeting.

We were breathless and panting when we reached the school at one minute to three. We hardly had time to gather ourselves together, because Arnau's teacher arrived punctually on the hour, gave each of us a couple of kisses and asked us to accompany her to the staffroom.

"I'm very worried about Arnau," she declared in the tone of voice that a doctor who has discovered you have an incurable disease might use.

She read out a long report that Montse and I suffered in silence. According to the teacher, Arnau was a fidgety child (she actually used the word "hyperactive") who found it hard to concentrate because he spent the whole time chatting to his friends and winding the girls up. His interest in football, and in Barça in particular, was verging on an obsession, she added, as you could see at playtime when he found it impossible to interact with the girls because all he ever wanted to do was play football.

"You must realize that if Arnau continues in this vein he will be facing failure in life," she warned, looking as severe as a judge delivering a death sentence.

Arnau is five years old. At home he is a loving, communicative child, as they say nowadays, and, like most kids his age, rather mischievous. At the annual meet-the-teachers session with the other parents at the start of term, the teacher had lectured us on the dangers of television, video games, football and Barbie dolls, that, according to her, transformed girls into anorexic adolescents first, and sex objects second. At the time, Montse and I felt she'd laid it on rather thickly, but the majority of parents were in agreement and applauded.

"But what is Arnau doing exactly? Does he hit other children? Does he break things? Does he show a lack of respect towards you?" I asked.

"He never sits still and spends the whole time chatting. And sometimes uses swear words," said the schoolmistress in a hushed voice. "Obviously, children normally pick up swear words at home…" she added pitilessly.

I looked down, shamefaced, and Montse remained silent. I initially interpreted her silence as an act of contrition, as implicit acceptance that we had failed as parents and had no idea how to bring up our son. I was wrong. When I looked up and saw the expression on my wife's face, I realized Montse was so angry that her silence was caused by the effort she was making to stop herself going for the teacher's jugular.

"So what do you suggest?" Montse asked curtly, not returning the smile of commiseration the teacher had given us when she finished her little speech.

Her advice was to ban Arnau from playing football and to give him a course of homeopathic medication. Many children in the class are already taking some, she said. The other option was to start on Bach flower remedies that worked extremely well.

I'd been shocked to hear that Arnau ran the risk of becoming an illiterate, foul-mouthed, male chauvinist piglet, and was at a loss for words. Montse, who is feistier, thanked the teacher dryly and reminded her she was a professional psychologist and that, in her view, Arnau's behaviour wasn't abnormal in the slightest. In any case, she would take her remarks on board, she added, though she didn't feel it necessary either to have recourse to medication or to ban him from playing football.

"You are his parents. You must make these decisions," said the teacher, raising her eyebrows, with a knowing smile that meant we were to blame for Arnau's problems and she was washing her hands of the whole business.

"Indeed," Montse retorted as she got up. "My husband and I will do whatever we think necessary. Thank you for your concern."

"That's a stupid teacher, if ever there was one!" Montse grunted as soon as we were outside the school gates.

"Yes, I do think she was exaggerating rather…"

"What does she mean when she says Arnau is hyperactive because he likes playing football? He's only five years old, for Christ's sake!"

"Anyway, I think he's too young to start taking pills…"

"Forget it! I know my son. There's nothing wrong with him."

Montse was beside herself. I suggested going for a coffee, although what my wife needed right then was a herbal infusion. We sat at a small café terrace and, while we were waiting to order, Montse asked me for a cigarette. I took out a packet and gave her one, but said nothing. She's been trying to kick the habit for three years, and that was her first in five days.

"The fact is," she explained after a couple of drags had calmed her down, "leftist teachers now think it's trendy to recommend homeopathy or Bach flower remedies."

"I thought you were all for that kind of thing…"

"Not any more. Besides, you shouldn't experiment on kids," she asserted as she savoured her sinful cigarette.

I'd suspected for some time that my wife was beginning to doubt the effectiveness of some of the so-called alternative therapies, from when some children in the school who had bronchitis developed pneumonia after their parents put their trust in some esoteric juice or other. Montse was also quite against the idea that vaccinations were simply an evil conspiracy by the pharmaceutical companies to boost their profits, and was worried by the tendency of her radical acquaintances to refuse to give permission for their children to be vaccinated and hand them homeopathic rather than antipyretic pills when they got a temperature.

"There's only one way to keep a kid quiet in class, and that's fear," she continued. "That's why priests and nuns are so good at keeping order."

"So what should we do? Change Arnau to another school?"

"No, it's almost the end of term and they say the teacher he'll have next year isn't so dopey. Anyway, I don't think there's a single school in Barcelona that doesn't have at least one specimen of that kind."

"What are you getting at now?"

"They have a thing about authority and don't know how to instil discipline. On the one hand, they are against punishment and expect kids in kindergarten to behave like little adults. When they realize they can't keep control halfway through the year, they start blaming television or parents who don't spend enough time with their children…"

"I don't think they're so wide of the mark in that respect," I retorted. "Arnau *does* watch too much TV. In my day —"

"Exactly, that's what they always say: in our day we did this or didn't do that. That old refrain about things not being what they used to be."

"We all fall for that…"

"But the world has changed and you can't bring up kids nowadays trying to tell them that the TV and video games don't exist, as the way to get them interested in books. And whatever they say, kids today are much more aware."

"I agree."

The waiter came and put the bill on the table.

"Are you missing your old job?" I asked as I searched for my wallet. "It's been almost two years since you…"

"Not at all, and even less so after that little chat with Arnau's teacher!"

In the days when I was still earning my bread in a bank, before Pep returned to Barcelona transformed into Borja, Monte worked as a school counsellor thanks to her degree in psychology. She too was bored with her job, and, as soon as she could, she did what I had done and changed her lifestyle. She and some friends opened up the Alternative Centre for Holistic Well-being in Gràcia, close to the plaça de la Virreina where, apart from selling beauty treatments using organic concoctions, they provided anti-smoking group therapy and yoga and meditation courses.

"I must be off. I have a session," she said, looking at her watch and putting out her cigarette.

"I expect I'll be back late tonight. We're going for a drink with that girlfriend of Borja's."

"Merche?" she scowled.

"No, Mariona Castany. It's to do with our new case."

"Your partner's affair with Lola will end in disaster. You do realize that, don't you?" she sighed.

"Don't be such a spoilsport."

5

As it was still early, I took a leisurely stroll home and had a delicious siesta. When I woke up, it was almost six o'clock. I didn't want to be late, so I leapt out of bed and scrambled around in the wardrobe for something decent to wear to cocktails with that sophisticate Mariona. I rolled up at Borja's at a quarter to seven and he, too, looked as if he'd just got out of the sack.

"You by yourself?" I asked when he opened the door.

"Yes."

"So, was it lunch with Merche?"

Borja nodded.

"We went to the Port Olímpic. I think she's rumbled me."

"About you and Lola?"

"She suspects there's another woman. And I thought Merche wasn't the jealous kind!" he sighed.

"What did you expect? You'll have to choose sooner or later. You can't sustain this situation for much longer."

"It's late. I need to have a shower," he replied, changing the subject.

While Borja was sprucing himself up, I switched on the TV and zapped for a while. The princess in town was over the moon with her latest face; a footballer had cheated on his teenage sweetheart with a famous model; the octo-genarian Duchess of Alba was as happy as a lark with her young, proletarian fiancé. More of the usual. The usual circus programmed to keep our eyes on the box. Our daily ration of fantasy.

A few minutes later, Borja appeared showered, dressed and scented – overly so, for my taste.

"Like my shirt?" he asked.

"Very smart. Where did you pick that up?"

Borja had opted for black jeans and a mauve shirt.

"I snaffled it the other day in Gonzalo Comella on the Via Augusta," he confessed.

"Pep!…"

"It cost a fortune."

"One of these days they'll catch you."

"I don't think so. I'm a dab hand at it," he said, smiling as he admired himself in the mirror.

I sighed. Designer wear is one of Borja's vices, but he can't afford such luxuries, so instead loots expensive shops. His other vice is taking other people's overcoats and umbrellas from restaurants when he lunches out, and he has an impressive array in his flat. Still smiling, he put on a sea-blue jersey and took another look in the mirror to be sure he liked his ensemble. Then he gave me the once-over and nodded.

We decided to take the car, but rather than driving straight to the Gimlet we made a detour via the office to look at the lie of the land. The police cars and bystanders had gone, and we didn't stop. We reached the cocktail bar early and, while waiting for Mariona, ordered a couple of gin and tonics, light on the gin. Our friend arrived at five past eight, in jeans and a tight-fitting T-shirt that emphasized her svelte body, which remained in good shape. After giving us a couple of pecks on the cheek, she flopped down on a chair and tetchily ordered a Singapore sling.

"I am up to here with my friends!" she huffed. "All they can talk about is who has just died or who is about to. It is *awfully* depressing."

"You need a boyfriend, Mariona. Or two," quipped Borja, shaking his head. Mariona has been a widow for three years although it's rumoured she's been having an affair with a famous city architect for the past fifteen.

"Shut up about boyfriends! What are you two into at the moment? A new case?"

"Not exactly a case, Mariona. You know we're not detectives," replied Borja with another shake of the head. "But we do have an assignment. We've been contracted to... How should I put this?…"

"To do some research?" she suggested.

"Yes, something of the sort. It's Teresa Solana, that writer I asked you about the other day. She wants to write a novel about alternative therapies and has contracted us to do her field work."

"About alternative therapies?" queried Mariona, raising her eyebrows, as if she didn't understand.

"Well, the ambience in places that programme these therapies. Or more precisely the feel of one such centre on the upper side."

"I get you. And that's why you wanted to speak to me, I imagine?" she asked, gulping down the cocktail that had just arrived.

"Well, Mariona rules above the Diagonal. You're the queen."

Mariona burst out laughing and ran her fingers through her long, silvery waves of hair. Then she threw herself back, like a *grande dame* of the stage, and said, "There's a centre near my house that is very fashionable. It's called Zen Moments. By the by, an architect friend of mine designed the building. He even got a prize for his pains."

"And what do they do?" I asked.

"Oh, a bit of everything: meditation, yoga, massage. But it's a serious establishment, you know? No happy endings. The doctor that runs it is Horaci Bou." And she added, with a Cheshire-cat grin: "*He* is peculiar."

"This sounds like just what we're after," I replied.

"They rake it in," speculated Borja, always keen on the financial angle.

"I suppose they do. They have lots of takers."

"Are you one of them?"

"I have very occasionally accompanied a friend for a spot of meditation, but the truth is I find these things very boring. Besides, I have a gym at home and a personal trainer who is most becoming."

"Ah, so you know the people who run the place?" Borja asked.

"Of course! I bump into Dr Bou and his wife at parties. They aren't one of *us*," she specified, "but are very well connected and never miss an opportunity for self-promotion. What's more, they belong to the tennis club." She was referring, of course, to the Royal Tennis Club, that much I knew because I'd been there a few times with Borja.

"Where is the centre?" Borja asked.

"It's on Escoles Pies. I told you it was practically next door to my house."

"And do you know if you need a recommendation to get in?"

"No, it's not a club," answered Mariona, shaking her head. "I think you simply need to be well-heeled, as I believe they charge the earth. In any case, if you need endorsing you can mention my name. I am sure they will be thrilled if you say I sent you."

"You're wonderful, Mariona. I don't know what we'd do without you."

Mariona insisted on ordering another round and, as it was a warm evening, she suggested sitting on the terrace so she could smoke. Borja and I exchanged anxious glances because the advance from Teresa Solana had flown and our current capital amounted to forty euros.

"Now, that's more like it!" chirped Mariona after a couple of puffs.

The second glass brought with it the inside story on various individuals I'd never heard of and on places that I'd never set foot in. On the other hand, Borja seemed to know the lot and hung on Mariona's every word with genuine interest while I tried to hide the fact I was bored out of my mind and fought off my yawns. When we finally finished our drinks and the time came to pay, Mariona took the bill and insisted on paying. Borja made gentlemanly noises of dissent, but was sensible enough to be less assertive than usual.

"All right, this time, I'll allow you to be an emancipated lady and pay for us," he said, almost as if he were doing her a favour.

Mariona paid with her magical gold card and we all three got up from our chairs. As it was her chauffeur's day off and she had come by taxi, Borja offered to drive her home in his Smart. Initially, Mariona refused, arguing that the three of us couldn't cram into the car, but I said I felt like a walk and they shouldn't worry on my account. In fact, I was tired and the gin and tonics had gone to my head, and the last thing I felt like was a long walk home. As soon as they were out of sight I went off to catch the bus, hoping that Montse had taken pity on me and got dinner ready. The bus dawdled and when I walked through the door, the Spanish omelette Joana had cooked was no more and I had to make do with a miserable sandwich.

6

The next morning Borja was due to pick me up on the way to visit the centre Mariona had recommended. We had an appointment for eleven and it was a quarter to when the bell rang. I assumed it to be him and I answered "I'll be down right away!" not thinking to ask who it was, but the second I opened the door, I regretted I hadn't. The man waiting in the street wasn't my brother but a young, tall, burly *mosso d'esquadra* who immediately asked if I was Mr Eduard Martínez. When I finally stammered that I was he, he said that Inspector Badia wanted to talk to me and invited me in a threatening voice to get into the patrol car parked opposite.

While I walked towards the car, praying that no neighbour was watching and rushing to phone Montse or, even worse, my mother-in-law, I saw Borja was already inside, trying to keep a stiff upper lip, as the English say.

"Are we under arrest?" I whispered after I'd sat down next to him.

"No. At least I don't think so. Apparently the Inspector wants a word with us," he whispered back.

"Did they say why?"

"They don't know. The Inspector told them to take us to the headquarters on Les Corts, and that it was urgent."

"Shit!"

We were back in it. I scowled out of the window and muttered that this was the last time I took any notice of my brother. How could I let him dupe me like that? I should have known Borja's bright ideas are never the solution, but simply the quickest way to create more hassle.

"We still don't know what it's all about," he hissed when he saw me looking so appalled. "So please, let's not get into a stress. And you leave the talking to me."

We didn't say another word and both of us pretended to look out of the window. I am sure Borja was also speculating that the police might have found out we'd been to the American's flat on Monday morning and, reasonably enough, deduced that we were involved in his murder. On the other hand, I couldn't help thinking it was really strange that Brian Morgan had entrusted my brother with the keys to his flat, and that Borja, to complicate our lives even more, had decided to hide an antique there that was surely stolen or smuggled goods.

"Above all, you have never heard of Brian and have never set foot in his flat," repeated Borja before we alighted.

My legs felt weak. It was my second visit to the police station on Les Corts in six months, and I was scared we'd both leave in handcuffs. Inspector Badia's frosty manner and extreme politeness gave me the shivers. Ever since that day he summoned us to his office to tell us he knew Borja was using a name that wasn't the one on his ID card, and that he and I were brothers and that the fraud consultancy we claimed we ran was a company that didn't exist, I knew that sooner or later he'd have it in for us. On that occasion, the Inspector had more important matters to attend to, but the fact he had us taped was hardly comforting. Borja was also stressed out. Quite unawares, he'd started biting his nails.

The secretary told us we'd have to wait because the Inspector was on the phone and she pointed us towards some chairs. Borja and I obediently sat down next to each other under her beady eye. After ten minutes that seemed like an eternity, the office door opened and the Inspector stuck his head out.

"Please do come in. I am so grateful you were able to make it," he said affably, disconcerting us even more.

"Always ready to be of help, Inspector," replied Borja, trying to recover his sangfroid and shaking the Inspector's hand.

"I hoped you weren't alarmed because I sent a patrol car," the Inspector smiled. "I thought it would save time. But do come in, I beg you."

When you aren't sure what it's all about, best keep your mouth shut. That's what Borja always said and we both knew we should say nothing until the Inspector showed his cards.

"I suppose you've heard what happened in the building where you have your office," he began, watching to see how we reacted.

The Inspector stared at Borja and, immediately afterwards, trained his cold, blue eyes on me. Unlike my brother, I couldn't stand his accusing look and cowered like a little kid who'd been caught up to no good.

"What happened?" asked Borja, sounding surprised.

"Ah, so you didn't know?"

"No," we both chorused.

"So when *was* the last time you went to your office?"

Borja put on his innocent angel face and looked as if he was remembering hard, trying to gain time to formulate a plausible response that wouldn't make life difficult for us.

"We were there Monday morning," he said finally. "We had an appointment with a writer. A friend of yours, I believe, Teresa Solana."

"But, of course, Teresa…" replied the Inspector, sprawling back in his chair. "I hope you didn't mind me mentioning your name to her."

"On the contrary," said Borja. "We are always delighted to help out when we can."

"She sometimes drops in when she wants information for one of her books. She told me her new novel is something to do with alternative therapies and I thought you might be able to give her a hand."

"Yes, we did see eye to eye," Borja replied enigmatically.

The Inspector sprawled back yet again and rubbed his hands together.

"So you've not been back to the office since Monday morning?" he continued.

"The fact is we were intending to go yesterday afternoon, but in the end we had a drink with Mariona Castany at the Gimlet and it got very late," explained Borja, reminding the Inspector of his friendship with one of the wealthiest women in Barcelona. The Inspector took note.

"A neighbour of yours has been murdered," he let drop. "By the name of Brian Morgan."

Borja and I pretended to be shocked.

"Really?"

"First I've heard of it," I lied.

"What on earth happened?" enquired Borja, slightly overreacting.

"The concierge found him a couple of evenings ago. He'd been dead for over a week."

"Poor woman! She must have got the fright of her life!" said Borja, shaking his head as if he was really upset.

"You didn't notice anything that morning when you went to your office?" The Inspector's gentle tone contrasted with his icy glare.

"No," we both shook our heads.

"When the concierge started her afternoon shift, she noticed there was a stink on the staircase. She walked upstairs to see where it was coming from and found the door to your neighbour's flat wide open. The stink was coming from inside."

"Well, we didn't notice a thing," Borja replied hastily. "Did we, Eduard?"

"No, nothing at all."

"The concierge says there was no smell in the morning," continued the Inspector. "When did you two gentlemen leave the building?"

Borja stared up at the ceiling, making it plain he was still trying hard to remember.

"It must have been half past one, because the concierge had gone for lunch," he said in the end. In fact, we can't have left the flat until about four, what with cleaning Brian Morgan's flat and waiting for the locksmith.

"That means the door to the victim's flat must have been shut and someone must have opened it between half past one and five," deduced the Inspector, jotting on a sheet of paper. "That was why the stench had reached the staircase."

"Have you caught the culprit?" asked Borja.

"Not yet. My men are pretty good, but not that good!" the Inspector exclaimed with a smile. "In fact, Mr Masdéu, that's why I had you brought in."

When the Inspector persisted in addressing Borja by his fictitious name, although he knew he was a Martínez and that we were brothers, I felt we were done for. I was sure he had it in for us.

"Mr Masdéu, a neighbour living in the building opposite swears she saw you opening and closing the windows in the victim's flat on Monday morning." The Inspector suddenly changed his expression and looked extremely severe. Borja went bright red. I turned white.

"Come off it!" was my brother's immediate reaction. "The only windows I opened were in our office. The neighbour must have mixed them up."

"Mixed them up?"

"Yes, as our office windows are right under the windows in the dining room of that Brian…"

"So you have been inside Mr Morgan's flat. Or at least his dining room…" retorted the Inspector.

"Well, yes, I mean no, obviously not," mumbled Borja nervously. "I imagined the windows overlooking the street are in the dining room. Or am I mistaken?"

The Inspector stared through Borja, but said nothing.

"Did you know the victim?" was his only response.

"Not really. We may have passed him on the stairs now and then," said Borja.

"What about you, Mr Martínez? Did you know Mr Morgan?"

"I just said 'Good morning' to him a couple of times," I replied, shrugging my shoulders to underline the fact that I couldn't care less that a total stranger was dead.

The Inspector consulted his dossier.

"Do you know what his line of business was?" he asked, keeping his eyes trained on his sheaf of papers.

"I was under the impression that he worked for an American company and was always on the hoof. I believe it had to do with electrical components," replied Borja in a tone that indicated that he wanted to cooperate.

"The fact of the matter is that Mr Brian Morgan was really Brian Harris and worked for the government," the Inspector explained.

On this occasion, our shocked expressions were for real.

"The government? Which government?"

"The government of the United States, naturally."

"Oh, you mean he was in the FBI?" asked Borja, sounding frightened.

The Inspector sighed.

"The FBI is the federal police force. Don't you ever watch television?"

"That must mean he was in the CIA, right?" I asked.

The Inspector smiled, but said neither yea nor nay.

"We have to handle this case with kid gloves," he said finally. "We must of course investigate Mr Harris's death, and that is what we are doing, but I am under orders to collaborate with the Americans and not to interfere in their investigations unless I am asked to."

"So what you are saying is that the Americans will take over the case," said Borja as if he were *au fait* with police protocol in such situations.

"Not at all. This is our business. Though it does complicate matters considerably," he admitted. "If I brought you here it is because your office is in the same building, and I know how very observant you both are…"

"If you say so…"

"I thought you might have come across the occasional foreigner or suspicious-looking individual over the last few weeks. Do try to remember."

My brother and I glanced at each other and shook our heads.

"The truth is we've hardly been to the office recently," said Borja. "You know, with the crisis we have very few clients. In any case, the person you should speak to is Paquita, the concierge. She knows everything that goes on in the building. Who goes in, and who comes out…"

"We've done that. But she's only there from nine to one and five to eight. And never at the weekends," replied the Inspector.

"It may even have been an inside CIA job. How do you know *they* didn't shoot him?" I piped up, thinking aloud.

The Inspector stiffened slightly and stared into my eyes.

"And how do *you* know he was shot?"

I'd put my foot in it big time. I felt myself going bright red and Borja looking at me panic-stricken. I took a deep breath, trying to calm down and do what Borja would have done, namely, come out fighting.

"Well, Inspector, if he was in the CIA, he must have been a spy, mustn't he? And spies are always shot in the head, right? At least in films…" I argued in a shrill voice, hoping the Inspector would be convinced by my logic.

"Indeed, Mr Martínez, you are quite right. Mr Harris died from a shot to the head. But there is something that doesn't quite fit. Are you both sure you know nothing about all this?"

Borja, who'd guessed the Inspector was shooting in the dark, lolled back in his chair and smiled.

"Inspector, we devote our lives to doing favours for people with money, as you know. And, sometimes," he added, "a writer comes to see us claiming she is a friend of yours. But the CIA? Don't make me laugh! Eduard and I don't even speak English!"

"Rest assured, Mr Masdéu. I'm not accusing you of anything."

The Inspector got up out of his chair. "In fact, this wasn't an interrogation. It was an informal conversation. Deputy Inspector Alsina-Graells is leading this case, not me," he continued with a crafty smile. "In any case, if by chance you do find something, I hope you will tell me straight away."

"But, of course," replied Borja, getting up and shaking the Inspector's hand. When the Inspector shook mine, I could tell from the suspicious look in his eyes he'd noticed mine was a cold and sweaty palm.

I looked at the floor and gulped.

7

Out in the street the sun was shining brightly, but after the fright Inspector Badia had just given us I'd have thought the weather was wonderful even if thunder and lightning had been booming and flashing overhead. We hadn't been arrested, and, despite that statement from the neighbour who'd said she'd seen Borja opening and closing the windows of Brian's flat, it was evident the Inspector didn't seriously suspect we were involved in the murder. Still shaking with fear, Borja and I lit up and started to stroll silently down the road, crossing Les Corts. We needed to exercise our legs and release the adrenalin that had accumulated in our veins.

"That bastard Badia!" Borja exclaimed after a while. "He gave me a real shock! I thought he was on to us!"

"Perhaps we *should* have told him the truth. If he finds out we've been lying, he won't let us off lightly."

"He'll never find out. That's quite impossible."

"What about the neighbour opposite?"

"Bah, the Inspector accepted she simply got the wrong flat. Besides, don't you ever forget we are in no way involved in Brian's death. We simply happened to find him – by chance."

"Well, by chance, because you've got the keys to his flat. And I recall we interfered with the scene of the crime…"

"Forget it. I bet even those CSI guys would never notice. I gave everything a good clean."

"That is precisely what most worries me," I groaned.

It was almost two o'clock, so I suggested we catch a taxi to get us on our way. I'd promised Montse I'd be home for lunch and, taking advantage of the fact Joana had gone to a friend's and that we'd be alone in the flat, we would see if we couldn't find a solution to the bank's refusal to give them the loan they needed to keep their business on the road. The crisis meant many of Montse's leftist clients were unemployed, and that had forced them to give up the treatment they were getting at her Alternative Centre (that was entirely dispensable, in my view). Without a cash handout to see them through until the situation improved, she and her two partners would go bankrupt. Usually a spirited, optimistic woman, Montse had been depressed for the last two days, as I told Borja.

"Change of plan," he now told the taxi driver. "Let's go to the market on València."

"To the market?"

"We'll take her a bunch of flowers. I've yet to meet the woman who doesn't cheer up when she's given a bouquet of flowers. But don't worry, I'll only drop by for a moment and then I'll leave you to have your lunch in peace."

"Pep, we're in no state to spend money on flowers…"

"Don't you worry, this one is on me. Or rather, on Merche," he replied with a wink.

I sighed and let him get on with it. Once in the market, Borja scrutinized the different varieties of flower and finally chose five sprays of red, crimson, pumpkin, pink and yellow African daisies that made up a spectacular bouquet that cost him forty euros.

"Don't be so mean," he reproached me. "Do things well or don't do them at all!"

Montse's face lit up when she saw us walk in with that colourful bouquet. She wasn't expecting it and I'm sure she immediately guessed it had been Borja's idea. When I went into the dining room, I was surprised to see Joana and Lola setting the table. I discreetly asked my wife what they were doing there.

"My mother's friend is ill and they had to cancel lunch. And you know Lola, she came to the Centre this morning to cheer me up, and then invited herself to lunch," she whispered.

"Now I'll have to ask Borja if he wants to stay and eat a bite with us…" I growled.

"What do you bet he says yes?"

So there would be five of us for lunch, and Joana had decided on a menu of Cuban rice followed by sausages. While the women were busy in the kitchen, Borja and I finished setting the table and opened a couple of cans of beer. I still hadn't got over our big scare.

"We'll go to Dr Bou's centre this afternoon," Borja declared. "It's best if we can keep to the schedule we planned."

"You mean in terms of the Inspector?"

"No, I mean in general. After all, we were *not* involved in Brian's death."

"That's quite a coup to have a CIA spy for a neighbour."

"Merche, who is a friend of the British consul, tells me Barcelona is teeming with them. It's all to do with al-Qaeda."

"Wonderful! What with the spies and the tourists, we'll never get a look-in!"

"In any case, his death wasn't connected with the statue I hid in his flat," he reminded me.

"I suppose not," I had to agree. "But if the guy was a CIA agent, that might make things a bit livelier. And if they ever find out we were in his flat…"

"They never will! You saw how the Inspector didn't suspect us."

Over the course of lunch, we explained that a man had been murdered in the building where we rented our office, but avoided mentioning the episode of our conversation with the Inspector and, naturally, the fact that we had found Brian's corpse. On the other hand, as it was no secret, we made the most of the curious assignment from Teresa Solana and how we intended enrolling at a Zen centre.

"The peculiar things you two get up to!" said Joana, who still hadn't digested the fact I'd left a secure job at the bank to work with Borja and that Montse had abandoned her job as a school counsellor to set up an Alternative Centre in Gràcia.

"But the place we are going to investigate is not at all like Montse's," Borja made clear.

"You mean it's an establishment for the well-to-do, don't you?" asked Montse.

"I hope so," said Borja with a smile. Lola grimaced.

"Homeopathy is a much more natural form of medicine," my sister-in-law suddenly declared, even though she was immediately on the defensive. "All chemists sell it. I take it too."

Borja said nothing and Montse and I simply goggled at Lola. We were surprised because if Lola is a fan of one thing it is antibiotics, ibuprofen and paracetamol, which I knew she hadn't given up because I'd caught her swallowing a pill just before lunch.

"Well, it's all yours," interjected Joana. "I reckon all those things are a lot of tosh."

"But lots of people believe in it. So I reckon it must work."

"The fact that a huge number of individuals believe something to be so doesn't imply that it is so," I suggested tentatively.

"Doesn't it? Well, if people believe in it, it must be for a good reason," came her defiant response.

"Come on, Lola, lots of people believe in horoscopes, in kidnappings by beings from other planets or in UFOs, but that's no proof that they actually exist."

"People believe in UFOs because so many have been sighted."

"So if people have seen them, how come there is no definite proof they exist? At the end of the day, all we have as evidence is what the people who claim to have seen one say," I replied.

"That's because governments keep it from us, just like they do with alternative therapies. They would rather people stuffed themselves with medicines that damage their livers or kidneys, so that pharmaceutical companies can make a bomb."

"Oh, that's all we needed! The famous conspiracy theory!" I retorted sarcastically. But Montse kicked me under the table. "The problem, Lola, is that before antibiotics were discovered, people simply died, if you remember."

"Many illnesses can be cured by homeopathy, without antibiotics," she countered. "That's a well-established fact."

To be frank, as far I was concerned, the jury was still out on homeopathic medicine, and I decided to end the discussion right there and let Lola have the last word. Borja very deftly channelled the conversation to noir novels and Teresa Solana, whom only Montse had read, on the recommendation of one of her customers. After coffee, Joana said she was going to stretch out and disappeared into her bedroom. Montse and Lola also got up and slumped on the sofa, but not before they had subtly invited us to clean the kitchen. Borja and I obediently donned our aprons and started washing up.

"The next present you get from me will be a dishwasher," grumbled Borja. "I've a friend down in the port who —"

"No thank you very much! I don't want to hear another word about any of your friends! I bet it's illegal!"

"Shush! Not so loud, or the girls will hear you…"

"And talking of risky business, have you heard from your statue friend?"

"Not yet. But he said it would be at least a fortnight…"

"You know I'm not keen on hiding it here," I carped.

"Take it easy, kid. I said it's only a matter of days."

We finished the washing-up in silence, dried our hands and went into the dining room to say goodbye to Montse and Lola and announce that we were going to Zen Moments to meditate a while and purge our sins.

8

The Zen Moments centre was on Escoles Pies, above the boulevard Bonanova, very close to where Mariona lives. It was a three-storey designer building, cube-shaped and painted in several shades of grey. Unlike the exuberant, chaotic gardens that one could glimpse around the nearby mansions, where creeping plants spilled over walls and offered the street their wisteria and magnificent clusters of deep-purple bougainvillea, the garden surrounding the meditation centre was so prim and proper that all its plants looked man-made. There wasn't a single leaf on the gravel, and I noted that all the flowers were pallid – not one was red. The pale mauve petals of two huge hydrangeas welcomed visitors from their earthenware pots on either side of the front door.

"Good afternoon," we chorused as we walked in.

Borja smiled and walked towards the young woman sitting behind a shiny black marble counter that was flanked by an artificial waterfall under an elegant, equally black, stone Buddha that must have been at least a metre and a half high.

"We are looking for information," said Borja. "My business partner and I are interested in finding out about your centre's activities."

"Is this your first visit?" she asked, returning his smile.

"Yes."

The young woman got up from her chair and emerged from behind the counter. She was dark-haired and stocky, in pastel pink trousers and a short-sleeved smock that reminded me of the uniforms nurses and girls in beauty centres often wear, though not entirely.

"If you would be so good as to follow me," she instructed us.

A tinted glass door opened automatically and led into a wide, door-lined corridor. There were two offices at the end with signs that said respectively, "Dr Horaci Bou" and "Dr Bernat Comes". Two doors next to them were labelled "Seminar 1" and "Seminar 2". The receptionist opened the only door without a sign and ushered us into a waiting room with a window that overlooked the garden. The room was empty, with no chairs; only two long concrete benches without backs that were placed in parallel either side of a small rectangular table decorated with white flowers and white candles. Six white cushions were arranged in perfect harmony on each bench.

"If you would take a seat, someone will soon be along to help you."

The receptionist left, shutting the door behind her. A soft, subdued New Age melody began to waft from a small loudspeaker.

"This place is spooky," I said, surveying the empty space.

"What do you mean?"

"Well, you know, I was expecting to find the usual paraphernalia you get in this kind of centre. It's all very sober, dispiriting, if you ask me."

"There's a Buddha in the entrance," retorted Borja.

"Yes, but it's stone and not gilded."

"So what?"

"I'm not sure," I replied, shrugging my shoulders. "Montse's centre is quite different and so colourful…"

The only adornments in that spotless room with white walls and a grey fitted carpet were a standard lamp with a white paper shade, a bonsai by the window and a huge white canvas where black brushstrokes represented what I imagined was an Oriental character. When we'd been sat there for five minutes eyeball to eyeball, the door opened and the same dark-haired girl from reception came in with a tray, two cups, a steaming teapot and a dish of those thin biscuits you find in the slimming section of supermarkets. The teapot and cups were also white.

"Somebody will be with you right away," she said with a saintly smile. "In the meantime, I thought you might like some green tea."

"That's most kind," said Borja.

So as not to be rude, and because Borja gave me a vicious look when he saw I was wondering how much liquid the bonsai soil could take, I drank the tea, which I hate. Five minutes later, the door opened once again and another dark-haired woman appeared wearing black fishnet tights and an off-white smock that barely reached her knees.

"I apologize for keeping you waiting," she began as we stood up, on our best behaviour. "I was saying goodbye to some students. I hope you liked the tea."

"Yes, it was excellent," I lied.

"I am Cecília, the yoga teacher," announced Cecília, shaking our hands. "Maribel told me you wanted information on the activities we have on offer at the centre."

"We need something to fight stress," said Borja, sighing mournfully. "My partner and I thought this might be just the place we are looking for. We have heard nothing but good…"

"Oh, really?" she replied as she sat down and scrutinized our faces. Just like the girl in reception, at first glance she didn't seem to be wearing make-up, but a closer inspection revealed the lightest touch of face cream that worked wonders for her complexion and a lipstick that made her lips glow.

"They say that meditation and yoga are excellent ways to fight stress," I added.

"Indeed, a lot of executives come here to meditate and learn relaxation techniques. Here you have a brochure with information about our services," she said, putting the brochure on the table in front of us. "As well as meditation and yoga, we have a homeopathic consultant and a specialist in Bach flower remedies. And, naturally, the centre offers reiki and shiatsu massages, and we also run short feng shui courses and introductions to Buddhism and Hinduism. You'll find all the information you need here," she said, pointing to the brochure.

Borja picked it up and, on the sly, we took a peek at the prices. Mariona was right: they were executive class.

"Yes, we would be interested in starting meditation," said Borja. "Mind over body and all that…"

"I'm afraid our meditation sessions are full for the moment," she said with a smile. "You'll have to wait several months given the length of our waiting list. I do apologize."

"But we can't wait all that time!" exclaimed Borja, clicking his tongue. "Isn't that right, Eduard?"

I nodded.

"If you give us your details, we'll let you know as soon as —"

"I'd like to say," interjected Borja forcefully, "Mariona Castany, a friend of the centre's director, recommended it. We were hoping to speak to Dr Bou in person."

"Oh, so you know the doctor?" she asked, raising her eyebrows and changing her tone.

"Well, not exactly. But our friend, Mrs Castany, assured us that if we said we came on her recommendation, he would be so kind as to see us."

"If you could wait just a moment," she replied in a voice indicating it was all change.

Cecília shut the door behind her as she left, and we were alone again, accompanied by that tune that was starting to grate on the nerves of a man who preferred the Beatles and the Stones. A few minutes later, she came back to say that Dr Bou was busy leading a meditation group, but if we could wait, he *would* be pleased to see us. She offered us another pot of tea, but Borja and I said we'd rather stretch our legs and would be back in a short while.

We went for a stroll and smoke around the vicinity, and Borja swore to God that one day he'd be wealthy enough to live in one of those fantastic mansions that are still the hallmark of streets that enjoy the privilege of living with their backs turned on the hustle and bustle of the city's cars and crowds. We returned to the meditation centre twenty minutes later and the same pink-uniformed, dark-haired girl showed us back into the same sitting room. On this occasion, we passed a group coming downstairs, their faces radiating bliss. Most were our age and some even older.

"The meditation class has finished and the doctor will be with you right away," the receptionist informed us.

He didn't keep us waiting. At half past six on the dot, the girl was back and asked us to follow her.

"Dr Bou will see you in his office. Please come this way," she said as she pointed us down the corridor.

Borja and I jumped obediently to our feet and followed her. Dr Bou's office was at the end of the corridor and the girl knocked on his door.

"Come in!" boomed a male voice.

I was slightly shocked by the appearance of the man who was getting up to welcome us. After soaking up Zen Moments' state-of-the-art filthy-rich designer atmosphere, I had imagined he would be one of those globetrotting doctors who hawk their wares in bespoke suits, silk ties and a glowing tan. The man before us certainly had the tan but he looked fresh out of an ethnic clothes store. A closer glance revealed it must be the expensive, exclusive kind, because his garb was nothing like the ragged outfits worn by the greying radicals in my neighbourhood who love cheap exotic garments. Dr Bou wore a traditional, cream-coloured Indian kurta, with matching silk embroidery, over straight jeans that could only have been Levi's. His comfortable, brown Clarks made me green with envy because they are shoes I really go for, but I can never find my size when shopping in the sales.

"I hear that Mrs Castany sent you here," he said, vigorously shaking our hands, with a smile as warm as it was fawning.

His teeth were far too white and perfect for someone in his late forties, and he was smooth-shaven. His skin had a slight sheen as if he used one of those moisturizing creams that are now so fashionable with men, and not a hair on his head was out of place, as if he'd just visited the hairdresser's. Neither too short nor too long, and dark brown except for the shock of white hair over his temples. The elegance and symmetry of those silvery temples reminded me of Stewart Granger in *King Solomon's Mines*, his African tan, aristocratic air and equally perfect white teeth.

"I am Borja Masdéu," my brother introduced himself with the swagger that comes with a recommendation from Mariona Castany. "And this is my business partner, Mr Eduard Martínez."

"Pleased to meet you," I responded.

"Mariona said this was just the place we were looking for," continued Borja.

"Oh, really, Mariona… And how is the good lady? We've not seen her for some time."

"You know her. She is busy with her artists, as ever," responded Borja with a shrug of his shoulders, as if to say that Mariona was a hopeless case. One of her recent hobbies was acting as patron to a group of plastic artists, either as an investment or for tax-relief purposes, I imagine. She found it passed the time.

"Do please sit down," said the doctor, pointing to a sofa at the back of the room, no doubt purchased from Vinçon. He sat down in a Fifties-style chair opposite us.

I glanced round as discreetly as I could. Dr Bou's office wasn't as austere and monochromatic as the lobby and waiting room, but it didn't much resemble a doctor's consultancy either. There were no shelves of medical books, although a huge framed poster on one wall displayed a nude man criss-crossed by lines that grew into circles buried under words, letters and figures I couldn't decipher. A couple of Persian rugs, a trio of bonsais and another small Buddha on the desk completed the decor.

"My partner and I are extremely interested in some of the treatments on offer at your centre," began Borja. "We run a think-tank for entrepreneurs that fortunately has yet to be affected by the crisis. Moreover," he added with a smile, "our problem is that we have more work than we can handle and are run off our feet."

"I do understand," responded the doctor laconically.

"It's high time we stepped back and did something for our stress levels before we have a heart attack. And Mariona, who is a peach of a lady, told us that meditation and yoga are the best alternative to conventional medication."

"Mariona is absolutely right. Indeed we only use treatment based on homeopathy and Bach flower remedies, that is, completely natural therapies. Meditation and yoga are pivotal, but sometimes we have patients who need reinforcing, particularly at the beginning. In your case," he swung round slightly and addressed me, "I am sure you have problems with the fifth chakra."

"Oh, really?"

"Have you been putting on weight recently?"

"True enough," I was forced to admit.

In fact, ever since I'd hit forty, to the tune of four pounds a year.

"Weight increase is usually related to stress," the doctor opined. "Your friend, on the other hand, should be worried by the second chakra. My impression is that it is underperforming."

"You can detect that simply by looking?" I asked in good faith.

Dr Bou smiled, rather dismayed. Borja looked at me as if my comment was bad form.

"The problem," Borja continued undeterred, "is that we have just been told we will have to wait several months because the meditation classes are full and there is a waiting list."

"Yes, that's right. We only accept twelve students per session in our yoga and meditation classes. But I imagine," he added with yet another smile, "we might make an exception in the case of friends of Mrs Castany."

"This is fantastic news, because my partner and I must really do something to de-stress *now*." Borja emphasized that "now" with his best north-of-the-Diagonal accent. "So when do you think we might begin?"

"One requisite," said Dr Bou, resting his elbows on the arms of his chair and clasping his hands together, "is participation in one of the weekend 'initiation into meditation' courses we run at the centre. They start on Friday night and finish on Sunday evening. It is a kind of voluntary, what we might call, spiritual confinement."

"You mean we have to sleep here?" I asked. I wasn't exactly thrilled at the idea of spending a couple of nights in these surroundings.

"Yes, we have bedrooms for residents on the third floor. It is the best possible start, an immediate cleansing of body and mind. In fact, many of our clients come back and repeat the experience. You'll see how gratifying it is."

"We'll do whatever you advise us, doctor," rejoined Borja. "We're placing ourselves in your hands."

"Please, don't stand on ceremony. Call me Horaci," he asked, beaming a huge smile at us. He immediately went to his desk and picked up the phone. "Just let me have a word with Maribel to see how we stand."

A couple of minutes later, the girl from reception walked in without knocking and carrying a black A4 diary.

"We've got two rooms free this weekend," she said, pointing at one of the pages. "Then we're full up until the end of June."

"This weekend would be perfect, wouldn't it, Eduard?"

"Yes, I suppose it would…"

"So you're all set," concluded the doctor, inviting us to leave. "You'll be our guests over this weekend. And I must say goodbye for now because I'm late for a yoga session. If you would be so kind as to accompany Maribel, she will tell you all you need to know."

"Thank you, Horaci," replied Borja, shaking his hand. "My partner and I are most grateful to you."

"See you Friday then."

The word "guests" that Dr Bou had used to refer to our weekend stay at Zen Moments was what you would call a euphemism, because enrolment cost a handsome two thousand euros per head. That sum, Maribel informed us, must be paid in full upon arrival. On the other hand, the instructions were simplicity itself: we only had to bring pyjamas (optional) and a couple of changes of underwear, because the centre, the girl explained, would supply comfortable clothing. During our stay we couldn't use mobiles or any electronic gadget, but we could give the centre's telephone number to family in case any emergency arose.

"You do realize we can't go, don't you?" I told Borja the moment we were in the street.

"Why?"

"Because this little escapade costs four thousand euros that we don't happen to have!"

"Teresa Solana will pay, don't you worry," answered Borja, shrugging his shoulders.

"Yes, but she's not around. And she might find it on the expensive side. Four thousand euros, I ask you!"

"Nah, it could be worse. Besides, I like the look of this place."

"What *exactly* do you like the look of?"

"Didn't you notice the aroma of wealth given off by the people we passed in the corridor? We are bound to make good contacts for the future here."

"I repeat that we do *not* have four thousand euros."

"I know. I'll have to ask Merche for another handout," he sighed. And he put his hand into his pocket and added, "That means I can't dine with Lola tonight."

Borja hurriedly took out his mobile and rang my sister-in-law.

"Please, do at least try to make your excuse sound plausible," I hissed.

9

On Thursday morning, Borja rang to say he was going to his hairstylist's (his blond highlights needed retouching) and would be attending the launch of some exhibition or other in the evening. That meant I had the day free and, as I was curious to learn more about the treatments and therapies on offer at Dr Bou's centre, I decided to use my time to do research on the twins' computer and give the flat a bit of a pre-weekend clean. Given that tomorrow I'd be off for the weekend and that at breakfast Montse seemed to think my stay at the meditation centre was tantamount to dereliction of family duties, I thought it would be a good idea to go to the Llibertat market, buy an anglerfish and cook her a tasty supper. However, anglerfish was priced sky high and in the end I bought sardines. Fried with garlic and parsley, and accompanied by a good salad, that would also do the job.

Montse appreciated the gesture and was even more understanding at supper time: clearly the sight of me at the sink, gutting sardines, cutting heads off and removing bones warmed the cockles of her heart. For my part, I had no desire to spend three days practising spiritual exercises surrounded by strangers and attending talks on the mysteries of chakras or the therapeutic virtues of Bach flower remedies, especially as Barça was playing

València on Saturday and I imagined the centre didn't have a TV. At half past twelve, with the twins, Arnau and Joana in bed, I suggested to Montse that we should open a bottle of cava.

"We drank wine at lunch. We'll have hangovers in the morning," she remarked, heading to the kitchen to collect the bottle and a couple of glasses.

"No worries. I'm going to spend the weekend drinking tasteless tea and eating tofu hamburgers."

"A spot of diet will do you good. Apart from getting dinner, what have you got up to today?" she asked, handing me the bottle of cava to open.

"I've been researching homeopathy and Bach flower remedies."

"And did you reach any conclusions?"

"I think your mother was right. They are taking the piss, whatever Lola might say."

"To be candid, a couple of months ago I'd have agreed with my sister, but after what happened to the Rosselló boy I'm not so sure. Luckily, in the end, his mother backed down and took the kid to hospital…"

"You know they sell homeopathy and Bach flower remedies as alternative medicines to the conventional sort without any kind of scientific proof they really work," I said, pouring out the cava and getting into my stride. "They're based on a whole set of beliefs and premises that are centuries old and have been overtaken by scientific discoveries."

"But homeopathy is taught in our faculties of medicine," replied Montse, filling her glass. "In the United Kingdom, homeopathic hospitals are part of the public health system. And none other than Prince Charles is a big fan…"

"Come on, love, the fact you are a prince doesn't automatically make you an expert on the subject. And he doesn't exactly have a reputation for being a brainbox…

Really," I added on a more serious note, "most scientists are adamant there is no basis in science to justify the claims of homeopathy and, if you think about it for a second, you'll see it's a simple matter of common sense."

"What do you mean?" asked Montse, sipping her cava.

"Homeopaths believe that the more often you dissolve an active principle in water and shake it, the more powerful the resulting medicine is. However, the fact is that when you dissolve a substance in water several times, let alone the exaggerated number of times they do it in homeopathic preparations, the substance that is theoretically supposed to cure you has in fact disappeared."

"How can you be so sure?"

"We know that any substance has a finite number of molecules. It's known as Avogadro's law," I replied, sipping more of the cava that always lubricated our late-night debates.

"Sounds familiar."

"Consequently, if you dissolve a substance a lot, the moment comes when it ceases to exist as a substance. It's simply not there any more."

"So how do the homeopathic people justify themselves?"

"Now, we come to the best bit of all. They believe that water has a memory that preserves the properties of the substances that are dissolved in it."

"And is that possible?"

"Scientific experiments carried out in laboratory conditions say it isn't. The theory that water has powers of memory is bullshit."

"It's incredible."

"It's the same with Bach flower remedies," I continued. "No rational criteria exist to prove the effectiveness of preparations based on steeping wild flowers from a region in Wales in watered-down brandy."

"So what is it all about then? A money-making exercise?"

"I don't know," I said, shrugging my shoulders. "I imagine a little bit of everything. People who believe in the stuff in good faith, like Lola, and people who earn thousands from it."

"You know what?" asked Montse, refilling her glass with a smile that suggested we'd not just be going to bed simply to sleep that night, "I think we'd better drink the cava before its molecules dissolve and no longer have any impact on us."

Montse was right: we got up with a headache. After I'd taken Arnau to school, I came home, took an ibuprofen and stretched out in bed again. When I woke up, it was almost midday, and even though the headache had gone, I still felt groggy. In a spirit of dutiful resignation, I showered, then packed pyjamas and underwear in a bag and went out. Borja had insisted on inviting me to lunch to compensate for all the times he invited himself to our place, and I didn't want to ring him and make an excuse. We had to be at Dr Bou's centre by five, and the plan was to have lunch, grab our bags and head there.

"There's a restaurant near here with an excellent set lunch," he said, hardly hiding the fact that he was euphoric. "We can leave our bags in the flat and collect them after-wards."

"So Merche handed over the four thousand euros, no questions asked?"

"Well, I'd hardly say she didn't ask any questions... But this time I did promise to return them."

I left my bag at Borja's and we went off. As soon as we stepped out, we saw it was drizzling, but, as the restaurant was only a couple of streets down from where my brother lives, we didn't bother to go back to the flat for our um-brellas. We hadn't gone twenty metres when a complete stranger wearing huge sunglasses stood in front of us and blocked our path.

"You *are* Mr Masdéu, aren't you?" she whispered, addressing my brother.

"That depends," replied Borja, smiling sweetly.

"Carry on walking. We don't have a lot of time," said the stranger, looking all around and breaking into a brisk walk next to Borja. "They might be trailing me."

"I'm sorry, but you are?…"

"What business of yours is that? You have something that doesn't belong to you," she continued.

She was thin, average height, with dark hair that was cut pageboy style. She was dressed so as not to draw attention to herself, but even so couldn't hide the fact she was svelte and shapely. The small area of her face her rain-splashed glasses allowed a glimpse of was youthful and soft-skinned, and her small nose and highly sensual lips gave me a hard-on. I didn't register this at a first glance, but I am almost definite she was wearing a wig.

"Yes, I think I know what you are referring to," Borja snapped, winking. "But must we really keep walking?"

"I told you they are probably following me. It's dangerous."

"Dangerous?" Borja stopped dead in his tracks. "Hey, nobody ever said anything about —"

"I've come to give you this." She took a mobile phone from her pocket and gave it to Borja. "And to say that someone will be contacting you. Be prepared…"

"Be prepared? But you just listen, I —"

"I must be off. Don't try to pull a fast one, or you will regret it."

And she left us gawping into space, rushed across the street, and left in her wake a trail of scent and mystery until she vanished from sight.

*

"Dangerous! She said it was dangerous," I yelped, forgetting I was screaming at Borja in the middle of the street. "And who the hell is she?"

"I don't know. My contact for the business over that statue, I expect. But I don't understand why she gave me this mobile, if they already have my number," my brother mumbled, not bothering to hide that he, too, was bemused.

"And that damned stone statuette is in my home!" I growled.

"I'm sorry, bro. I didn't think that... But don't you worry. They don't know you've got it. They can't possibly know."

"And who are *they*? If you don't mind!"

"I don't have a clue. The antique dealer in Amsterdam said it would all be very straightforward: a person would contact me via my mobile and give me a time to hand over the statue. There must have been a change of plan."

"Well, you'd better phone him and find out what the hell is going on!"

"It doesn't work like that. He contacts me. I don't have a way of ringing him."

"You've got to find another hiding place, Pep. I don't want that statue in my house."

"Quite right," he replied. "I'll drop by your place on Sunday night when we leave the meditation centre and take it with me."

"And where will you hide it?"

"In my flat, I suppose. At least, until I can think of somewhere better..."

"Do you know what? I have just lost the little appetite I had."

"Me too."

Even so, we had lunch in the restaurant. Borja gradually recovered his sangfroid and by the time the second course had arrived he had convinced me it was all a wheeze to frighten him and prepare the ground to pay him less money than he'd agreed with the antiquarian. While we were drinking our coffees, he took the mobile out and put it on the table.

"It's not what you'd call the latest model, is it?" he remarked with a smile. In fact, I hadn't seen a model like that in a long, long time.

"So what are we going to do?"

"Nothing much. Wait for them to call," Borja replied, shrugging his shoulders.

"But mobiles are banned from the meditation centre," I retorted. "I left mine at home…"

"You're a real baby! I don't expect you can smoke either, but I don't intend going three days without a smoke."

"And what if they catch you?"

"Eduard, we're big boys now. This chakra and cosmic-harmony business is baloney to soak the rich, can't you see that? And what's more, we're going of our free will and paying a fortune for the ride. I intend on smoking the odd cigarette. Whatever they may say," he added, shrugging his shoulders yet again.

"Know what? I'll be back in a second," I said, getting up from the table. "I'm off to buy a packet of cigarettes."

PART II

Alícia Cendra had long since given up trying to pick up boyfriends in bars. That was the past. Now she was about to hit fifty, the only men who approached with a saucy glint in their eyes when they spotted her sitting with only a glass for company were solitary seventy-year-olds with the stink of alcohol on their breath and a box of Viagra in their pocket. She no longer interested men, or at least the ones she fancied, so no need to lose any sleep over it. As the women's magazines that she read at work or the hairdresser's explained, she had simply become invisible. The hint of cellulite her clothes revealed and the incipient crow's feet no cream could erase disabled her from competing against the skinny, soft-fleshed bodies of the young girls who marked out the night-time territory to the lilt of the latest hit song. No, picking men up in bars was no longer an option for her. She had gradually been forced to resign herself to that sad fact.

Winning the love of a man was a slow, painstaking task in this new pre-menopausal stage in her life. A long-term project that required time, patience and hours in the beauty parlour and, above all, planning. Alícia Cendra had assumed by now that going out at night in the hope of coming across a second Prince Charming – her first had been the husband who'd abandoned her for one of those silly young things – meant coming home drunk and depressed, and, worst of all, alone. Consequently, on the rare occasions when she did go to a bar for a drink, she did so without high hopes, only to sip one of her favourite cocktails, and, jostled by a noisy crowd, she would fantasize secretly about the man who had recently become the great love of her life, Dr Horaci Bou.

When she left the cinema that night, she decided to go to the Dry Martini for a drink before going to bed. She felt like a margarita. Nobody was expecting her home, apart from her cat, and, even though she'd have to be up early in the morning to go to work, it wasn't that late. Now spring was in the air and longer days were here, she found home oppressive. She had few women friends, and those she did still have had husbands and better things to do on a Thursday night than go out with a divorcee who lived absorbed in a very different mental world. Alícia's friends felt envy rather than pity. They imagined her childless and without commitments, happily enjoying a life that was beyond their reach as married women.

Reality was somewhat different. True enough she entered and departed relationships without having to explain herself to anybody, but at the end of the day she couldn't get used to living by herself. The silence that dominated her flat, a silence too eloquent to be broken by the sound of television or radio, overwhelmed her and translated into attacks of anguish Alícia fought off by frequent visits to her refrigerator and bouts of cleaning that wiped her out. But she could hardly tell her girlfriends that, because she felt that if she confessed she couldn't stand so much freedom they'd think she wasn't a modern woman and would phone her even less.

Dr Bou had been a stroke of luck, and for some time he'd been the focus of her nocturnal fantasies and kept her brain busy with romantic dreams during the day. Dr Bou, the man known to her and the rest of his patients simply as Horaci, was her therapist, the man dedicated to healing her body and soul in this new and crucial stage of her life. She had met him through Abril, a work colleague on a six-month temporary contract, who was always buttering her up in the hope it would be made permanent, because Alícia was administrative head of the department where they worked. Abril was hooked on alternative therapies and always singing the praises of the centre for meditation that Dr Bou ran in Sarrià and all things you could learn there. One afternoon, they both went there after finishing at the office. It was a turning point in Alícia's life.

Dr Bou inspected her chakras and solemnly stated, with the hint of a smile on his lips, that her second chakra, Svadhisthana, wasn't working harmoniously, and her seventh, the Sahasrara, was totally gummed up. As she hadn't a clue what chakras were, the doctor embarked on a long explanation of how these were the body's centres of energy, according to Vedic philosophy, and how, consequently, people's physical and mental well-being depended on them working properly. Yoga and meditation, Oriental disciplines that went back thousands of years, would help her re-establish the proper functioning of her chakras, or so he said. What's more, if she applied the principles of feng shui to the arrangement of her furniture at home, principles Abril had mentioned to her more than once, she'd corral positive energies and block out negative ones. They held short beginners' courses in the centre and the results were spectacular, the doctor assured her, dazzling her with his dentist's smile.

Alícia left the centre in a spin. Apart from being charming, Horaci was sensitive and handsome. Beneath long eyelashes, his dark myopic eyes radiated magnetic power saturated with a mystical allure she found hypnotic and difficult to shake off. She immediately felt drawn to him and without a second thought signed up to the Zen Moments meditation centre and became a devoted pupil of Dr Horaci Bou.

Horaci was personally responsible for the meditation classes, and Alícia was quick to turn him into the second love of her life. An impossible love, like all great loves, because the doctor was married and, as he confessed to her one day, he remained faithful to his wife. As she was so in love with him, Alícia was always at a loss to know what to say, and, whenever she opened her mouth, she realized what a fool she must seem. Nevertheless, one day when she'd stocked up on red wine at the supermarket and on incense and candles at the ethnic products shop, she found the strength to invite him to her flat with a view to seduction. However, her plan was thwarted.

Dr Bou turned down her invitation in a highly intelligent manner. He apologized, saying that his marriage was going through a rocky patch and he wasn't sure he could survive the test of spending an evening alone with such an attractive, sensitive woman as her without falling in love. In truth, he sweetly snubbed Alícia with his flattery, but from that day on, as his words had half-opened the door of hope, she kept fantasizing about a mortal illness or timely accident that would remove his wife from the scene and turn her dream of becoming the second Mrs Bou into a reality.

She had taken the first sip of her margarita when she saw him sitting at a table at the back of the bar. He wasn't alone and she wasn't his wife, whom Alícia knew. Even so, it wasn't difficult to see that the emotional intimacy between this woman and Bou had been spawned in bed: his hand on her thigh, his passionate looks, the words he whispered in her ear. Alícia gulped down her margarita and asked the waiter for another, feeling her voice shake and her cheeks redden.

Horaci had deceived her. He hadn't rejected her because he wanted to remain faithful to his wife, as he'd said, but because he already had his bit on the side. The rumours that were rife in the centre were true. And this other woman, the object of his attentions, was no youngster with a lithe, supple body, but a woman her age, and nothing out of the ordinary. That made her even more furious. What did that bitch have that she didn't? More class? More cash, perhaps? She knocked back her margarita, asked for the bill and walked out of the bar with a broken heart, blurry eyes and a snotty nose.

Once in the taxi she started to wrestle with an idea. By the time she opened the door to her flat, she had reached a decision. That was it. The time had come to give up, to accept she'd never find a man with whom it was worth the turmoil of falling in love, that she would never be happy again. The most she could hope for at her age was to grow old eating ice cream and drinking vodka in front of the TV, like the woman in that film. Faced by such an unappetizing future, she might as well end it. It was time to bring the curtain down.

She went to the chemist's and bought the pills, then opened a bottle of vintage Rioja and put an opera on her CD player at home. She didn't really like the opera but she felt *La bohème* was a more appropriate soundtrack to suicide than Julio Iglesias, her favourite crooner. She sat on her sofa, took her shoes off and started stuffing pills, washing them down with Rioja. There were almost two hundred, in small bottles, and it took her some time to empty them. Luckily, they were small and easy to swallow.

At around two a.m., after seeing off the Rioja and starting on a Penedés, expecting death through overdosing on homeopathic pills at any moment, she got terrible stomach ache. She felt the need to vomit and shit all at the same time, but, as she was drunk and her head was in a spin, she didn't make it to the bathroom in time. Prostrate on the floor in the hallway in her flat, she realized the light had gone out on the theatrical scene she had been imagining. The forensic investigator would find a pathetic, drunken fifty-year-old swimming in her own sick and shit in the hallway at home, and that would be the only thing that everyone, Horaci included, would mention at her funeral.

Feeling miserably sick, she managed to reach the phone and ring a girlfriend for help. Half an hour later, an ambulance was rushing her to the emergency ward at the Sant Pau hospital, its siren wailing away. The results of the tests they did showed that the vomit and diarrhoea were caused by alcohol and the huge bag of sweets she'd crunched at the cinema. The two hundred homeopathic pills had made no impact whatsoever. The doctor who saw her didn't take her attempted suicide at all seriously.

"By the way," she told her as she signed her discharge form, "I'll give you a prescription for an ointment to cure mange. You should use it over the course of three days."

"Mange?" exclaimed Alícia, totally at a loss. "What *are* you talking about? Those blotches are brought on by a psychosomatic illness!" And as she ran her eyes over the red patches on her arms and legs, she added, "Don't you see? It's nerves."

"No way!" retorted her doctor, shaking her head. "It's mange. We've had a few outbreaks recently. But no need to worry: use this ointment and give your sheets a good wash. It'll all be gone in three days."

Alícia had been suffering from blotchy skin and itches all over her body for over seven months. Horaci had examined them and assured her that they were stress-related, and would disappear as soon as balance was restored to her chakras. That was when he had prescribed those homeopathic pills – six a day – that she'd used in her attempted suicide. The doctor couldn't have been so far out in his diagnosis.

"Hey, I can't possibly have mange," she insisted, choked and deeply embarrassed. "Do you think I'm some dirty slut living like a down-and-out? You could damned well eat your dinner off the floor in my flat!"

"That's neither here nor there," replied the doctor as she signed the prescription. "You could have caught it anywhere you've been in contact with someone who's got it. Do you go to a gym?"

No, Alícia did not go to a gym, but all of a sudden she remembered the grey fitted carpet where they did their yoga exercises and the itching Pietat, a fellow pupil at the centre, was always complaining about. Horaci had also told her it was stress and prescribed the same pills, though they didn't seem to make any impact on her either.

She thanked the doctor and got up from the bunk. What if that young doctor was right and the problem that had been torturing her for months could be solved in three days by applying an ointment? And what if that whole chakra scene was simply stuff and nonsense? Her head still in a spin, she took off the hospital gown, put on the dirty clothes she had been wearing on admission and left her little cubicle in a state of shock. As she walked through the emergency ward, her brain kept buzzing. How could she have been so gullible? Why hadn't she listened to what everyone had told her and gone to see the dermatologist in the local medical centre?

She left the hospital half sleepwalking on the arm of her friend. What with the hangover and the diazepam she'd been given to fight off her next attack of anguish, the world had become a very confused place. However, inside her head, a word started to ring as forcefully as those absurd mantras she had to learn at the meditation centre. Her friend tried to calm her, but she didn't feel like chatting and, in the end, they walked to her place in complete silence. Once in her flat, she showered and let her friend prepare a cup of camomile tea and put her to bed.

"I feel much better. But I'm tired and need some sleep," she told her. "You go, and don't worry about me."

The fact is Alícia simply wanted to be alone. She had a lot to think about and a new reason for living: she wanted to make Horaci pay for the ridiculous farce she'd been part of during all those months. What was it people said? That vengeance was a dish best served cold? Hot or cold, Dr Bou would regret all his lies and hypocritical smiles, his sugary pills and gross incompetence. If it was the last thing she did, she would find a way to wreak her revenge on that man who'd made a real fool of her by taking advantage of her ignorance and trust.

So what if she was then reincarnated as a beetle.

10

After lunch we went back to Borja's flat to pick up our bags and go to Zen Moments. When we walked into the meditation centre we found four people in the queue at reception. In front of us were a pair in their late twenties, who seemed to be friends because they were so deep in conversation, a very courteous, silver-haired, well-preserved gentleman who immediately caught Borja's eye, and a woman around the fifty mark carrying a bag that looked on the big side if it only contained the pyjamas and two changes of underwear we'd been instructed to bring. In the meantime, people kept entering and leaving the building; some who walked past had just had a shower and their hair was still damp.

Borja and I stood and waited in the lobby. When it was our turn, the receptionist handed us forms where we had to provide our details while they collected the two thousand euros per head that the weekend cost and gave us our room keys. Unlike the people in front of us, who paid with their credit cards, Borja and I were forced to pay in cash, a wad of notes, and that was thanks to the generous loan Merche had granted us from her providential reserves. Once the red tape was dealt with, a lad who looked like a university student, in a sky-blue uniform like the pastel-pink one worn by the girl in reception, asked us to go with him into the lift.

The residents' bedrooms were on the third floor where, as Alex, a student of journalism, explained, we would also find the kitchen and dining room where we would eat our meals. There were a total of twelve single rooms with windows overlooking the garden. Borja was in number four, and I was next to him in number three, towards the back of the building. They weren't what you would call big, but were spotlessly clean, and each had an en suite bathroom. The walls were painted white and there was a futon under an equally white duvet cover. The fitted carpet was grey, a lighter grey than the carpet in the corridors and lobby. The final decorative touches were a bunch of candles and incense holders, a standard lamp with a parchment shade and a framed poster of a Hindu deity who brought the only hint of colour to the bedroom.

Alex said we should put on the clothes we'd find in the wardrobe, where there were also a dressing gown, bath towels and bathroom slippers. He asked us for our shoe size and said he'd be back straight away.

"Well, it's not exactly a five-star hotel," grumbled Borja, giving the room the once-over and seeing, much to his annoyance, that there was no bath in the bathroom. "No minibar, no TV, no jacuzzi... I hope at least we get the occasional massage!"

"I doubt it. We've come to meditate, not luxuriate, if you remember."

"Well, the grub had better be tasty!" he sighed.

A couple of minutes later, Alex came back with two plastic bags containing two pairs of new slippers, the kind gymnasts use, in a cheap brand.

"You're expected in the meditation room at six thirty for the welcoming session. On the second floor," he informed us.

"How come you work here?" Borja asked, giving him a ten-euro tip.

"No, please…" he protested, not sure what to do with the note. "You know, this really isn't a hotel."

"Take it," Borja insisted. "Do you come here to meditate as well?"

"Not really. I earn a bit helping out on the weekends when they have residents. That way I can afford to go to the Faculty during the week."

"Sounds good. It's very important to study and be equipped for life. The contacts you make there come in very…" my brother remarked sententiously. The lad smiled, thanked him and pocketed the note.

The moment he left, Borja asked me into his room and shut the door. He went over to the window, opened it, lit a cigarette and offered me one.

"Pep, they'll catch us," I said, refusing.

"Nah, there are no smoke detectors in the ceiling. Besides," he added, glancing through the window, "nobody's in the garden at the moment. And look," he pointed to one of the windows to our left, "I'm not the only smoker."

True enough. At the very least smoke was coming out of one other window. In any case, as breaking rules stresses me out, I decided to go to my room and change and leave Borja to savour his clandestine cigarette.

The comfortable clothing we had to change into consisted of a white kimono, the kind judoka and karateka wear, with a belt round the waist that, in this instance, was grey. There were three identical changes in the wardrobe, one for each day. I wondered how they got the right size and guessed it was down to the receptionist's sharp eye.

As the room had no table or chair, I sat on the futon to while away the time. I have never liked this kind of bed that is so very uncomfortable to sit on: it was like sitting on the ground. Finally, I got up and opened the window to let in the evening sun. Birds were singing.

I decided to kill time by revisiting my morning shave and brushing my teeth. When it was twenty past, Borja knocked on my door and we both went down the stairs to the second floor. We immediately saw a large room, its doors open, full of people dressed exactly like ourselves. Next to the door, a sign indicated we were in the Samsara Room.

As we walked in, we both said, "Good evening."

It was a large, rectangular room, the sole decoration being the views of the garden through the glass wall. They had set out a table with drinks and food at the back of the room. Borja and I soon spotted the elderly man we'd seen in reception, the two young women – now chatting to two men at least twenty years older than they were – Alex, the yoga teacher and Horaci, who was talking to a middle-aged couple. Everyone was conversing very quietly and it was impossible to hear what they were saying. The woman with the big bag we'd bumped into in reception arrived just after us and headed straight for the food table.

Alex came over and asked if we were hungry. We saw that everybody was holding a cup or a glass, so, to join in the spirit of the occasion, I asked for juice and Borja, tea. I nibbled one of the pastries that were exquisitely arranged on a designer plate, but it was tasteless and difficult to swallow. As I'd taken a bite and didn't know what to do with it, I hid it discreetly under the plate.

"Ah, welcome, Borja and Eduard," Horaci greeted us. "Do come and let me introduce you to Bernat, our Bach flower remedies specialist."

We followed him across the room.

"Bernat, please meet Borja and Eduard. They have stress-related problems and want to start meditation," the doctor explained, smiling.

"Delighted to meet you," Bernat shook our hands. "You've come to the right place."

"I've heard that Bach flower remedies are just the thing for fighting stress," I replied, opening the conversation. "You recommend them, I believe, sir?"

"Forget the 'sir'," Horaci grinned. "We're all friends here, aren't we, Bernat?"

"Yes," Bernat responded curtly. He was a good ten years younger than Horaci and displayed the same glowing tan.

"Now you can get to know your fellow residents this weekend," said Horaci, glancing around the room to check everybody had arrived. "We can start as soon as we're all here."

I felt slightly ridiculous dressed like that, surrounded by people in the same karate outfit, though, true enough, it was comfortable. On the other hand, only residents wore kimonos: Horaci was in a sky-blue kurta and Cecília, the yoga teacher, a very pretty pumpkin-coloured sari over a red silk T-shirt and trousers. The Bach flower remedies doctor was the only person in western dress, jeans and a short-sleeved apple-green shirt that reminded me of some Borja kept in his wardrobe. Everyone was wearing the same gym slippers, so as not to dirty the carpet, I imagine.

"Would you please sit round in a circle so we can begin introductions," said Cecília with a smile, raising her voice so we could all hear.

Everyone quickly put their cups and glasses down and imitated Cecília, who sat on the floor in the lotus position. I tried, but couldn't, and finally adopted what was a painfully contorted posture. The journalism student left the room, shutting the door behind him. Horaci and Bernat also sat down next to each other.

"Ladies and gentlemen, a very big welcome to you all," Horaci began. "It's a pleasure to have you here with us."

After formally introducing Bernat and Cecília, who, according to him, were highly experienced and qualified, he embarked on a little speech about the aims of these weekend stays at Zen Moments and how all participants thoroughly enjoyed them. As if revealing a deeply personal secret, he told us how he'd first taken an interest in meditation and homeopathy after studying in the faculty of medicine and discovering that the pharmaceutical industry was one big confidence trick. While some participants nodded their heads in approval, he asked us to introduce ourselves with first names only and any other information we thought relevant.

The elderly, silver-haired gentleman went first. He'd sat next to Horaci and, unlike me, had assumed the lotus position with no problems at all.

"I'm Sebastià, seventy-two years old and a sculptor," he announced, raising his chin. "I've had a lifelong interest in philosophy from the Orient."

"I'm Marta, and I'm twenty-nine," continued the girl next to him. "I've just separated and feel quite devastated."

"I'm Mònica, and Marta and I are childhood friends. I am an infant teacher and have been practising yoga for years, but I persuaded Marta to come here this weekend and experience for herself the benefits of meditation, and see whether it will help her over the bad time she's experiencing at the moment."

Of all the women in the room, Mònica was the most made-up, with the smartest hairdo.

It was Borja's turn next.

"I'm Borja, I'm forty-five and a business consultant. I'm here because of work-induced stress, naturally," he said smiling. Everyone laughed politely.

"I'm Eduard Martínez, and I am Borja's partner… And I'm also rather stressed out. And forty-five and married," I added to avoid any misunderstandings.

"Very good," said Horaci. "Next one, please."

The woman next to me was the sourpuss with the big bag.

"I'm Alícia, and I have been a pupil at this centre for more than a year. This isn't the first time I've participated in these encounters, is it, Horaci? I am sure this weekend will be particularly fascinating," she added in a tone that suggested a hidden agenda.

"Thank you, Alícia. It's fantastic to have you back," commented Horaci with a condescending smile that reminded me of the Jesuits at the school Borja and I attended as kids.

"I'm Xavier and I'm here because of the wife," scowled the man sitting next to Alícia.

"My husband is an entrepreneur," said his wife, seated next to him, with a smile. "Hello, I am Carme. I've also been coming to Zen Moments for some time to meditate. I wanted my husband to see what it's like, as he's not really into this kind of —"

"Well, I have come, haven't I?" retorted her husband.

"I was only telling them…"

"You don't need to tell them anything."

Cecília interjected subtly to stop what was threatening to turn into a marital squabble. Those two needed therapy for couples rather than meditation classes.

"We'd better continue," suggested Cecília affably.

"I'm Ernest, and I'm forty-eight. I work for an NGO with several ongoing projects in India."

"I'm Carles, and I'm an engineer," said the man sitting on his right. "I'm fifty-seven and like sport and anything connected to nature."

"I'm Valèria…" declared the woman sitting next to Carles, smiling broadly, "and there's no way I'm going to say how old I am!" There were titters all round. "No, seriously, I became a widow seven years ago, I went to India and my life changed. I've been practising meditation ever since."

That left one person, a redhead around fifty, who looked sickly, and didn't seem quite all there.

"I'm Isabel, I'm fifty and suffering from cancer. But I don't want any medical treatment because I don't trust conventional medicine," she added in a tone that suggested she considered herself a superior being.

Borja and I looked at each other askance as an uncomfortable silence fell over the room. Horaci immediately spoke.

"Thank you for that, Isabel. I am sure you will win through," he said gently. "Now we all know each other, I suggest you look at the programme Cecília is about to hand out."

Cecília dutifully got up and fetched sheets of paper that listed the activities we would be carrying out over the next three days. After giving them out she sat down next to Bernat again.

"As you can see," continued Horaci, "we will start today with a lecture on the relationship between yoga and meditation. Then we will have dinner and you can get to know each other better. All the activities will take place in this room, or in the garden, if the weather is good. The Nirvana Room has been arranged in a way to help you to chat comfortably after dinner. But I will let Cecília take over at this point. She will be with you over the three days and will stay and sleep in the centre, and she will now go through the rest of the programme. If you have any doubts or problems, please refer them to her."

The vaunted programme comprised lectures, meditation sessions, yoga classes, yet more lectures and tea breaks. Breakfast was at eight thirty, lunch at one and dinner at eight. No massages whatsoever.

"Before Cecília's interesting talk that will open our programme, I would like to invite you to drink a cup of red tea that will help clear the poison out of your system," said the doctor. "We'll meet again at dinner."

Horaci left the room, followed by Bernat, and Alex took the opportunity to come in and pour us the red beverage. Some participants had a second cup, and Borja rather overdid the praise. I left mine untouched in its white china.

We had to sit back in a circle in the same lotus positions. When Cecília saw I was in difficulties, she kindly came over to show me what to do. I didn't dare tell her I thought the posture was uncomfortable and tried to brave it out, but in the end my leg went to sleep and I had to shift it. Xavier, who was sitting next to me, smiled sympathetically.

The lecture was interesting enough, although on the long side for my taste. I became aware of a whole raft of things I never knew, for example, how dogs can practise yoga now, and how, thanks to yoga, you can make love for eight hours on end every day, as Sting claims he does. In my case, I couldn't imagine Montse devoting eight hours a day to a lot of what you fancy, and, from the looks of panic on the faces of the women there, I don't think they were exactly bowled over by the idea either.

At seven forty-five Cecília looked at her watch and asked if there were any questions, but there were none because we all wanted to rush to the loo to piss out that tea; we applauded politely and stood up. As dinner was at eight, we had just enough time to go to our rooms before going to the dining room. A mobile phone rang in a room that wasn't my brother's.

"We'd better spread ourselves around a bit and talk to the participants, and see if we can find any material for Teresa Solana's novel," Borja whispered to me as we went upstairs.

The dining room was immediately opposite the meditation room, on the other side of the corridor, and was a rectangular room with one very long table with chairs on both sides. At the back, there were trays of food on a counter behind which one caught a glimpse of a small

111

kitchen. The menu was vegetarian and it was self-service, with a very limited range of cold and hot dishes that looked as if they had been brought in by a catering firm. There was organic rice with lentils, organic spaghetti, spinach and soya salad, boiled beans, tofu hamburgers and vegetable sausages. Desserts were a couple of trays of fruit and the usual non-fat yoghurts. All washed down with juices or water.

Everyone took a tray and helped themselves to what they liked. I decided to try the spinach salad and organic spaghetti; I didn't like it one bit. I sat down next to Alícia (or, more accurately, she decided to sit next to me), with the young schoolteacher on the other side; opposite were the married couple, Xavier and Carme. For his part, Borja chose to sit next to the young woman who had just separated, and Valèria sat next to him on the other side. Horaci arrived late and sat at one end of the table next to Isabel, and selected a salad of soya sprouts, beans and sausages.

Everyone said it was very good and some even went back for seconds. The moment one of the two girlfriends got up to get a dessert, I hurried behind her to grab a banana, apple or yoghurt before they ran out. The bananas and yoghurts soon disappeared, but the rice and lentil salad had no takers. The fact is they looked most unappetizing.

Alícia, my table companion, also seemed very half-hearted. She seemed anxious and miles away, and barely nibbled the minuscule rations they doled out. Though she was talkative at first – she told me she worked at the town hall in Sarrià, and was a civil servant and divorced – the moment I said I was happily married with three children, she lost interest in me and spent what was left of supper chattering to Ernest, who worked for an NGO, and to the engineer. The married couple opposite were so busy quarrelling that it was impossible to have a conversation with them.

Shortly after nine o'clock we left our trays on the counter and Iolanda, the girl who saw to cleaning and supplies, started tidying the dining room as we headed towards the Nirvana Room.

Cecília and Horaci accompanied us, but Horaci immediately excused himself, saying he had to leave and that he'd be back in the morning. Bernat, who looked more like a rich boy whose worries were financial rather than spiritual, hadn't even stayed for supper.

"I reckon poor Cecília is the only worker here," commented Borja quietly.

"I'll try to get her to come and talk to me while you try to talk to Alícia. I get the feeling she knows how this place is run."

"Thank you very much, but I talked to her during dinner. And she lost interest as soon I mentioned I was married. If you like, I'll give the married couple a spin; the wife's also been a customer here for a long time. Let's see what she has to say."

The Nirvana Room lived up to its name, because, like the Samsara, it was simply an empty room. Cushions were scattered over the floor and everybody sat down on a cushion and soon made a little group. However, no one seemed interested in talking to Isabel, the woman with cancer, but Cecília sat next to her and did start talking to her.

It was all very strained, and, without the necessary protein to digest, or alcohol to help us lose our inhibitions, the conversations soon began to founder. Indeed, that was really what it was all about; as Cecília had explained, one meaning of "nirvana" is "to be extinguished". Only Borja and elderly, silver-haired Sebastià seemed to have anything to say to each other. At eleven thirty, most decided to call it a day and go to their bedrooms. The only ones who stayed on were the young women who were friends and Ernest and Carles, who turned out to be an item.

Borja and Sebastià came over to me and announced they were going into the garden for a smoke. I was still rather hungover and tired, particularly of listening and talking, and I decided to do what Borja had done: I would open a bedroom window and have a quiet smoke by myself. I really felt like a spot of TV, but had to make do with making a start on Teresa Solana's novel that Montse had stuffed in my bag. However, the bed wasn't designed for reading, and I developed backache after half an hour and decided to switch off the light and try to sleep. It wasn't easy: my hungry stomach kept rumbling, I was missing Montse and couldn't get the sensual lips of that mysterious young woman who had accosted us in the street with her strange foreign accent out of my mind. When I did finally drift into a deep sleep, the light of dawn was shining through the window and the skylarks were singing.

11

It was a struggle to get up in the morning after such a bad night's sleep. I didn't make an appearance in the dining room until a quarter to nine, the last to arrive and afraid I had missed the first meal of the day. However, the table where breakfast was theoretically served wasn't set, and some participants, who said they'd been up since seven, were complaining about being hungry. Borja was standing by the window talking to Valèria, Xavier and Carme. I went over.

"What's up? Where's breakfast?" I asked.

"There's a problem with the front door," Borja explained, "Iolanda, who's in charge of getting breakfast ready, couldn't get in and Cecília had to ring a locksmith."

"You mean we can't get out?" I reacted, suddenly feeling claustrophobic.

"They'll sort it out straight away, don't worry," he said with a smile.

Xavier, Carme's husband, kept grumbling and not exactly quietly. He said it was all one big con, and he and his wife could have gone on a luxury cruise for what the weekend in the meditation centre was costing.

"But this is something quite different," his wife retorted, trying to calm him down. "You wait... Just be a bit patient!"

Cecília and Iolanda appeared a quarter of an hour later, the latter weighed down by the bags containing our breakfast. The two of them quickly put out a few baguettes and a bag full of wholemeal croissants, and, while Cecília put it all on a tray, Iolanda headed towards the kitchen. She raided the fridge for boxes of fruit juice, yoghurts, vegetable margarine, non-fat jams and a dish of cream cheese, which she put next to the bread and croissants with the fruit left over from yesterday and transparent glass jars of muesli and various kinds of cereals. She then brought tea bags and went off to heat the water.

"Isn't there any coffee, or even decaf?" I asked Iolanda.

"I'm very sorry," she answered, shrugging her shoulders. "Coffee is banned."

When we had all served ourselves, Cecília apologized, saying that Iolanda had had a problem with her key and leaving it at that. Sebastià, who'd disappeared from the dining room while we queued at the counter, came back and sat next to Borja.

"Someone put silicone in the keyhole," he whispered. "That's why Iolanda couldn't open the door."

"How incredible. Even this neighbourhood has got its hooligans!" sighed Borja.

"Somebody stuffed it in from the inside," Sebastià went on. "I reckon the vandal is here among us!"

After lunch, we all went to our rooms to brush our teeth and then went down to the Samsara Room where Bernat was waiting. This time he was dressed like us in a white kimono that enhanced his dark tan and deep blue eyes. Mònica, whose hair looked as if it had come straight from the hairdresser's, started to flirt with him, and that made him uneasy. Conversely, the rumour that someone had put silicone in the keyhole had spread and everyone was discussing the incident. Cecília said it was true, but they had solved the problem.

We had to sit on the floor again.

"I'm not sure if you know what Bach flower remedies are all about," began Bernat. "Let's have a show of hands. How many of you have heard of them?"

Everyone lifted a hand, with the exception of Xavier and Borja.

"And how many of you have tried them?" he went on.

The only ones who didn't raise a hand were Xavier, Borja, the girl who had just separated and yours truly.

As most people knew what Bach flower remedies were, Bernat gave a very short presentation and said that anyone interested in finding out more could ask him whatever they needed to know, in private or public, or could even ask for an appointment. He told us about the life of Dr Bach and his theory – he called it his discovery – that illnesses are caused by negative mental states and a lack of harmony, and explained how the doctor conceived the idea of using pure water in the preparation of his floral cures.

"Early one morning he went for a walk in a dewy meadow and it occurred to him that each sun-warmed drop of dew contained the curative properties of the plant on which it was resting. He then went on to develop thirty-eight preparations with thirty-eight wild flowers that had the power to cure all illnesses."

"All illnesses?" I interrupted, not intending to be impolite or impertinent, but because I was so surprised by the categorical nature of his statement.

"To cure all the negative states of mind that prompt illnesses," Bernat finessed with a smile.

"Oh!"

"He explains all this in a book he wrote called *Heal Thyself*," he continued. "If you are interested, you can buy it in our shop."

"Lucky he didn't write anything called *Operate on Thyself*," Xavier whispered in my ear. "My wife would have butchered herself!"

"In any case," added Bernat, looking at us out of the corner of his eye and raising his voice slightly, "it is always best to have recourse to a professional for advice on what is the best cure to re-establish harmony in each individual case and for a prescription of the correct dosage. That, as you now know, is precisely my field of expertise."

I remained a doubter.

"So why are they wild flowers? I mean, what do flowers have that other plants don't?" I asked, as I raised my hand.

"Dr Bach discovered the vibrational characteristics of particular flowers," came his pat reply. I could see Valèria and Mònica nodding in agreement.

"But there isn't any scientific proof that these preparations work, is there?" Alícia suddenly piped up. Everyone stared at her, surprised by the sour tone of her voice.

"Oh, yes, there is!" said Bernat. "But you all know how scientific tests are designed for conventional pharmaceuticals and tested by cruel experiments on animals that make them suffer. That is why some people refuse to admit that Bach flower remedies work."

"But isn't it rather naive to trust in what was basically a vision – for that's what your Dr Bach had almost a hundred years ago, when he was walking through a meadow – and to take it at face value?" continued Alícia in that same cutting vein. "I have read the studies carried out by Dr Ernst that cast doubt on —"

"Come now, Alícia, I'm not sure where you want to take us…" Bernat stopped her in full flood, "You yourself have benefited from Dr Bach's cures…"

"Precisely," responded Alícia dryly.

A murmur rippled round the room. Cecília got up, looked

meaningfully at her watch and announced with a broad smile that it was time for a break. As the weather was fine, she said she was inviting us to take tea in the garden and enjoy the sunshine. Before we got to our feet, she reminded us that smoking was banned at the centre.

"And after tea we will start the yoga session that I will lead," she added, still smiling broadly.

The tea break lasted a good three quarters of an hour, and we were standing the whole time. Then we all went to the Nirvana Room, except for Alícia, who said the tea hadn't agreed with her and she was going to rest in her room. I was tempted to do the same, but Borja stopped me with one of those thunderous glances of his.

"Don't even think of skiving off!" he whispered.

Cecília asked us to take our shoes off. I noted that all the women in the group, except for her, had painted their toenails in different seductive shades of red. Mine looked awful and I had to agree with Montse, who sometimes reproaches me for neglecting certain details. Borja gave me a withering look.

After taking several deep breaths in and out, Cecília told us to sit on our heels and rest our elbows on the ground, level with our shoulders. Then we had to draw out our knees (or at least attempt to), lower our heads and put our arms in front of us.

"This is known as the dolphin position," she said, demonstrating how to do it. Some people, yours truly included, simply rolled over.

As I was trying to right myself, I noticed my whole body was itching. Initially, I tried to scratch myself discreetly (Borja had told me it's very rude to scratch in public), but the itching got worse and became intolerable. I saw Cecília had started scratching herself and that everybody around me was scratching furiously.

119

"What the fuck is all this about?" bawled Xavier, standing up, still scratching himself. We all followed suit and stood up. The itching on the soles of my feet was torture.

"I can't stand this!" yelped Marta, her neck sore and red from so much scratching.

"This is an allergy," commented Valèria. "We've all got food poisoning."

"I think not," reacted Carles pompously. "I am rather of the opinion they cleaned the carpet with a product that provokes nettle rash."

"Look!" whooped Borja, bending down and examining the ground. "There's something on the carpet and I think it is itching powder."

"I don't get it," said Cecília, aghast. "Last night we all sat here and we had no after-effects… I think we should go to our rooms, have a shower and a change of clothes."

There was a general stampede towards the door.

"I'm getting out!" roared Xavier as we went upstairs.

"There must be an explanation…" piped Carme, his wife. "Let's wait for Horaci to get here."

"That's true. Where *is* Horaci?" Ernest suddenly asked.

"He'll be back after lunch," replied Cecília, scratching away. "His meditation class is at three."

There was a mumble of disapproval. Why the hell wouldn't Horaci be back until this afternoon? Why didn't he participate in the activities? In any case, as everyone was rushing to take their clothes off and dive into the shower, attempted mutiny was temporarily shelved, and Cecília gave a sigh of relief.

I spent ten minutes splashing myself with cold water and put on a clean kimono. When I went back into the corridor, I saw that, in the end, no one had deserted. And as nobody felt like a repeat of the yoga experience and we were all too much in turmoil to listen to any spiel about the virtues of feng shui, Cecília suggested we rest in our rooms or in the garden and meet up in the dining room at one.

"I'll try to investigate what happened," she added.

A gaunt Cecília went downstairs and slammed behind her the door to the office of Bernat, who'd disappeared after his early-morning talk on Bach flower remedies.

Most people decided to retreat to their bedrooms, but Sebastià, Borja and I went to a far corner of the garden to light up. Marta saw us smoking and sidled over to ask if we could spare her a ciggy.

"This is all very odd," said Borja as he offered her a light.

"Alícia was lucky, because she missed out on the itching," he said, recalling that she'd not joined the yoga class on the excuse that she was feeling poorly.

"Yes, hers was an extremely opportune indisposition." Sebastià's tone suggested he believed it was a fraud.

"You're not suggesting Alícia…" Marta interjected. But she had to break off mid-sentence because an annoyed Ernest had come over to remind us that smoking was banned throughout the centre.

"I'm sorry, we didn't want to upset you," Borja apologized. "As we're in the open air…"

"Well, your smoke is annoying me at this very minute," said Ernest huffily.

"Well, if you must stand right next to us…"

"I have a right to stand wherever I want to!" he rasped back.

Sebastià, Borja, Marta and I moved several metres away from Ernest.

"I will speak to Horaci!" he shouted, turning round, walking into the building and snarling, "Smoking is banned here!"

All four of us sighed and decided to extinguish our cigarettes. As it was almost one o'clock and we were hungry, we headed straight to the dining room. The married couple, Xavier and Carme, had beaten us to it: he was in a bad mood and she was trying to calm him down. Isabel, the woman with cancer who didn't want treatment, was there too. She was by herself, as usual, in one corner, and nobody was paying her any attention, so I did.

"Are you feeling OK?" I asked.

"I've got cancer. But I'm curing myself," she replied with a resigned smile.

"The other day you said you didn't want treatment…"

"I'm curing myself. I never go to doctors. I don't trust them. They only want to prescribe medicines and get their hands on your cash," she added.

"So, if you never go to the doctor, how did you find out you've got cancer?" I asked.

"I *know* I've got cancer, I don't need to go to any doctor to find that out," she replied confidently.

"You mean you made the diagnosis yourself? That you've not had any tests or check-ups?"

"I don't need any tests. I told you I am sick. But I will cure myself."

"And how will you do that?" I enquired, intrigued.

"Through my mental powers and eating asparagus."

"Asparagus?"

"Yes, purée of asparagus: it's the best cure there is for cancer. I found that out on the Internet."

"Oh!"

I now understood why Isabel was always alone and nobody spoke to her: she was as mad as a March hare. I beat a discreet retreat to where Borja and Marta were standing as I wondered whether some people who have cured themselves using home-made remedies might not be people who've been wrongly diagnosed or, as in Isabel's case, have never been diagnosed medically.

"Yuck! This is inedible!" I heard Sebastià shout, who'd sat down at a table and tucked into the pumpkin purée he'd served himself.

Xavier and Carme, who'd also sat down with their respective trays of chaotically stacked food, tasted their helpings.

"It's very salty," said Carme, spitting out what she'd put into her mouth.

"So what kind of joke is this?" roared Xavier, throwing his fork down on his plate. "Are they trying to poison us or what?"

Cecília, who had just walked in, asked what the matter was and Xavier gave her a spoonful from his plate. She immediately wrinkled her nose and went to the counter where Iolanda had set out the trays with lunch. She started trying all the dishes with a spoon.

"It's true. It is all far too salty," she said. "As if someone had added pounds and pounds of salt." And she turned to Iolanda and asked her, "What the hell did you do to the food?"

"Nothing at all," replied Iolanda, looking scared. "What I always do. I took the Tupperware containers out of the fridge, heated everything in the microwave and served it up on the usual dishes."

"Well, this is quite inedible," declared Sebastià.

"So what are we going to eat for lunch?" asked Valèria with a sigh.

"We can bring out cereals, yoghurt and fruit…" suggested Cecília.

"I don't intend eating anything that has come out of this kitchen!" concluded Xavier. "There's something fishy going on!"

"Perhaps the microwave has gone haywire…" ventured Cecília, as if there could be a connection between a broken-down microwave and the fact the food was salty.

"I reckon someone is playing jokes in bad taste on us," Borja chipped in.

"No, no…" replied Cecília. "I am sure there is a good explanation. When Horaci comes this afternoon —"

"And, in the meantime, what are we going to eat, eh?" asked Xavier.

"I'm hungry!" said Sebastià.

"Me too!"

"And so am I!"

Cecília couldn't think what to do, and Borja suggested sending Iolanda off to get hamburgers and chips from the local McDonald's. Initially, Cecília wouldn't agree, arguing that the centre's philosophy was vegetarian, but Xavier called for a vote and Borja's motion was passed with ten votes for and two against, Mònica's and Ernest's.

"I want a double-decker with cheese," ordered Marta.

"Me too," said Mònica. Ernest gave her a withering look, indicating she'd betrayed the cause.

"And what are you two planning to do?" Valèria asked Xavier. "Are you leaving or staying?"

"We'll stay. At least until Horaci comes back and gives us back our four thousand euros."

"Well, we're off right away!" said Ernest, who clearly wore the trousers in that relationship. "This place is a joke, and I'm still all itches!"

He and Carles walked out in a huff. Cecília didn't even try to stop them.

"I prefer chicken nuggets," said Valèria. "And onion rings."

"I don't want any gherkin on my burger. I hate gherkins…" Cecília added timidly.

Iolanda made a list and rushed off to a chorus of rumbling stomachs. While we were waiting for her to come back with our burgers, I took Borja into a corner and asked him, "You're not behind what's happening, are you?"

"Of course not. How could you think such a thing? Do you reckon I've gone mad or what?"

"I don't know, all this is very peculiar. What if somebody is trying to poison us, as Xavier said?"

"Silicone in the keyhole, itching powder, salty food... I think it's somebody playing tiresome practical jokes at our expense," sighed Borja.

"Do you suspect anyone?"

"Alícia. She's the only one who's been behaving strangely."

When Horaci walked into the dining room and saw the table covered in cold chips, packets of ketchup, glasses of Coca-Cola and burger boxes with the McDonald's logo, his mouth gaped so wide that any passing fly would certainly have paid him a visit. Cecília dragged him out of the room and explained the situation. A few minutes later, Horaci returned, apologized profusely and in a deadpan tone declared that Cecília would ensure we had a decent dinner that evening.

Xavier immediately squared up to him and demanded his money back, but Horaci took him aside and said something we didn't catch that seemed to calm him down.

We had an hour for a siesta and came back to the Samsara Room at four. Just in case, Iolanda ran the carpet-cleaner over the floor before we went in, and Cecília checked that everything was as it should be.

"I imagine," said Horaci in best schoolteacher manner, "that one of you has been playing these little pranks on us. I don't want to know whom. I'd only ask the person if he or she is still with us to have a little respect for the people who have come here to learn. And now let's begin the meditation class."

There were no more japes or incidents that afternoon, and, in the evening, as Horaci had indicated, we had to

make do with a vegetarian dinner like the previous evening's, and that made me long for the hamburgers we'd
eaten at midday. This time I decided to try the sausages,
which I didn't like, and had my second helping of spinach
salad. Bernat, Cecília and Horaci dined on our table, and,
as soon as we finished, Bernat said he was going home, and
Horaci said he had things to see to in his office.

As we decided it wouldn't be very sensible to go down
to the garden for a smoke because Horaci would see us
from his office, Sebastià invited Marta, Borja and me for a
whisky in his bedroom.

"Hey, this is like being back at school!" quipped Sebastià,
taking the bottle out of his bag. "Who'd have thought I'd
have to hide to smoke and drink a Scotch at my age?…"

"Well, no one forced you to come," I retorted. "You're
here because you want to be!"

"It's not quite as simple as that," said Sebastià, winking
at me.

Borja and I exchanged glances: we'd been too hasty in
making Alícia our main suspect. So, what if it turned out
that this apparently benign, venerable old guy, fond of his
whisky and tobacco, was behind all these annoying japes?

Guessing what was going through our minds, Sebastià
simply smiled.

12

At a quarter past eight on Sunday morning, a distraught Borja dashed into my room.

"Eduard, I think you'd better get dressed."

"What's the matter?" Breakfast was served at half past eight, and as I had had another bad night I had just got up and was still in my pyjamas.

"Horaci is dead. He's been murdered," he said. "We just found him in his office, with his head split open."

"Is this another joke?"

"If only." Borja's distraught face confirmed it was no prank. "We've informed the police. The *mossos* are on their way," he said as he lit a cigarette, his hands shaking.

"So what happened?"

"Sebastià heard me drinking a glass of water in the kitchen and came to see if I wanted a smoke in the garden. We went down in the lift, and when we got out, we saw that the walls and floor on the ground floor were covered in red blotches. At least, that's what Sebastià said, because, as you know, I —"

"Blood?"

"No, it's paint. You can still smell it. But we noticed Horaci's door was half open and went to investigate. We found him on the floor in the middle of his office, with his head bashed in."

"Did you touch him to see whether he was still alive?"

"Sebastià did and said he was dead. I didn't have the… He phoned the *mossos.*"

"Couldn't it have been an accident? Perhaps he fell and hit his head…" I ventured, wanting Borja to have got it wrong.

"If you'd seen him, you wouldn't be asking. No, Eduard, they did Horaci in."

People were shouting and running in the corridor. We both peered around the door and saw residents in pyjamas rushing frantically down the stairs. They had just heard the news.

"I'll get dressed," I said, going to my wardrobe.

"I'm going to change." Borja was still in his kimono. "Better put your own clothes on, bro, I reckon our time at Zen Moments is over!"

Borja shut the door behind him as he left. I hurriedly dressed and stuffed my belongings in my bag that I put on the futon. Before going out into the corridor, I washed my face in cold water to wake myself up, but didn't bother to shave. My brother was waiting for me in his new jeans and designer shirt. He was chatting to Valèria and the disgruntled couple. They, too, were in their everyday clothes.

"They've also put graffiti on the first floor," said Borja, turning round to me. "They've made a real mess."

"Does the graffiti mean anything?"

"I'm no graffiti expert, but from what I could see they were just meaningless blotches," said Xavier.

"Maybe they are the symbols of a Satanic sect. Or squatters," said his wife, trying to embrace her husband. He wriggled away.

In the meantime Marta and Cecília were trying to calm Mònica down at the end of the corridor. She had an attack of hysteria and couldn't stop sobbing.

"Calm down. Take deep breaths. The police will be here any moment and then you can go," I heard her say. Just then Iolanda came out of the kitchen and took her a cup of steaming tea.

"What we need is a cognac," announced Borja. "Pity I left my flask at home!"

"I heard that. It's the first sensible thing I've heard since I arrived here," said Xavier, shaking his head.

"Why don't we go downstairs?" I suggested.

Borja and I went downstairs, followed by Xavier, his wife and Valèria. When we reached the first floor, we stopped to contemplate the spectacle offered by walls, doors and floor. Xavier was right: they were just blotches, I imagined made by one of those spray cans graffiti artists use. They didn't represent any symbol or seem to inscribe any kind of message. It was as if the entire act of vandalism was about making the biggest mess possible.

"It's the same on the ground floor," said Borja. And he asked me quietly, "Is this paint red as well?" Borja is colour-blind and can't tell red from green, but for some reason or other wants to keep it a secret.

We walked down to the ground floor, where everyone had spontaneously assembled. The only person I didn't see was Alícia. The same splashes of paint were on the floor and walls, and I saw that the reception counter and Buddha in the entrance had also fallen victims to the spray. Sebastià was blocking the entrance to Horaci's office to stop anyone from going in and disturbing anything. Borja preferred to keep his distance, though I stuck my nose round the door to confirm that, in effect, his death had been no accident. The small, bloodstained statue of the Buddha the doctor kept on his desk was next to the body, with a tuft of hair stuck to it.

"What about Bernat? Where's Bernat? Somebody go and get him. He's a doctor, isn't he?" I heard Carme say.

"He never sleeps here," said Cecília, who'd just come down with the two younger women.

"Besides, Dr Comes is no medical doctor," added Iolanda, unable to hide the satisfaction she derived from making such a revelation.

"What do you mean, he's no medical doctor? It clearly says 'Doctor Comes' on his door!" growled Xavier.

"He's a doctor of philosophy," Cecília went on uneasily.

"That's right. He's not a medical doctor," the young girl reiterated in case anyone still was in doubt.

I heard shocked mumbling all around me.

"What cheek!"

"This is a fraud!"

"I want to go home! Someone open the door!"

"You do realize they could have killed any of us?"

Luckily the *mossos* arrived before there was an outbreak of collective hysteria. As the steel door that gave access to the precinct from the street was shut, Cecília went to the control panel in the lobby to enter the code and let them in. After that, she opened the security lock so they could enter the building.

"Whoever did it didn't force the door," I observed. "They must have got in somewhere else. What did you and Sebastià do the other day to get into the garden?" I asked Borja.

"There's one of those emergency doors behind the lift that open inwards," he replied. "You just need to wedge so it doesn't close, because you can't open those doors from outside."

As soon as Cecília gave them access, the *mossos* burst in like a whirlwind and asked us to stand to one side. The graffiti was the first thing they noticed, though they immediately went into the office to make sure Horaci was dead and not in need of medical help. Then one of the police, who was in plain clothes, introduced herself as Deputy Inspector

Alsina-Graells from the murder squad and asked about the sprayed paint.

"They did it last night," Cecília explained. "There wasn't any when I went to bed, at around eleven."

"And who are you?" asked the Deputy Inspector, who seemed very young, taking a notebook out of her pocket.

"My name is Cecília Ros, and I'm the yoga teacher. I was in charge of this group this weekend," she added, pointing at us.

"How many people are in the building?" she asked.

"Twelve residents plus the girl responsible for the meals and myself. Dr Comes will be here later on," she answered.

"And who is Dr Comes?"

"He's our specialist in Bach flower remedies. He should be here mid-morning to give a talk."

"He's no doctor!" shouted a voice that didn't belong to the girl who ran the kitchen.

"He is a doctor of philosophy," Cecília said to clarify the situation. Her cheeks blushed deep red.

"Ah!" was the police officer's only response.

A group of four plain-clothes *mossos*, feet wrapped in plastic bags, walked towards Dr Bou's office. Another group in uniform cordoned off the area with plastic tape and created a kind of passage from the entrance to Horaci's office.

"So then, tell me what happened," barked the Deputy Inspector.

Sebastià hurriedly introduced himself and explained how he and Borja discovered the graffiti and the body. He also described the string of incidents from the previous day. Sebastià, who hadn't moved from the office in all that time, was still wearing his white kimono, and the Deputy Inspector was staring at him in bemused fashion.

"But we didn't touch anything," Sebastià assured her. "And we didn't let anyone in."

131

"And where is this Borja character?" asked the Deputy Inspector, giving us all a look-over.

"This time I can't wriggle out of it!" whispered Borja, stepping forward and raising his hand like a good boy at school.

Borja repeated more or less what Sebastià had said.

"Is anyone still upstairs?" asked the officer, staring at the ceiling.

We looked around, checking that nobody was missing. I saw the two girls who were weepy-eyed friends, the unhappy married couple, Sebastià, Cecília, and the girl who ran the kitchen…

"Alícia isn't here," I heard a voice say.

"Yes, Alícia is missing," said someone else.

"Is she the only one in the group not here?" asked the Deputy Inspector.

"Yes," Cecília confirmed, doing a recount of the faces present.

The Deputy Inspector simply raised an eyebrow and a group of *mossos* went up the stairs while the rest of us stayed in the lobby and answered questions. A few minutes later, we saw a *mosso* come down looking scared and carrying a travel bag I was very familiar with. In his wake came three policemen with Alícia in her nightdress, her hair uncombed.

"Hey, chief, we found this in this woman's room," one of the *mossos* shouted.

The Deputy Inspector stepped back and opened the bag. Although she was trying to do it on the sly, we could all see it contained at least half a dozen spray cans of red paint.

"And take a look at this," said the *mosso* in uniform as he forced Alícia to show her hands to the Deputy Inspector.

Alícia's hands were covered in blotches of red paint.

"I don't understand. I swear I didn't kill him…" she said, bursting into tears. "I only wanted —"

"Tell her what her rights are, handcuff her and take her to the station," the Deputy Inspector ordered with a sigh. And added, turning to us, "Good news. I think we'll soon be able to let you go home."

Just as Alícia was leaving, the forensic investigator arrived. Everyone shut up and moved to one side to let him through, as if he were the high priest of an ancient religion keen on human sacrifice. The forensic investigator walked silently towards Horaci's office, not deigning to give us a glance while some of us scrutinized his face for a sign that betrayed his macabre profession. It's not every day you get so close to a forensic investigator and I'm sure several of us shuddered in horror when he walked past.

13

The *mossos* took note of all our details and finally gave us permission to leave. What with one thing and another, it was well past midday. On our way out, we passed, on their way in, Sònia Claramunt, Horaci's widow, and Bernat Comes, the specialist in Bach flower remedies who turned out not to be a real doctor; their sorrowful faces showed they'd heard the dire news. Some participants who knew Sònia Claramunt offered her their condolences, but she strode on imperturbably, not stopping to thank them.

"Poor woman! She must be quite distraught!" said Valèria. "I can remember when I lost my husband…"

My brother and I inelegantly skipped the dramatic story she was about to unfold and, once we were in the street, Borja gave me his mobile so I could tell Montse I was on my way home. I wanted to reassure her, because journalists and TV cameras had begun to arrive at around eleven, and I was afraid she or Joana might hear the news on the radio or TV and get the fright of their lives. Borja then phoned Merche and Lola, who'd taken advantage of our stay at Zen Moments to go to Madrid with some girlfriends to visit the Prado.

"We've had a real run of bad luck," I muttered as we walked along the Bonanova, trying to find a taxi. "Everything we touch goes haywire."

"We'll have to think what we're going to do about Teresa Solana's assignment. And how we're going to reclaim our four thousand euros!" sighed Borja.

"Do you think we'll get a refund?"

"Well, that's the least they can do."

"I'd never have said that Alícia woman was a murderer. She must have planned it all from the start."

"I guess so. Come on, let's go home, I'm starving!" my brother shouted as he waved at a taxi with a green light.

I was famished too. Even though the *mossos* had let us into the kitchen in the middle of the morning to get something to eat and drink, as they didn't even serve decaf at the centre, my stomach was empty. The second we reached our place, I quickly prepared aperitifs with crisps, olives and slices of chorizo and cheese. The crisps disappeared immediately and the twins offered to fetch more from the local corner store run by a couple of Pakistanis.

"Bring us a couple of tins of *berberetxus*," said Borja, handing Laia a twenty-euro note.

"*Escopinyes*, proper Catalan, if you don't mind!" Laia replied, wincing at his mix of Spanish and Catalan for the word for cockles.

Joana and Montse joined us for aperitifs and insisted we described what had happened in lurid detail. The twins also wanted to be in on how Borja found the corpse of Dr Bou and all the gore he added to spice his story; for the first time in ages they stayed with us for aperitifs rather than disappearing into their bedrooms. Arnau seemed to be the only person who was completely uninterested, and he simply asked, "Daddy, how can Dr Bou be a vegetarian if his name says he's an ox?"

Borja and I had told them how we'd gone hungry because of the vegetarian menus they served. It was lucky Montse had cooked macaroni and meat and cheese pasties for lunch, and Borja had insisted on buying a cream sponge cake for dessert. Unusually for a weekend, when we usually start lunch after three, that Sunday we were all tucking in well before two.

After lunch, Borja said he was going home to rest, and I was all ready for a long siesta. On this occasion, Montse let me off doing the washing-up, and, discreetly, while she and Joana were busy in the kitchen, I went to our bedroom and extracted from the trunk the small statue Borja had asked me to keep for him.

"Here you are," I said, putting it into his El Corte Inglés bag. "I'm sure you'll find a good place to hide it in your flat."

"Of course, don't you worry," said Borja.

"And get some rest, right?"

"You too."

14

The following morning, the telephone rang just before ten. It was Borja.

"What the hell are you doing awake?" I asked, surprised to hear him so early in the morning.

"I didn't get any shut-eye last night."

"Well, in the end I slept like a log! I needed to. And I was lucky because I still have backache from that blasted futon..."

"Eduard, we've got to recover the four thousand euros."

I noted a nervy edge to his voice that is quite unlike my brother and felt uneasy.

"Is anything wrong?"

"No. But I'm not going to let the Zen Moments people hang on to Merche's money."

"Right, I agree, but they killed the director yesterday, if you remember..."

"I regret what happened to Horaci, but money is money," he insisted.

"So what do you suggest?"

"I suggest you come here and we'll both go to the meditation centre and demand an immediate refund."

"Do you think anybody will be there this morning? After all that shit yesterday, I expect it will be shut and the *mossos* will be busy looking for clues and all that jazz."

"I expect someone will be there. Bernat, the Bach flower remedies guy, was one of Horaci's partners, wasn't he?"

"Yes. And his wife Sònia was the other partner, so it seems. Alícia told me that on Friday when we were having dinner. Who'd have thought it?… She didn't look like a murderer." I felt a shiver go down my spine when I remembered that she'd sat next to me.

"We'll press them and demand they refund our cash," Borja responded, ignoring my comment. "Can you be quick?"

I sighed. I knew I didn't have any choice.

"I'll get dressed and I'll be with you in half an hour."

I didn't expect we'd find anyone at the centre, and was even less optimistic about Horaci's partners handing back the four thousand euros we'd given them so blithely and that had probably disappeared from the centre's safe. Nevertheless, as Borja had sounded so touchy on the phone, I thought there was no point arguing and that it would be more sensible to go to his place and make him see the light there. As it was Montse's turn to take Arnau to school this week, I was still in my pyjamas. I showered and dressed as quickly as I could. Before leaving, I told Joana something urgent had cropped up and that I would go to the supermarket in the afternoon. As Borja's tone of voice had been worrying, I grabbed a taxi to save time.

Borja opened the door all ready to leave. He didn't even ask me inside. He looked in a bad state and I told him so.

"I said I didn't get any sleep last night," he growled.

"Hey, bro, just as well it wasn't your money. You look terrible…"

"Come on, let's be off."

As we went down in the lift, I got the impression my brother was feeling too rough to drive and I suggested we took a taxi. However, he argued we would certainly need the car to ferry back and forth. If nobody was at the centre, he said, we'd try to get the addresses of Bernat or the widow, and, as a last resort, pay him and her a visit at their homes. I'd never seen Borja so beside himself, and concluded he urgently needed the money back. Perhaps Merche had given him an ultimatum, which wasn't like her, or he had a creditor who'd lost his patience.

"You sure everything is all right?" I insisted.

"Quite sure," he rasped. But his "sure" implied quite the opposite.

Borja had parked the Smart by the entrance to the Catalan Trains station in Putxet that is five minutes' spirited walk from his flat. We started down Balmes and, while waiting for the green light to cross the road by Castanyer, we were accosted by three men in tracksuits who towered a good metre above us. The sky was cloudy but all three wore shades.

"Come with *nosotros, por favor,*" said one of them, while the other two surrounded us and pinioned our arms.

"What are you after?" Borja asked, trying to disentangle himself.

"Come."

One of the men spoke to his colleague in a language I didn't understand that sounded like Russian or another Eastern European language.

"He *tambien* come," he shouted, referring to me, as his colleague pushed me in the direction of a black Transit van parked in front of Borja's block.

"Hey, what the hell do you think you're doing?" I yelped, trying to resist. "Hel—!" but a hand was stuffed into my mouth before I could finish the word I was trying to shout.

It all happened in a flash. In a matter of seconds, Borja and I were tumbled in a heap inside the Transit. Resistance or escape was impossible, because our pathetic limbs, the product of sedentary existences, were no match for biceps flexed by weights and circuit training. Once inside the Transit, one of the men put a cloth to my nose, dripping with a substance I guessed was chloroform; I tried to fight and kick, but it was no use. Before hitting the floor unconscious, I saw Borja also struggle to stop them from anaesthetizing him.

When I woke up, my head ached and I was sitting in a chair with my hands, but not my feet, tied behind me. I didn't know how long I'd been like that, but, wherever we were, it was almost pitch dark. I gradually recalled the men with shades, the black Transit van and the cloth soaked in chloroform. When my eyes got used to the shadowy light, I saw we were in a very big room decorated like a Chinese restaurant.

"What's happened? Where are we?" I heard Borja ask sleepily. I then realized that we were back to back, I was facing a small barred window, and he faced a wall.

"I don't know," I whispered. "Are you all right? Are you hurt?"

"No, but I've got one hell of a headache."

"So have I. That must be chloroform they gave us."

"Yeah, but where are we?"

I was slightly more awake by now and surveyed the room again. A closer look revealed that the objects were nothing like the tacky items you find in the Chinese restaurants Montse and I sometimes visited. These seemed the genuine article. The beams in the ceiling were polychrome wood, and two square columns painted red flanked a wooden door that was closed. There was a sign written in gold Chinese characters above the door and, by the window, at ground level, were a bed, a trunk that looked antique and two chairs leaning against the wall that also had an antique flavour.

The only light in the room came through the small barred window opposite me.

"What can you see?" I asked Borja in a hushed voice.

"Nothing at all. It's very dark in here. Wait," he said a few seconds later. "There's something that looks like an old suit of armour. But it's not like our medieval armour. The helmet is different... There's a bow and quiver with arrows next to it!" he whispered.

"How extraordinary. It's as if we were inside a Chinese house," I muttered.

"Look at the lanterns in the ceiling," said Borja. I looked up. "You're right. They do seem Chinese. What about you? Can you see anything else?"

"A small window," I answered, stretching my neck as much as I could to see outside. However much Borja turned his head, he couldn't see the window.

"And?"

"I don't know. It looks as if we're in the countryside."

"In the countryside?"

"I can see the sky. And mountains. And a very long stone wall... Hey!" I paused to make sure my eyes weren't playing tricks on me and then stretched my neck further. "Hell, I don't believe it!"

"What do you mean? What's wrong?"

"I don't believe it! It can't be true!" I muttered as I felt my heart racing.

"Eduard, say something, for Christ's sake!" Though Borja was making every effort to twist his neck, he could only see the window out of the corner of his eye.

"You won't believe this, but I can see the Great Wall of China," I whispered. "Pep, I reckon we're in China!"

"China?"

"Shush! Don't shout!"

"China? Are you sure?" repeated Borja incredulously.

"Lower your voice. Yes, I swear what I can see through the window is the Great Wall, and we're in this room with all this oriental furniture… Welcome to China, Pep. To China!"

"Damn me…"

My head went into a spin and I took some deep breaths. China. That meant Borja and I were thousands of fucking miles away from home. How long had we been asleep? Ten hours? Twenty? And why had they bothered to transport us so far?"

"Eduard, I meant to tell you something," Borja said all of a sudden.

"Go on, fire away."

"On Sunday evening, when I got back to the flat, I found it had been turned upside down. I suppose someone was looking for the statue."

"Bloody hell…"

"That's why I needed the cash. I wanted to go to a hotel until this was all cleared up."

"You should have told me. Look at the mess we're in now!"

"I'm sorry, bro. I swear I had no idea things would turn out like this. I'm sorry I got you involved."

We said no more. I was angry and Borja was shamefaced. Our breathing was the only sound. I tried to wriggle free, but hurt my wrists.

"How do you know they weren't ordinary burglars?" I asked after a while, trying to sound hopeful. "You know, with the crisis, burglars are back big time…"

"They didn't steal anything, my plasma TV, Rolex, crocodile-skin briefcase… I checked them out. They just made one hell of a mess."

"So it probably wasn't the burglars who raided our office either," I said, thinking aloud. "It was people after the statue."

"I'd come to the same conclusion. Though I don't understand why they have brought us to China if it's the sculpture they're after," argued Borja.

I was as confused as he was and as at a loss for words.

"Perhaps it's an extremely valuable Chinese antique," I suggested a few seconds later. "Perhaps it's a deity of theirs and you've committed sacrilege…"

"Sure, but the guys who stuffed us into that Transit weren't Chinese!" Borja responded. "They seemed more like Russians. Besides, I don't think the statue was Chinese. Oriental at a pinch, but not Chinese."

"Oh, so now you're a specialist in antique art, are you!" I grunted. "I seem to remember you failed every single exam in art history at school. And if I hadn't let you copy me in the final exam…"

"So what? You copied your maths answers from me…" he countered as we both tried to free our hands.

We heard voices approaching and shut up immediately. The door opened and three men walked in. I recognized two of them from the trio who'd shoved us into the Transit; I'd never seen the third man, who looked like he was the boss. Although they hid behind shades, they didn't bother to switch any lights on.

"OK, you fuckeeng bastard! Your time is up! Give me the fuckeeng memory steek or your brother is dead!" shouted one of the men, squaring up to Borja and slapping him in the face twice to encourage him to answer.

"What the hell is he on about?" Borja asked me in a hushed tone.

"I don't know. I don't understand him either!"

The man was speaking English, but he had a strange accent that betrayed the fact English wasn't his mother tongue.

"I won't ask you again!" the guy said, punching Borja. "The memory steek! Now!"

"No English!" screeched Borja. "No English!"

"No English?" The three men burst out laughing. "Come on, man, don't try fooling me!"

"No English!" repeated Borja. "*Français. Est-ce que vous parlez français?*"

"I told you ages ago we should learn English!" I whispered. "Nowadays, you can't get anywhere without English."

I heard him swear in his mother tongue.

"*Cosa querer* you *tienes*," said the man who'd addressed us in jumbled Spanish in the street before kidnapping us. "You *buscar* and *traer*. Or bang, bang, him *muerto*!" He aimed a finger at my head as if he was about to shoot me.

"I don't know what you're on about!" hissed Borja.

"I reckon he was saying you should go and get the statue and bring it here, or they'll do me in," I muttered.

He clouted Borja, again.

"OK, OK!" shrieked a whimpering Borja. "*Me traer cosa!* No hurt *mi amigo.* Not him *culpa.*"

The guy who seemed to be the boss of that gang of mafiosi, curiously the smallest of the three, signalled to the younger one, who nodded. He went over to Borja and cut the string tying his hands with a knife that was no Boy Scout affair.

"*Ir!* Now!" shouted the man who spoke Spanish, giving Borja a push.

I could see his drawn face and bleeding nose. Borja clutched at the door frame and asked in a pleading voice, "Hey, Eduard, if we're in China, how will I go home and come back here?"

"*Ir!*" repeated the man.

I had never seen Borja look so scared. For my part, I was terrified and could only think of Montse, Arnau and the girls.

"Pep, do whatever you have to, but bring that statue back here. Montse, my children…" I implored, a knot in my throat.

"I'll be back, Eduard. I swear I will..." he said, as they dragged him out of the room. "Don't worry. I won't let them..."

His voice faded into the distance and the man who'd cut him free came over and gagged me, I imagine, in order to ensure I couldn't shout for help. The fact was I was so shit-scared that if I had tried to scream right then, my voice would have failed me. Before he shut the door and left me by myself in that peculiar room, the man laughed and said something I didn't understand. My whole body was shaking. I made one last effort, pulled myself up slightly and looked through the window, where the impressive stone mass of the Great Wall reminded me that I was in China. And at that point I fainted.

15

When I came round, my first thought was that it had all been a nightmare and I still hadn't woken up. However, that fantasy only lasted a few seconds, because the stabbing pain I felt in my arms and wrists, and the panic attack that overwhelmed me the moment I realized my mouth had been gagged, brought it all back to me: I had been taken prisoner by total strangers and, even worse, they spoke languages I didn't understand, so I couldn't communicate with them. The scared look on Borja's face gradually came back to me, as did the punches, his bloody nose and the way he'd been dragged out of the room by men who'd forced him to go back to Barcelona to get that damned statue. I also recalled we were a long way from home, in China, a country where I wouldn't be missed if I disappeared, because, apart from Borja and our kidnappers, nobody knew I was there.

I could still see the Great Wall through the window and the tears clouding my vision, and it was a chilling reminder that nobody would come to my rescue in such a far-flung spot. I was more alone than I'd ever been in my whole life, and I felt completely numb. I was incapable of thought: all I wanted was to return home and for none of this ever to have happened. Why the hell couldn't my brother be a normal person with a normal job, as they said in that beer advert? Why did he have to be a Walter Mitty and get involved in these kinds of mess, rather than being happy to contemplate the lives of the wealthy in glossy magazines and on the TV, like the rest of us mortals?

I found it hard to breathe with that gag over my mouth, and my heart was racing. I realized that putting the blame on Borja wasn't going to help me out of that situation and that I should calm down. I tried to slow my rhythm of breathing for a few minutes by taking deep breaths in and out of my nose; almost imperceptibly, my heart started to beat at a more reasonable rate and I gradually calmed down. My situation was too serious to risk a fatal heart attack.

I took one last deep breath and glanced around me. I concluded I hadn't been unconscious for very long after they'd taken Borja off: the light coming through the window, an afternoon light that was gently, monotonously turning into dusk, hadn't really changed. Although I was sitting down, the stance I had been forced to adopt was excruciating, because my arms were tied behind me to the back of the chair and the rough string knotted around my wrists cut into my skin; I could move my feet, which weren't tied at all, but had pins and needles in my hands and that indicated they were about to lose all feeling because of the lack of any blood flow. What's more I was very thirsty, and I suddenly realized I'd not eaten or drunk anything for hours. Not that I was hungry… After the long journey I'd been forced to make, my brain had ignored my stomach and concentrated on keeping me alive. Nonetheless, it was so hot in that room that I now felt alarmed when I realized that, if my kidnappers didn't soon give me water, I would start to dehydrate and hallucinate. I tried to shout to attract their attention, but saw straight away it was very unlikely that my gagged cries would penetrate the stone walls imprisoning me. I listened hard: I could hear nothing on the other side.

In my situation, all I could do was think. At best, I worked out it must take ten to twelve hours to fly from Barcelona to China, and that meant Borja would require more than a day for the round trip, assuming he was travelling by private jet and didn't have refuelling stops or air-company timetables to worry about. That was a massive number of hours to be stuck in a chair, and the prospect of waiting all that time before Borja appeared with the statue and those men set me free numbed my brain once again. I had no other options. To cap it all, the guys who'd kidnapped us didn't look like the kind who had scruples. How could we be sure that once they'd got their clutches on the statue, they wouldn't shoot us in the head and bury our bodies in no-man's-land?

At the same time, I couldn't work out why the hell they'd taken us to China if the statue they wanted was hidden in Borja's flat? It was obvious they were keeping me prisoner as a kind of guarantee that my brother wouldn't simply make his escape, but I couldn't for the life of me see the sense in forcing us to make such a long journey that, in Borja's case, had to be endured three times. Perhaps they thought the statue wasn't in Barcelona and that he'd hidden it in that corner of the planet, but that didn't make any sense either, because, as I well knew, my brother had never set foot in China. It was true he had worked on a merchant-navy vessel at some stage in the twenty years he worked abroad and had thus seen the world, but that was years ago, when Borja was still called Pep and didn't have the contacts he now had. No, it was complete madness. There had to be a simple explanation.

Sitting opposite the motionless landscape framed by that window, I gradually began to lose all notion of time. I suddenly realized I didn't know what time or day it was, and the monotonous light coming through the window was no clue at all. Perhaps sunset took longer in China than in Barcelona, and afternoons were longer, I pondered, or perhaps only a few minutes had passed since I'd come round from my fainting fit, a few minutes I felt had been never-ending. From childhood, I'd always thought that time passed very slowly in China, a name that still evoked for me the era of the mandarins and great emperors, and that had all belonged to the two thousand years of their feudal period. I am sure my perceptions were shaped by the cliché-ridden films made in the West that I had watched from childhood, but nevertheless the word "China" immediately brought to mind images of ferocious warriors on horseback, women with bandaged feet wearing exquisite silk kimonos, and Fu Manchu. I had to make an effort to remind myself that contemporary China, where we were now, had gone through a first revolution that ended the imperial era, and that the country was presently going through a second revolution, a slow, inexorable transition to rampant capitalism. On the other hand, China still had the death penalty. What if those men handed us over to the Chinese authorities once they'd got their statue back, and *they* decided to sentence us to death for trafficking a statue that was part of their national heritage?

The sound of approaching voices halted my ramblings. The door opened and in walked Borja, flanked by our kidnappers. He looked scared and came over to ask me how I was. I nodded to the effect that I was fine, perplexed but happy to see him back so quickly. He used words and gestures to ask our captors to remove the gag from my mouth, which they did.

"You all right?" he asked anxiously. His nose had stopped bleeding but looked very swollen.

"I'm fine," I said soothingly. "What about you? What happened?"

"I'm all right too… Everything is fine, don't you worry."

"*Amigo* good," interjected the kidnapper with a smattering of Spanish, grabbing Borja by the arm and pulling him away from me. "Now you give the *cosa* to him," he added, pointing to the man who was presumably the boss.

Borja nodded and put his hand in his pocket. He carefully took the statue out and handed it to the man, who took it, looked at it in a state of shock, and finally shouted, "What the fuckeeng hell is that?"

He inspected the piece closely from every angle. Turned it round, upside down and weighed it in his hand. The expression on his face showed his mounting anger.

"You must be kiddeeng me? What the bloody sheet is that?" he bawled.

"What's up with him? What's he saying?" Borja asked.

"I don't know. I think he was expecting something else," I whispered.

"It's what you wanted, isn't it?" asked Borja, looking disconcerted. "*Nosotros* go *ahora. Marchar*," he added, pointing at the door.

In a rage, the man threw the statue to the other side of the room. Luckily, it fell on the bed and didn't break. I was nonplussed, even more so by how Borja had managed to do the China–Barcelona round trip so quickly. Could I really have been unconscious for over twenty-four hours?

The man produced a pistol and put it to my head. Borja started shouting hysterically.

"No, no! Please, please! I brought you the *estatua*! You *querer más*?"

"You pulled a fast one, you *bastardo*! You friend *muerto* now!"

"Eduard, I don't understand! I've… brought them the statue… I don't understand what they want now…" he clamoured, bursting into tears.

"Fuckeeng *bastardo*! That's the last straw!" he shouted, quite beside himself.

"But the statue is *verdad*! Not *mentira*!" Borja yelped again while the two men pinned him down. "Please! He not *culpa*! Please! What the fuck do you want?"

I felt the pistol's cold barrel against my temple and started to shake. Borja flushed a bright red, and his eyes bulged out of their sockets as he struggled to get free of the men pinning his arms down. They were too strong for him and all his efforts were futile.

"Let me go, you shits!" cried Borja. "If you harm my brother I will kill you! Get that? I will kill you!"

"*Si* us *plau*, please…" I begged. "*Tengo mujer e hijos…* Wife. Children…" I added, trying to remember the words I knew in English.

"Bye, bye, *amigo*!" said the guy holding a pistol to my head.

"No!" shouted Borja.

The guy held the gun steady. His hand began to move and I knew he was about to shoot. I closed my eyes, realizing my pleas were to no avail, and suddenly Borja stopped shouting and the curses of my executioner faded, as if the world had suddenly hit the silent mode key. Images began to churn through my brain: the first time I held Arnau in my arms, the day the twins were born, the first kiss I gave Montse in that pumpkin-coloured 2CV, and Pep and me paddling on the beach with my father while my mother shouted and waved to us from under the sunshade to come and have lunch. My mother's face was all smiles and freckles, an eternally young thirty-something because the car accident meant she and Father would never grow old. Turning points in my life.

I felt someone trying to free my hands and the sound returning. I opened my eyes. There were shouts and shots outside, and the man aiming his pistol at me had gone.

Borja was the only person in the room and he was trying to cut the string tying my hands to the chair with a small, blunt knife.

"Are you all right, Eduard? Are you all right?" he repeated. By the time I managed to say "yes", he added, "Almost there. We've got to scarper and fast!"

"What on earth has happened?"

"I don't know. Some men ran into the warehouse, those guys left the room and started a right shindig!"

"Are those shots?"

"Yes, they are. We should beat it quick. Follow me! I know where there's an exit!"

As soon as I got up from the chair, I felt my legs were still responding even though I'd been sitting in that same position for hours. I followed Borja and could see my prison was inside a big warehouse that was in complete darkness. There was a smell of gunpowder in the air.

"This way!" whispered Borja. "I know a place where we can get out of here!"

We saw two of our kidnappers lying in pools of blood on the ground, but didn't stop to find out whether they were dead. I could still hear shouting and shooting. The hangar we'd entered was full of strange objects, the pitch black hindered our escape operation and it was easy to stumble over. We decided to crawl over the ground, to dodge the bullets and avoid being spotted, and we reached a corner where a small door was concealed behind some boxes. It wasn't locked and Borja opened it. The sunlight was dazzling.

"What the hell!..." I exclaimed in astonishment.

The door led to a street that was very familiar. We weren't in remote China, but in Poblenou, in the small area that had been refurbished for the Olympic Games and where old hangars and warehouses had survived.

"We're in Barcelona!" I shouted, tears in my eyes and jumping for joy. "Pep. We're in Barcelona! In Barcelona!"

"We'd better clear off," he said, looking both ways and walking on. "There are two cop cars over there and I'm sure more are on their way."

"We're in Barcelona!" I whooped.

"Yes, lad, we're in Barcelona. And we are still alive and kicking!" he added with a smile.

16

It was four p.m. After all that sweat, I calculated we'd been kidnapped for just four hours. Borja and I started walking briskly through Poblenou to get away from the *mossos* and, luckily, we hit on a very busy street. My brother suggested we took a taxi and that I should shower and clean up in his flat before going home: I looked dreadful, or so he said. In fact, we were both in a bad state. We were exactly what we looked like: a couple of dirty, dishevelled and bruised fugitives. Borja told the cab driver to park in front of a Chinese restaurant and, while I waited in the taxi, he got out to buy some lunch (ironically, we both fancied fodder from the Orient) because we were hungry. I phoned Montse to make sure everything was all right at home.

"Everything is OK here. Why shouldn't it be?" she asked, disconcerted.

We reached Borja's flat without further mishap. We showered and my brother let me have a clean shirt that was big on him, but I couldn't change my trousers because all of his were too small. As soon as he was out of the shower, Borja put an ice pack on his nose, which was swollen, though not broken, and on his eye, which had started to turn purple; his jaw had also been punched hard. As his face was hurting a lot, he took a painkiller. My whole body ached, so I followed suit.

While we had lunch and waited for the paracetamol to take effect, we switched on the TV to see if they were reporting the shoot-out we'd seen with our own eyes. And, it turned out, the TV3 twenty-four-hour news service was reporting the news that the *mossos* had arrested a dangerous gang of mafiosi comprising ex-members of the disbanded security forces of the former Soviet Union that they'd been tracking for some time. The criminals had resisted and opened fire on the police, and only two mafiosi were in hospital because the other three members of the gang had died in the shoot-out. Two *mossos* had been wounded, but none killed.

"I don't get it," Borja muttered, switching the TV off.

"You sure you've told me everything?"

"I swear I have, Eduard," he said, sounding distressed. "You know as much as I do."

I knew he wasn't lying and that he felt guilty he'd involved me in risky business that could have turned out badly for both of us. However, we were too tired to talk or think, and, after lunch, I suggested we ought to stretch out and have a siesta. Borja took the phone off the hook, lowered the shutters and, good brothers that we are, we shared his king-size bed. As we'd drunk cognac for dessert, I fell asleep immediately.

It was eight o'clock when we woke up. I'd slept like a log. Borja was already up and in the dining room, sitting on the sofa, silently contemplating the small statue that was wreaking such havoc in our lives. I sat next to him and took another look at it. The statue's head was twisted to one side, and the muscles on its body, which was human, stood out. Its front legs started off as arms but turned into legs, claw on claw, like a wrestler preparing for a fight. Its eyes were open and its expression was at once determined and tranquil. It was beautiful in a disturbing kind of way.

"It's got a cat's face, don't you think?" Borja asked, training his eyes on it.

"More like a lion. Or a lioness, because it doesn't have a mane. It's got the body of a wrestler. And is very small…"

"Maybe the problem is that its hind legs are missing…" speculated Borja. "I expect those guys got angry because the statue is broken. But I swear it was like that when they handed it over."

"I don't think so. By the look on the face of the bastard who was the leader of that pack of wild animals I reckon it wasn't what they were after. Remember how he threw it to the other side of the room…"

"Perhaps it's a fake and he could see that…" surmised Borja.

"I'm not so sure," I responded. "The guy didn't look much like an expert. And I think this item is a genuine antique."

"The TV news said it was a dangerous gang of Russian mafiosi. They didn't say it was a gang of art thieves."

"That's what I don't get: since when did the police engage in shoot-outs with art thieves? Maybe with drugs or arms dealers, but not with crooks who thieve or deal in stolen antiques… And I reckon the *mossos* weren't looking for us. I don't think they even knew we'd been kidnapped."

"You're right. If they'd known, they'd have kept an eye on my flat and would have seen us come in," argued Borja.

We sat in silence for a while, staring at the statue until finally Borja got up and said, "I don't know about you, but I need a drink."

"And what are we going to with the statue? Leave it in your flat?"

"No, I'll take it with me. I'll think of something."

Harry's had just opened. Borja and I sat at the back of the bar and ordered a couple of gin and tonics. The waiter, who knew us, stared at Borja's battered face but brought our drinks without making a single comment.

"Let's suppose for a moment that the men who grabbed us weren't after the statue," I said. "What else might they have been looking for?"

"I haven't a clue." Borja gulped on his gin and tonic and suddenly burst out laughing, "Hey, you do get some bright ideas, don't you? So we were in China…"

"Well, I could see the Great Wall through the window…"

"That was a diorama," he chuckled. "We were in a film studio."

"And how was I supposed to know? Remember they put us to sleep for the journey, and, to begin with, you thought we were in China too," I growled, feeling upset. "By the way, how did you know there was a door that led to that back street and that the *mossos* weren't lying in wait on the other side?"

"I didn't know the police weren't there," he replied, shrugging his shoulders. "But I knew about that door because I once worked as a film extra for a spell in that studio."

"You worked as an extra? Do tell me more!" I asked, surprised.

"It was a horror film called *Perfume* and starring Dustin Hoffman. If you remember, they filmed it in Barcelona. I was in the orgy scene at the end."

"It's news to me… How come you never told me?"

"Well, it's a long story. The truth is we spent hours and hours there and I made friends with one of the production assistants. She showed me that door that was so hidden away that few of the people on the shoot knew about it. We sometimes skived off there for a cigarette."

"I reckon it saved our bacon!"

"I'm sure it did. But I'd like to know what the hell that was all about."

The two gin and tonics soon disappeared, and Borja ordered another round.

"And I still don't understand why that woman gave us that mobile phone," Borja declared after a while.

"Fuck, Borja! Suppose they were after the mobile and not the statue?" I'd had a sudden brainwave.

Borja put his hand in his pocket and took out the mobile and a keyring with the one key.

"Did you change your keyring?" I asked.

"No, it's the one Brian gave me."

"It's only got one key."

"Obviously, it's the key to his flat. I've already got the key to the front door."

"The mobile is switched off," I said, taking the telephone.

"Yes, it needs recharging," he sighed. "I'll have to find the charger, but if it's got a PIN number, God knows how we'll ever switch it on…"

I put the mobile on the table and stared back at that solitary key.

"Perhaps they were after this key, and not the statue or the phone," I suggested.

"The key to Brian's flat?" responded Borja incredulously.

"Remember how we didn't understand what they were saying and the Inspector insinuated that Brian was working for the CIA. And I'd remind you that those men were Russian and former members of the KGB. It all fits."

"But the Cold War finished years ago and the Russians and Americans are friends nowadays," Borja retorted. "Even though…" he left his sentence hanging in mid-air. "But organizing all those shenanigans for a key hardly makes any sense. They could simply have bust the door open like they did ours."

"Unless this key opens another door," I said, taking the keyring and scrutinizing the small key.

It looked like an ordinary key. It didn't even open mortice locks.

"It's a nice keyring," said Borja. "I think I'll keep it."

It was elegant, chrome metal and oval shaped. But too big for a single key.

"Hey, what have we here? It looks like a small spring…"

I asked the waiter for a ballpoint pen and tried to force the mechanism. The keyring half opened. There was a pen drive inside.

"Shit!" I shouted.

"What the fuck is that?" asked Borja, frowning.

"It's one of these things you put in your computer to store information. A pen drive. The twins have got one."

"You mean it's a kind of chip like the ones spies used for hiding info?"

"I suppose so, the modern version. Now I understand!" I said suddenly. "This is what they were after, that's why they got so angry when you gave them the statue. That must have put them out no end."

"What kind of info do you think it's carrying?" asked Borja.

"I have no idea."

"Well, we'll have to find out."

Borja suggested we went to his place and stuck it in the twins' computer to see what came up. We rapidly downed our gin and tonics and went out into the street for a taxi. A quarter of an hour later we were in front of Laia's computer.

"It must be a code, because it makes no sense at all," I said as I saw what came up on the screen. "It's just letters and figures."

"Perhaps one of the twins will be able to decipher it," rejoined Borja.

"Do you think so?"

"It's worth a try."

"Laia! Aina! Come here for a minute," I shouted.

"What do you want, Dad?" grumbled Laia. Aina pushed me out of the chair and sat down.

"We don't have the right program to read this document," she concluded after a while. "And Windows hasn't been able to identify what program it is either. If you want to read it, you'll have to take it to a programmer, or better still, to a hacker."

I sighed and extracted the pen drive from the computer and put it in my pocket. Montse, who'd just arrived, came into the room and had a fright when she saw Borja's face.

"What the hell's happened to you?" she asked, her eyes leaping out of their sockets.

"Nothing really. I tripped in the street where there were roadworks, and bashed my face," he said, trying to laugh it off.

"In the street?" asked Montse, not believing one word. "You sure it wasn't a jealous husband that did that to you?"

"No, Montse…" said Borja, trying to smile, but his face hurt and the move ended in a grimace of pain.

"Have you been to the doctor?"

"No need. I've not broken anything… A little ice pack and I'll be fine in a couple of days."

Montse went into the kitchen and came back in nurse mode with a packet of frozen peas. After applying it to Borja's face, she asked us if we were hungry and offered to cook supper. Borja said he was tired and was going home, but I took up her offer. After accompanying Borja to the door, while Montse went to the kitchen to cook my omelette, I stretched out on the sofa and fell asleep dreaming of Fu Manchu.

17

I got up late next morning. I was exhausted, and Montse, who suspected something dire had happened, let me sleep in and didn't ask any questions. I was grateful. Borja had also declared he was going to spend the day resting at home, so when the phone rang at one o'clock, I wasn't expecting it to be him.

"The Inspector has just phoned," he fired away. "He wants to see us this afternoon."

"Both of us?"

"Yes. He asked us to go at around five. He said he wants us to do him a favour."

"A favour?" I repeated, slightly nonplussed.

"He was all over me. I don't know what it's all about."

"Something to do with what happened yesterday in Poblenou?" I suggested. It was the most logical conclusion to draw.

"I hope not. He said it was to do with the murdered doctor."

"You mean Horaci Bou, of Zen Moments fame?" I responded, rather surprised.

"That's what he said. He wants to talk to us because we were at the centre the weekend of the murder and we know the course participants."

I huffed and puffed.

"I don't like the sound of it."

"Nor do I."

We both knew the Inspector was too wily to try to pull a fast one and that we had no choice but to go along with his request. We said nothing for a few seconds, our mobiles silent next to our ears, and then I asked, "So where shall we meet?"

My brother drove by in the Smart at half past four and we went to Les Corts together. This time the Inspector saw us straight away.

"Good heavens, Mr Masdéu! Whatever happened to you?" he asked, as he invited us into his office, with a broad smile I thought verged on the sarcastic.

"I tripped on a street where there were roadworks..." Borja started to explain.

"Which street?" asked the Inspector, looking at him incredulously over his spectacles.

"All right..." Borja smiled wanly. "Perhaps I was too familiar with a lady whose husband happened to be a prizefighter," he continued, hoping that explanation would satisfy the Inspector.

"I'm with you," nodded the Inspector, inviting us to take a seat.

"Well, here we are, Inspector," began Borja. "You said it was in connection with the death of Dr Bou, didn't you?"

"That's right. And I am extremely grateful you were able to come so promptly," said Inspector Badia, doing his best to sound pleasant.

"So, what's the problem?" asked Borja, who, like me, was beginning to lose his patience because the Inspector was playing cat and mouse.

"My problem is that the case remains unsolved," the policeman said, becoming very serious all of a sudden.

"You're joking?" I exclaimed. "I thought the *mossos* arrested the guilty party on the day of the deed!" I added, recalling the sight of the miserable Alícia sobbing as she left the Centre in handcuffs.

"Yes, but the judge let her go. And we are sure it wasn't in fact her."

"How come? Her bag was full of paint sprays and more besides. I saw all the stuff she had!" I replied.

"Yes, so she could leave that graffiti and play all those practical jokes, as one might call them. She has confessed to that. But she did not kill Dr Bou. In fact, the doctor was already dead when she was plastering the walls."

"Can you be sure of that?"

The Inspector shut his eyes and nodded.

"The forensic investigator has put the time of death between twelve and one a.m., and Alícia Cendra was on the phone from half past eleven to half past one. She did her paint spraying after that, when Dr Bou was already dead."

"So, who was she on the phone to for all that time?" I asked, remembering that the use of mobiles was banned at Zen Moments and realizing I was the only one who'd taken the ban seriously.

"Oh, to loads of people!" said the Inspector, who had opened the dossier on his desk and started flicking through the papers it contained until he found what he was after. "First she spoke to her ex-sister-in-law, that was for fifty-six minutes; then she called a tarot number for them to read the cards for her – twenty-seven minutes; another girlfriend she spoke to for a mere twenty-two minutes and finally, at one twenty-five, she phoned back the friend she'd first spoken to, who had put the phone down on her."

"Couldn't she have killed him while on the phone?" Borja asked.

"No," the Inspector shook his head. "Mrs Valèria Camps was in the room next door with her window open and heard the conversations. Indeed, at one o'clock she went and complained and asked her to stop shouting so much because she couldn't get to sleep. Alícia Cendra has confirmed that. In fact," the Inspector added, "they are the only people with cast-iron alibis."

"What do you mean?"

"That currently we have a bunch of suspects who were asleep in their bedrooms without alibis!" exclaimed the Inspector with a deep sigh. "Including you two, naturally."

"So, you see us as suspects?" asked Borja, shocked. "You can't be serious?"

The Inspector stared at us for a few seconds with those cold, steely blue eyes that make me so nervous.

"Not really," he said in the end, unable to avoid smiling at our reaction. "We've carried out a number of investigations, and, in principle, I don't think either of you had any reason to murder him."

"That's lucky!" I yelped, relieved.

After all we'd been through over the last forty-eight hours, it would have been the last straw to be included on a list of murder suspects.

"We barely knew Dr Bou," clarified Borja. "And if it hadn't been for that assignment on behalf of Teresa Solana…"

"I know, I know. That's why I want to ask you to do me a favour," said the Inspector gently.

After a rather theatrical pause, the Inspector closed the dossier, sprawled back in his chair and wrung his hands.

"You won't believe this but we, too, are affected by the new government's cutbacks," he began.

"Oh, really?" said Borja.

"I've lost staff who haven't been replaced and have people off sick, and at the moment the murder squad can't cope.

164

I think we've got off on the wrong foot this spring. And to cap it all, I don't know if you heard about the battle royale in the Poblenou the other day that ended in a total free-for-all…"

"I think I got a whiff of that," replied a deadpan Borja.

"The truth is we're not coping, and I thought you two could give us a hand. Quite off the record, of course."

"Us?" I asked, astonished.

"Come, come, Mr Martínez, don't be so modest." The Inspector shook his head. "Additionally, I must declare a personal interest in this case."

"Could I ask what that might be?" enquired Borja, as perplexed as I was.

"Dr Bou was the younger brother of Dr Virgili Bou, who saved my life years ago on the operating table – no need to go into the sordid details. I am very grateful to him and am keen to solve this case as soon as possible. It's an open secret they couldn't stand each other, but Dr Virgili has been quite shattered by his brother's murder. Family is family, particularly when murder is involved…"

"So where do we come in?" I asked, not seeing what the Inspector was driving at.

"Unfortunately, as I've explained, my men can't cover everything. What with people on sick leave, unfilled vacancies, the bloodbath in Poblenou and gender violence against women, we're chasing our tails. And most of the eyewitnesses the detectives have interviewed clam up: nobody wants to talk to the police, let alone be mentioned on the television news."

"I find that really odd," Borja piped up. "People nowadays kill to get on TV."

"Be that as it may," the Inspector continued, "I'd thought that as you got to know these people when you were in the meditation centre the night Dr Bou was murdered, perhaps you could ask them a few questions and see what you get out of them."

"In what capacity would we do this?" I objected. "They are under no obligation to talk to us. Besides, as you know, we're not even licensed detectives…"

"Dr Virgili Bou is aware of that. Indeed, it was *his* idea to have recourse to a private investigator, because I am quite against bloodhound agencies. But you are different: you aren't professionals and don't have any of their vices. All you have to do is talk informally to all the suspects and see if you can find anything out."

"And all *gratis et amore*, I suppose," I asked.

The Inspector smiled slyly.

"I thought I wouldn't need to mention the fact that you and I have a deal: *quid pro quo*, or have you forgotten?"

I turned bright red.

"Could we please let Latin rest in peace?" Borja pleaded in irritation. "Which suspects do you want us to interview?"

"Well, the people who spent the weekend in the clinic, Dr Bou's partner, his wife…"

"So his wife is a suspect as well?" I asked.

"Currently we are investigating everybody at the centre when the murder was committed, with the exception of Alícia Cendra and Valèria Camps, who appear to have good alibis, and those who know the alarm codes and had access to the building. On Dr Bou's side, there are five individuals who knew him," he continued, reopening the dossier and reading aloud. "The yoga teacher, who spent the night in the centre, Dr Bernat Comes, Sònia Claramunt, the receptionist and the young woman who cleaned and cooked."

"Iolanda," I added.

"Sure, but what were their possible motives to kill him? Couldn't they help us reduce the list of suspects?" asked Borja.

"My men haven't come up with much. To start with, it seems Dr Bou owed that Sebastià money, and that one of the young women, Mònica, had had a fling with Dr Comes ages ago and it went badly wrong and she blamed Dr Bou. Iolanda complains she was paid a pittance and that he was a complete clown, and the gay couple… Well, it seems the younger guy was jealous of Bou. Bernat Comes has an alibi, thought it's quite weak. As for Dr Bou's wife, her horns reach as far as the Port Olímpic."

"Is that it?" asked Borja sardonically.

"Oh, I almost forgot," added the Inspector. "There is one final suspect, an American sculptress we might describe as Dr Bou's official mistress, one Edith Kaufmann. Mrs Kaufmann claims she didn't know the alarm codes, but we can't be sure she's telling the truth. Besides, Dr Bou himself could have let her in."

"An attack of jealousy and a lovers' quarrel that ended badly?" asked Borja.

"Very possibly. That's what I want you to find out!"

"You still haven't told us how he was killed," I reminded him. "Was it a blow to the head?"

"Several, actually. The forensic investigator reckons he was hit three or four times."

"But, Inspector, do you really think we'll be more success-ful than your men?"

"At the very least, I think your findings will speed us on our way to a conclusion. I may not approve of the way you make a living, but that doesn't mean I don't recognize you have a certain talent for sussing people out."

"There's still one thing you've yet to clarify in terms of the suspects," I said. "*Cui bono?*"

"For fuck's sake, can't you pack in the Latin?" growled Borja.

"His wife inherits the lot," explained the Inspector, "but it's no huge fortune. Indeed, they were still paying off the

167

mortgage on the clinic and there are more debts than anything else."

"And what about his partner, Bernat Comes?" asked Borja.

"He gets nothing. What's more, it does him no good that the widow now becomes the clinic's main shareholder. Obviously there are rumours about them being lovers, but they have denied it…"

"In other words, this is just one huge pile of shit…" Borja concluded graphically, with a sigh. The Inspector smiled.

"Here are the witness statements and everybody's telephone numbers and addresses." The Inspector handed over a sheaf of paper from the other side of his desk. "Of course, this is all highly confidential. Theoretically, I called you in to question you as witnesses, but quite off the record. The judge, who is leading the investigation, must remain in the dark concerning our little accord."

"And if he finds out?" I enquired.

"He *won't*. What's more, please remember you've been contracted by Dr Virgili Bou. I simply acted as an intermediary, because the doctor is very busy and doesn't have the time to see you."

"By the way, have you checked out his alibi?" I persisted.

"Yes, Mr Martínez," smiled the Inspector. "He was on duty from eight p.m. and spent nearly all night in the operating theatre."

"And does he suspect anyone?"

"He never really took to the widow."

"Fine. We'll talk to all the suspects and tell you what we think," said Borja, getting up and shaking the Inspector's hand.

As he was about to open the door, Borja turned to the Inspector and asked, "On another front, have you found out who killed Brian, our neighbour?"

168

"We've got one or two leads," the Inspector replied laconically, terminating our exchange.

We couldn't say no to the Inspector. We both knew that. When we'd walked a good distance away from the police station, we went for a beer.

"After all we've been through, I'd completely forgotten about the doctor's murder," I told Borja.

"Me too. Frankly, we could have done without this..." came his reply.

"You know, lately we just seem to have been treading in shit."

We were silent for a time, chomped on the crisps we'd ordered with our beers and put up with the deafening racket in the bar. Two tellies were switched on, broadcasting different channels on different sides of the bar. If that wasn't enough, a radio was droning on as well. A bad habit shared by lots of bars in Barcelona.

"Look at it from another point of view," Borja said finally, always looking for the positive side. "The Inspector's assignment will help us flesh out the report we have to write for Teresa Solana."

"So what do we do now?"

"What the man said: talk to the people on his list."

"Do you really think we'll find out anything new? Do you think the Inspector has got a screw loose?"

Borja shrugged his shoulders.

"How should I know, bro? In any case, we didn't have much choice."

We finished our beers and retraced our steps to get to the Smart. Borja offered to drive me home and, when we'd almost got there, he looked for a place to park the car.

"You want to come up for a moment?" I asked, bemused, because I thought he was keen to get off home.

"No, it's just that there's a very big Chinese bazaar near here."

"You're going shopping in a Chinese bazaar?" I asked again, even more bemused. The last thing I expected my sybarite of a brother to do was yield to the temptation of the cheap goods on sale in the Chinese bazaars.

"I've had an idea for a hiding place for the statue," he said. "I can't carry it around with me all the time."

"You mean you had it on you in the police station?"

"Of course I did. And Brian's keyring too. I'm not happy about leaving that at home."

"So what's your bright idea?" I asked, not daring to imagine what might have happened if the Inspector had suspected Borja was carrying on his person a valuable, smuggled statue and a CIA spy's pen drive.

My brother smiled and said I should go to the shop with him, if I wanted to find out. We went in, and Borja grabbed a basket and filled it with lurid objects with one thing in common: they were all more or less the size of the statue in his pocket. A total of eight euros and seventy cents of junk in bad taste.

"What are you going to do with all that?" I asked.

"I'll clear out one of the drawers in the dining-room sideboard and put these objects in there next to the statue. So, if anyone opens the drawer, they'll think they've found the odds and sods."

"The odds and sods?"

"Yes, you know, the odds and sods," he repeated as if it were obvious. "The presents you say are just more 'odds and sods' because you don't know where to put them. So you make a special place…"

"I suppose that might work," I admitted grudgingly. "And what are you going to with the keyring?"

"For the moment, I'll take it with me, as we don't know what's in the pen drive."

"But what if it's some kind of secret formula? Or the plans for a horrific weapon?" I said, contemplating the possibility that information that was vital to world safety had fallen into our hands.

"Don't be so melodramatic," responded my brother, throwing the bag of junk into the Smart. "If it were really important, Brian would never have entrusted it to a complete stranger."

PART III

Iolanda leapt out of bed when she woke up, without any prompting from an alarm clock. It wasn't quite seven a.m. When she realized she was out of work and had no reason to get up early, she slipped back in between the sheets, though she knew she wouldn't get back to sleep. Her six-month contract at Zen Moments had run out and not been renewed, and she was too angry with herself to turn over and snooze as if her life was continuing as normal. She kept telling herself she had only herself to blame. Why the hell hadn't she kept her big mouth shut? Would she never learn?

Iolanda had fixed her CV to get that cleaner's job at the meditation centre. Bitter experience had taught her that putting down her degree in biology guaranteed she wouldn't get any job she went for. At the moment, biologists weren't in demand, and you didn't need a university degree to work as a shop assistant, checkout operator, waitress or housemaid. What's more, Iolanda knew her university years counted against her, because the moment they saw she had a university degree they assumed she was far too clever and sent her packing. For certain jobs, young women without degrees were more vulnerable, and more easily cheated.

Iolanda felt guilty when she got the job at Zen Moments: she kept thinking her lies had allowed her to beat off an immigrant girl who, unlike her, had no academic qualifications and no chance of aspiring to anything better. She *had* been to university, but how did it help? All the effort made by her parents to give her a good education and university place, so she would have a better future than them, had been a complete waste of time. Everyone said that her only option was to study for an MA, but MAs were expensive, and her parents' savings had disappeared long ago. Iolanda was prepared to work at anything, except whoring, to pay for a course, but her big mouth had now lost her that job.

And she'd been very lucky because it was a doddle. As the building was new with decor designed according to the latest minimalist aesthetic, all she had to do was go round with the vacuum cleaner, dust the few objects on display, clean the windows, change the linen and clean the rooms of residents on Monday mornings. This was the most onerous part, but all in all it didn't amount to very much. She was young and energetic enough, and her job left her a few hours to go and clean a couple of houses a girlfriend had found for her.

Even so, the fact they'd contracted her because she was Catalan and spoke Catalan had annoyed her from the very first day at the centre. Lots of cosmic harmony and smooth talk, she thought, but, at the moment of truth, they preferred a local girl to anyone from India or speaking with an East European accent – and at the same low rate of pay. Iolanda had noticed that, apart from the gardener, who was Peruvian – and, naturally, never moved from the garden! – not a single employee was foreign. Then there was the centre's atmosphere of good karma and fake cheeriness that she couldn't stand. Iolanda was sick to the back teeth of that jumble of second-rate mysticism and Eastern philosophies, so sick that when they found the corpse of Dr Bou in his office with his head smashed in and someone had said Dr Comes ought to be alerted, she had simply felt the need to shout out something that was quite true: Dr Comes, however skilled he was with Bach flower remedies, or however handsome, wasn't a medical doctor, but a doctor of philosophy. Naturally, her comments soon came to the ears of Sònia Claramunt via Cecília, and Sònia Claramunt, apart from being Dr Bou's wife, was also the centre's financial director, and she soon informed her that her contract had run out, good riddance and *adéu*.

She soon tired of lazing in bed and got up at a quarter to eight. She'd agreed to meet Maribel, the receptionist, for a drink that morning. As they always caught the bus together after work and in the end had become friends, Maribel was annoyed Iolanda's contract hadn't been renewed. Maribel had worked at the centre for a year and a half and knew all the gossip; even though she was on holiday, she still had first-hand, last-minute information.

"They're going to make lots of changes," Maribel told her in that secretive tone she adopted when talking. "To begin with, they intend installing a spa and beauticians' rooms in the basement. And they will charge more for weekend courses that will now include massages and beauty treatment."

"I don't think the old director would have liked these changes one bit," commented Iolanda.

"Oh, they've also cancelled the rubbish vegetarian catering. Sònia wants to contract one of Ferran Adrià's protégés as a chef. And you can drink wine with your meals, because she says research has shown that a drop of alcohol is good for you."

"In other words, now that the old witch has sacked me it's getting lively!…" Iolanda lamented, sighing as she spoke.

"Well, you did stick your neck out…"

"So what? What I said was true!" she retorted, trying to act the innocent and not succeeding.

"Yes, but you said Bernat wasn't a doctor so sarkily," replied Maribel, who was no fool.

It was true. She had been very sarcastic. But the fact was that Bernat was an idiot. All that homeopathy and Bach flower remedies was nonsense. All the same, the bastard was handsome. Far too handsome. With that glowing tan and bright eyes, he was handsome in a virile kind of way that was quite genuine, and brought tremors to Iolanda's tummy whenever she bumped into him in the centre's corridors. What's more, Dr Comes (he'd never told her to call him Bernat) always smelled sweet and had the prettiest feet Iolanda had ever seen: Greek feet in line with classical ideals of beauty, with an index toe that was longer than the big toe. Iolanda also wondered whether his svelte body would be like those young bodies she'd seen sculpted in marble in books and museums, with the difference that Bernat was no downy adolescent, but a fully grown man who, unlike a lot of boyfriends Iolanda had suffered, would surely know how to run his expert hands over her body and excite her to an ecstatic climax. Iolanda got the shakes whenever she speculated about Bernat's amorous dexterity.

"The fact of the matter," said Maribel in a gentle, common-sense tone of voice, "is that you've got the hots for Bernat!"

"You're crazy."

"Oh, yeah?"

Fancy him? How could she fancy someone who spent his time cheating people?

"Homeopathy and Bach flower remedies are one big piss-take," continued Iolanda.

"That's what you think, darling. There is scientific proof that they work," retorted Maribel, who didn't share her friend's scepticism.

178

"There is *no* scientific proof, Maribel. The homeopathic belief in *similia similibus curantur,* that is, like is cured with like, is based on the medical ideas of Hippocrates, a Greek doctor who lived in the fourth century BC, in an era when they had only the vaguest notions about how our bodies work and doctors did what they could."

"You mean Hippocrates was a nincompoop?" asked Maribel. Her only contacts in the world of the ancients were *Gladiator,* Brad Pitt disguised as Achilles and a television series based on the exploits of Hercules.

"No, Hippocrates was a pioneer and many people think of him as the father of modern medicine because he transformed it into an independent discipline, separate from philosophy and religion, the opposite of today's homeopaths who think they are his descendants."

"Oh!" exclaimed Maribel, who'd lost the thread.

"Curiously enough," continued Iolanda, "Hippocrates was the first person to reject the idea that illnesses were caused by supernatural or divine causes, and he sought their causes in environmental factors, diet or way of life. It's true he believed that illness derived from an imbalance of bodily fluids, that is, blood, black bile, yellow bile and phlegm, what he called 'humours', but to continue to think all his theories are valid, without taking into account the discoveries and advances made over twenty-five centuries by his followers, is really ridiculous. Hippocrates himself must be turning in his grave."

"You are so knowledgeable," said Maribel with genuine admiration. "I am sure you'll get a job as a secretary. But, in the meantime, why don't you ring Bernat and apologize? He might persuade them to give you your job back..."

It was quite unfair the way they had sacked her. And, besides, she needed the work. Although she didn't go along with that philosophy for the idle rich they peddled at Zen Moments, she had to recognize it wasn't the worst job in the world. Considering she'd only been able to save six hundred euros towards the MA from the wretched pittance they paid her, it would be worth her while making the effort to apologize. Perhaps Maribel was right and she could persuade him she had only said he wasn't a doctor in all good faith, to stop them from swamping him. She'd go to the hairdresser's, spend an afternoon shaving and applying creams, put on a low-cut dress and on a work pretext phone him and arrange to meet for a coffee in a quiet café where she would tell him she was a biologist and not merely the girl who did the cleaning. After all, Bernat couldn't possibly be as nasty as he seemed, and, you never know, with a bit of luck and the right kinds of hints, they might end up dining together.

18

Two days after we escaped safe and sound from our kidnappers, the dailies and television news were still talking about the spectacular police raid in Poblenou, though fortunately the reports said nothing about any kidnapping. In fact, what struck me most was the way politicians and commentators said the *mossos* had gone too far, while others reproached them for not going in hard enough. Afraid an angry spy might retaliate if he handed the pen drive Brian had given him over to the authorities, Borja had decided to keep it hidden at home. In the meantime, my brother still hadn't heard from the person he was supposed to deliver the statue to, so the antique and the keyring had ended up in the drawer with the junk made in China he'd bought in the bazaar near our flat.

We thought the investigation the Inspector had assigned us was slightly peculiar, but in the end found it comforting because it meant Badia didn't think we were involved in Horaci's murder, or in Brian's, and didn't suspect we'd escaped by the skin of our teeth from the shoot-out at the film studio on Monday. On the other hand, we couldn't refuse his request because, if he wanted, the Inspector could really land us in it, so we had decided to forget the other business and focus on his list of suspects and eyewitnesses.

Sònia Claramunt, Horaci's widow, was the first person we had to speak to. She lived in Tres Torres, which is closer to Borja's neighbourhood than mine, so we agreed to meet at her flat. I rang the bell a few minutes before eleven, and Borja, who was waiting for me, came downstairs straight away, flourishing the keys to the Smart.

Tres Torres was in the well-off part of Barcelona, north of the Diagonal. Sònia Claramunt lived in a flat in a modern, three-storey building surrounded by a garden area that was unambiguously cultivated for aesthetic effect; it wasn't designed for children to play in or for neighbours to sunbathe or enjoy the cool shade in. The report the Inspector had given us indicated it was a building the Bous acquired before the property boom began, even though the price the Bous paid at the time was well beyond the budgets of most ordinary citizens. A uniformed porter in the lobby asked us which flat we were visiting, and before letting us in, rang Sònia Claramunt to check that we were welcome.

"Tell her we've come on behalf of Dr Virgili Bou," Borja told him.

Sònia Claramunt gave us the green light and the porter pointed us to the lift.

"Don't you think we should have phoned her before coming?" I asked Borja, as we zoomed up to the third floor.

"No way. I'd rather catch her by surprise and not give her time to prepare her answers!"

"Sure, but the police have already questioned her," I replied.

"It's hardly the same," countered my brother, very self-assured and confident of his skills as a detective. "You let me do the talking."

An uncombed Sònia Claramunt opened the door: in her dressing gown and in a temper. She wasn't made up, and I hardly recognized her because the widow in dark glasses

I'd seen walking into Zen Moments with Bernat Comes had looked to be an elegant beauty much younger than the woman standing in front of us now. When I inspected her from close-up, I saw she was well past the forty mark and had undergone a facelift: a pert little nose, full cheeks, puffy lips and a hieratic glare that betrayed the work of a plastic surgeon who'd meddled with her face and made a fine mess. She was tanned, but her skin was coarse and singed by the hours she spent in fake-tan establishments preserving that perpetual summer shade of brown. She was barefoot, and I was shocked to see that her two little toes were missing.

"We'd like to ask you some questions about your husband's death," remarked Borja after expressing his condolences. "Your brother-in-law has contracted us to give the police a hand in their investigations."

"Virgili?" she snapped, unable to hide the bad feeling the sound of his name provoked. She invited us to step into the lobby, but didn't seem about to offer us even a glass of water.

"His brother's death has left him distraught," continued Borja in the same mournful tone. "That's why we would like to talk to you —"

"Oh, really," interjected Sònia, assuming the same haughty air she'd displayed in the clinic on the day of her husband's murder. "Well, tell Virgili to leave well alone and let the police get on with it!"

"Surely, but the fact is —"

"Are you two policemen?" she asked, looking as if she was about to send us packing.

"Well no, but —"

"Then I have nothing to say." She opened the door. "Have a good day!"

She was adamant and we could hardly create a scene because the porter looked every inch a nightclub bouncer, and Borja and I had used up our annual quota of fisticuffs with thugs, so we left her flat, tails between legs and offering no resistance. Although Sònia Claramunt was under no obligation to talk to us, we were shocked by her hostile attitude and total lack of interest in helping to clear up her husband's murder.

"What a waste of time!" I sighed when we were out in the street.

"On the contrary," Borja contradicted me. "Her attitude was extremely eloquent. I bet you anything her brother-in-law is right and that she was the one who did him in."

"I'm not so sure. You like rushing to conclusions... Besides, the fact she can't stand her brother-in-law simply means the dislike is mutual. That doesn't make a murderer of her."

"In any case, *I* think she did it," insisted Borja, very sure of himself.

I looked at my watch.

"Half past eleven. What are we going to do now?"

"Ring Alícia," suggested my brother, smiling like Mephistopheles. "It would be interesting to hear her opinion about what happened to Horaci."

During our stay at Zen Moments, Borja and Alícia had only exchanged a few polite words, so we thought it would be better if I called her. Alícia was at home, depressed and on sick leave, and she sounded so pleased to hear my voice she said we could go to see her whenever we liked. As she lived in Sarrià and her flat was relatively near to where Sònia Claramunt lived, I suggested going that same morning. She was delighted by the prospect and invited us to come for pre-lunch drinks.

Alícia welcomed us, all spruced up and with the dining-room table all ready. Crisps, olives, strips of ham and a bottle of Martini Rosso were set out on serviettes. She asked us whether we preferred beer or Coca-Cola to Martini, but we were both happy with Martini.

"I got very angry when I realized Horaci had led me such a dance," she announced, telling us about her suicide attempt with homeopathic pills, which we knew nothing about. "How can medicine cure you, if it doesn't kill you when you take an overdose? And you know, I took one hell of a lot of pills that night!" she added, shaking her head.

"It's quite natural you should feel angry," said Borja.

"That's why I enrolled on the weekend course at Zen Moments. I wanted revenge, to ruin Horaci's reputation with all those annoying jokes. But I never thought of killing him. In fact," she continued, "I am sorry he is dead. I know I am naive, but I did have such high hopes. And when I saw him in the Dry Martini, with that woman, and when I went into hospital and the doctor said the blotches and itches weren't nerves, but a case of mange…"

"I'm not surprised you wanted to get back at him," I replied. "I imagine I would have reacted no differently."

"Do you have any idea how much money I spent at Zen Moments? I could be enjoying new tits and an unwrinkled face right now!" she mused.

"But you look wonderful…" soft-soaped Borja. "Most women would do anything to be like you when they're past forty!"

Alícia smiled gratefully because she was now well past fifty. Even so, Borja was right: she looked very well preserved for her age.

"If I have understood correctly," she went on, "you are detectives and investigating Horaci's death on behalf of his brother."

"That's right," said Borja, not wanting to enter into details.

"Where do I come in?"

"Tell us all the centre gossip. Anything that might give us a lead on who killed Horaci and why."

Alícia told us she'd heard rumours about Sònia Claramunt and Bernat being lovers, though some people also reckoned Bernat was gay.

"But I don't think he is," she added, sounding quite definite. "The fact he's such a handsome hunk doesn't mean he's necessarily queer. And I don't believe he's been carrying on with Sònia. In fact, it was Pietat, one of Horaci's students, who started to spread that gossip. Simply because she saw them together in the street one day…"

"What can you tell me about Cecília, the yoga teacher?" Borja then asked. "Do you think she had any reason to feel resentful towards Horaci?"

"I wouldn't know," she replied, shrugging her shoulders. "Though everybody knew she was in love with Bernat. That stuck out a mile," she continued, lowering her voice and leaning forward.

"So what about Horaci? Did he have, shall we say, a special relationship with any of his pupils?"

"Horaci's admirers were legion," Alícia smiled sadly. "Admirers as silly as I am, I imagine."

"Do you have any theory about who killed him?" I asked.

"If I were to lay a bet on it, I'd go for Sònia," she said. "She must have found out Horaci was having an affair with that American artist and must have been afraid he was going to leave her and take everything with him. According to Maribel, Sònia is one of the shareholders in Zen Moments, with Horaci and Bernat. She must now own Horaci's shares!"

The rest of the gossip she told us wasn't connected with Horaci's murder, but Borja and I listened politely and pretended to be genuinely interested. We finished our drinks, said no to another round and that we had to leave.

"So what will happen to you now? I mean as a result of the japes?" I asked when we were in the lobby.

"My lawyer says I can claim I was mentally disturbed at the time. He says I shouldn't worry about the salt I put in the food or the itching powder, but that it was a mistake to stuff silicone into the keyhole and spray red paint everywhere, because though the judge may accept I was temporarily mad, I will have to pay damages, and the repairs will cost a small fortune," she said with a sigh of resignation.

After we left Alícia, I suggested to Borja that we go to my place for a bite to eat. He said he couldn't because he was having lunch with someone.

"With Merche, I expect?" I asked.

"Cold, cold."

"Lola?"

"You're freezing now." And he winked and added, "It's a surprise. If everything turns out OK, I'll tell you this afternoon."

"All right, Pep, but don't get us into another mess, right?"

"Cross my heart…" replied my brother with a solemn expression that boded ill.

Montse had work at the Alternative Centre and my mother-in-law and I had lunch by ourselves. My mobile rang at half past four when it was time to go and collect Arnau from school. Borja wanted us to meet at five at Montse's centre.

"I've got to pick up Arnau. We'll have to meet a bit later."

"OK," he agreed, and hung up.

I went to collect Arnau and left him with Joana, who gave him his afternoon snack. Borja was already at the centre when I got there at five thirty. Montse was surprised to see the two of us and immediately told us that if we'd come for money the centre had none.

"No, no, Montse!" said Borja, bursting out laughing. "Don't always think the worst! I'm the bringer of good tidings."

"What kind of good tidings?" asked Montse in a tone that barely concealed her scepticism. "Have you split up with Merche at last?"

"Much better news than that. I found you a capitalist partner to save you and your partners from bankruptcy."

"A capitalist partner? In this day and age? You must be joking!"

"Not at all. She is prepared to invest up to sixty thousand euros," Borja revealed.

Montse was so astonished she was struck dumb.

"Sixty thousand euros? Have you gone mad?" I exclaimed, afraid that this generosity must come with draconian measures that would suck out the little blood we had left. "And how do you reckon they will ever repay sixty thousand?"

"There's no need. I said I'd found you a capitalist partner."

"You mean Merche…" piped up Montse, weighing up the implications such a move might have for her relationship with her sister, if my brother's official girlfriend became her Alternative Centre's partner and saviour.

"Don't you worry," said Borja, bursting out laughing again. "It's Mariona. She'll drop by tomorrow to meet you and talk through the details. If you and your friends are happy to have her as your partner, that is."

Montse was shocked into silence for a few moments more before she finally asked him, "Why does a rich woman like her want to invest her money in a business that is going down the pan?"

"It's not really a business decision. She is doing it as a favour because I asked her to. And because, as you have pointed out, she is so rich that the sum of sixty thousand euros is neither here nor there for her."

"This means we can pay our suppliers and hold out a bit longer, until things improve," said Montse, who was already doing her sums. "We've invested so much effort and energy in this project…"

"So, there you are. Problem solved."

"And you say she'll drop by tomorrow?" Montse suddenly blurted out, looking terrified.

"Tomorrow, around midday. Is that a problem?" asked Borja, frowning.

"No, of course not. But I do need time to clean and tidy everything," said Montse, glancing around. "We'll have to give these walls a lick of paint and —"

"No need to stress out. Mariona knows Gràcia isn't the Bonanova. And she's not coming to carry out an inspection," Borja reassured her.

"Even so, we've not got any time to waste. We need to get a move on. I'll ring Elsa and Solé right now," she announced, running to the phone. Elsa and Solé are her partners.

I was speechless. Once again, Borja had saved my bacon, as he always used to when we were kids. Knowing Mariona, I imagined it hadn't been easy to convince her to invest her money in the Alternative Centre.

"I'll be home late tonight," Montse told me after she'd put the phone down. "We won't rest till the centre is shining like a new pin!"

"Montse, it really isn't necessary…" Borja repeated.

"Now you'd better be off. I've not got a minute to waste!"

Montse threw herself round Borja's neck and kissed him twice loudly.

"Borja, you may be a snob, but you're wonderful!"

"You know Eduard is like a brother to me," said Borja with a smile.

"It was a real stroke of luck when he met you. Lola and I struck it lucky too!" she exclaimed, giving him another kiss.

We left a happy Montse to get on with her spring clean, and, as we were in Gràcia and near the plaça de la Virreina, Borja suggested we go to the Salambó for a drink.

"I don't know how to thank you," I began. "If they'd ended up shutting the centre, Montse wouldn't have found another job very easily. She's no twenty-something any more."

"I know. That's why I decided it was time to do something. Besides, I owed you one. What with that crazy idea about us being in China…"

"Don't rub it in. You believed we were too."

"Whatever, but now we've solved Montse's little problem I think we should focus on the Horaci case and the suspects who have a motive but no alibi. Get pencil and paper."

I obediently took my notebook out of my pocket.

"Take notes. First we have Sònia. She had a reason to kill her husband and doesn't have an alibi."

"Right."

"We can discount Alícia. And if we discount Alícia, we can discount Valèria too."

"But she might have lied," I retorted. "It may be true that Valèria heard Alícia talking on the phone, but she would only have taken ten minutes to go down to Horaci's office and kill him."

"True, but, according to the police reports, Valèria had no motive," argued Borja.

"All right, we'll discount her," I sighed. "And what about Sebastià? The Inspector said Horaci owed him money."

"Yes, we should talk to him. Add him to the suspects' column."

"Who else?"

"Edith, the American artist," said Borja. "It may have been a crime of passion."

"True enough. I think we should include Cecília as well. She worked at the centre and may have a motive the police haven't yet uncovered."

"That's right. Another one for our list."

"And what about the others?"

"Maribel, Iolanda and Bernat have solid alibis that the police have checked out," said Borja, reviewing the documentation the Inspector had given us. "Maribel lives with girlfriends who said she was at home with flu; from what it says here, a doctor from social security paid her an emergency visit at around one a.m. Her friends said she didn't move from her bed the whole day. And Iolanda went to a concert at the Palau Sant Jordi with friends."

"And Bernat?"

"He's also got a good alibi. He went out to dinner with friends in the Port Olímpic and they ended up in the Vela where they stayed until three a.m. What's more, the guy brought a woman home with him," Borja continued.

"Even so, he and Horaci were partners and I think we should talk to him," I suggested.

"All right. We can eliminate Carles and Ernest from our list: they went to dinner at a friend's place and were out until two a.m."

"The alibi given by Xavier and Carme is quite rocky," I concluded after reading the reports. "I think Xavier was jealous of Horaci."

"Very good, add them to our list. We'll pay them a visit."

"Do we discount Isabel?"

"Who is Isabel?" asked Borja.

"You remember, the woman who said she had cancer and didn't want any treatment."

"I really don't have a clue. Put her on the list, just in case. And then there are the two young women who are friends, Marta and Mònica."

"Do I put them on the list of suspects too?" I asked.

"It doesn't look as if either had a motive to do Horaci in. And I don't think they are friends enough to commit perjury. I think we can eliminate them."

"You're the boss."

We now had a list of seven suspects, and as Horaci's murderer or murderess didn't force the door or set off the alarm, the guilty person must be one of them. Borja asked me to read the list out aloud.

"We've got Sònia, Sebastià, the American artist, Cecília, Xavier and Carme and Isabel. What I don't know is what we can do to get more information than whatever the police extracted."

"Bah, it will be a walkover, you just see," said Borja, who always thinks everything will be easy.

That evening we decided we would interview Bernat Comes first, although he wasn't a suspect, and then go and see Cecília. As we had all their addresses, courtesy of the Inspector, we'd call on them at home in the morning without prior warning and catch them by surprise.

"And now we've sorted that, let's drink a toast to Mariona!" said Borja.

"Here's to the good health of Mariona… and here's to yours, kid!"

19

That night Montse got home just before two. She and her partners had set about tidying their Alternative Centre in readiness to welcome Mariona, who'd said she'd be appearing at midday that same morning. Although my wife was shattered, she was so excited she couldn't sleep.

"Put the alarm on for seven," she said after tossing and turning in the dark for a while.

"We always get up at a quarter past," I replied.

"Yes, but I've lots still to do. Oh, and could you see to Arnau and the twins? I won't be around."

"OK, now get to sleep."

The next morning I did everything Montse had requested. Joana, who kept repeating she'd always thought Borja was basically a good boy, got up earlier than usual, prepared breakfast and eased the twins out of bed. I took Arnau to school and then headed to the San Marcos where I'd agreed to meet Borja before we paid our visit to Bernat Comes.

Bernat also lived in Sarrià, but unlike Alícia, who lived in an old, very humble flat, Bernat's was a modern, spacious attic flat that confirmed my first impression of him as a spoilt rich brat. Borja and I knocked on his door at ten and caught him in his pyjamas.

"Very sorry. We didn't have your phone number, so we

had no way of contacting you," Borja apologized. Naturally, he was lying.

"How did you get my address?" he asked, annoyed and half-asleep.

"Horaci's brother gave it to us. In fact, he's contracted us to investigate his brother's death."

"I'd better put some coffee on," he said, rubbing his eyes.

"Oh, so you're partial to coffee?" I asked in surprise.

"Coffee is a great idea," chirped Borja, digging me with his elbow to get me to shut up.

Bernat went off to the American kitchen at the back of his lounge-cum-dining-room and prepared three cups of coffee on one of those automatic machines that are now so fashionable. Personally, I prefer the old-style Italian coffee-pots, but that ersatz brew was better than nothing.

"So how come you want to speak to me?" he said after gulping down his coffee. "The police have questioned me and accepted my alibi. I was with friends well into the early hours."

"Right, in the Vela, and, indeed, you aren't a suspect," said Borja.

"So what exactly do you want from me?"

"Well, we thought that as you two were partners you might be able to tell us if Horaci had enemies or if there was anyone who resented him enough to want to kill him," said Borja, trying to establish a fraternal upper-class complicity with the guy and leaving me somewhat in limbo.

"I don't know if Horaci had any enemies," he answered laconically.

"It does seem obvious that someone hated him enough to kill him," persisted Borja.

"Or could benefit in some way from his death," I added.

"All I know is that he and his brother, the surgeon, didn't get on at all well," said Bernat.

"You are 'right there, but Dr Virgili Bou isn't a suspect."

"So, it would seem I can be of no help," he rejoined, languidly shrugging his shoulders.

"We know the person who murdered Horaci was either in the centre that night or had keys to the building, because nobody forced the door open," Borja went on.

"Oh, really?" said Bernat as if he couldn't care less.

"Come on now, you must suspect somebody…" continued my brother.

"It's one thing to have suspicions and another to have proof. I have none."

"What about Sebastià? I gather the centre owed him money…"

"Horaci commissioned the stone sculpture from him that's in the lobby, but Sònia and I thought his fee was far too high. We are negotiating a solution."

"Do you think Sebastià was so angry he could have split his head open when they were arguing?" I asked.

"Frankly, I think it's unlikely. What would he have got out of killing him? Besides, the centre may owe him for the sculpture, but having it on display in the lobby means Sebastià gets lots of new commissions. Why did you think he was there at the weekend? He was hunting for new customers. And as we owe him money, it was all free."

"So who do you suspect?" persisted Borja.

"I'm sorry, but I'm not going to accuse anyone. I —"

At that very moment, a young woman who was half-asleep and wearing a bathrobe that was too big for her appeared in the doorway. It was Iolanda.

"What's the matter?" she asked. "Oh!" she added, stepping backwards the moment she saw Borja and me.

"Good morning, Iolanda. We were talking to Bernat about Horaci's death," said Borja, as if Iolanda's presence in that attic flat was the most normal thing in the world.

"Oh, I agree with Bernat. I think it was his wife," said Iolanda. And seconds later, when she smelled the aroma of coffee, she shouted, "Great! You've made coffee!"

"I imagine you'd like to shower and dress before breakfast," said Bernat icily. "You'll find clean towels in the bathroom."

"But, of course…" Iolanda muttered, rather subdued.

After lingering for a few seconds, Iolanda turned and walked out of the room, her cheeks a bright red. Right then, I'd have liked to identify Bernat as Horaci's murderer and march him off to Les Corts so the Inspector could lock him up in a cell.

"We just had a chat after a few drinks," Bernat explained defensively. "I'd like to make it clear I've not accused Sònia of anything."

"Not to worry, you're not the only one rooting for Sònia," smiled Borja. "Might I ask you if it is simply an intuition or whether you know something the police don't?"

"It's what seems most logical," Bernat rasped, walking to the door and inviting us to clear off. "I'm sorry, but I must get dressed too. I have an appointment and it's late."

As I'd promised Montse that Borja and I would be at the Alternative Centre before twelve to greet Mariona, we decided to shelve our list of suspects for a while and head for Gràcia. Montse and her partners had performed miracles: they had painted walls, framed posters and bought candles and flowers. The old sofa in the entrance had disappeared, and in its place were two wicker armchairs with a matching table.

"They belong to Elsa," said Montse. "We'll take them back to her place after Mariona's visit."

At twelve Montse and her partners began to eye the clock nervously. Everything was ready to welcome Mariona. The minutes passed slowly. They started to fret impatiently at a quarter past, and by half past even Borja was worrying that Mariona had had a rethink and that this might turn into a remake of *Bienvenido, Mr Marshall*. Finally, at a quarter to one, Mariona's silver Mercedes was purring outside the door.

"You must be Montse?" she asked after kissing her on both cheeks and greeting her partners with a nod. "I am very, very sorry, but I can't stop. I've spoken to my lawyer and he'll send you the necessary paperwork next week, so no need to worry. Now, as we can trust one another and I think you may be rather short of cash, I've brought you this on account," she said, handing Montse a cheque for twenty thousand euros. "When we sign the paperwork, I'll give you a cheque for the balance. And I'm so sorry, but I must go now as I have another meeting."

"But wouldn't you like to have a look at the centre, madam?" Montse asked, quite beside herself.

"My dear, please cut the madams, we're partners," replied Mariona, bursting into laughter. "I'll come another day with more time and you can show me everything. I'm sure it's absolutely delightful. See you soon."

Montse stood rooted to the spot, cheque in hand and gawping, while Marcelo, Mariona's chauffeur and butler, opened the door of the Mercedes and she quickly climbed in.

I don't know where Mariona was rushing to, but from the jewels and clothes she was wearing I imagined it must be an important reception. Montse was happy with the cheque, but upset and disappointed because she and her partners could have spared themselves all the effort they'd made to prettify their modest premises. She said she was going to the bank to pay it in straight away.

"That's typical Mariona!" Borja apologized. "The key thing is you've already got a healthy advance."

When Montse returned from the bank, we all went to celebrate with a cheap set lunch. Then she and her partners returned to the Alternative Centre, and we went in search of the Smart. We'd decided to go to Hospitalet that afternoon to talk to Cecília, and as my brother refused to go by metro and a taxi would have cost a fortune, we needed the car.

Cecília lived in a small, dingy, stale-smelling flat in a poor neighbourhood. Her mother opened the door and told us her daughter had just slipped out to the supermarket, but would soon be back. The lady, whose name was Dolores, invited us in for a coffee without taking the minimal precautions necessary with total strangers.

It was a small flat, and while Dolores boiled up the coffee in the kitchen and we waited in the dining room, she informed us without raising her voice that she was a widow and deeply grateful to her daughter, because her widow's pension didn't cover the rent. Cecília was a good girl, she said. She'd been lucky to find that job in Barcelona, where she earned almost double what she was paid when she worked on a supermarket checkout. Pity she'd not got a steady boyfriend, she added, because she was over thirty and, if she didn't watch it, she'd be left on the shelf.

"Don't you worry, Cecília is a pleasant, attractive girl. I'm sure she has lots of suitors," said Borja.

Dolores had just poured our coffees when Cecília walked in, dragging her shopping trolley behind her. She was wearing tracksuit bottoms and a long-sleeved, faded T-shirt. She must have left her silk saris and garments at the meditation centre together with a good deal of her beauty. Though she wasn't spectacularly pretty, the Cecília I'd seen at Zen Moments was an attractive girl who had little in common with the tired, dreary woman now standing opposite us.

"Mum, how could you let two complete strangers into your house? Don't feel offended, please!" she added for our benefit. "What if they'd been a couple of thieves? You are too trusting!"

"Look, dear, they seemed honest enough…"

"Your daughter's right, Dolores," I said. "You shouldn't open your door to strangers. Appearances can be deceptive sometimes."

Dolores sighed and offered to take the trolley into the kitchen and leave us alone with Cecília.

"We'll have a nasty shock one of these days!" the girl lamented.

"I'm very sorry. We had your address but not your number," Borja apologized.

"How can I be of help?" she asked, intrigued by our visit.

Borja told her Horaci's brother had involved us in the investigation and that we wanted to ask her a few questions.

"I suppose the police think I'm a suspect as I don't have an alibi?…" she asked, sounding frightened.

"I don't think you have a motive either," said Borja soothingly. "We've not come here to talk to you as a suspect, but because you've been working at Zen Moments for some time and have first-hand knowledge of how the place works. You might have your own theory about what happened to Horaci."

"You mean about who killed him? I don't know. Horaci was a good person," said Cecília, shrugging her shoulders. "Although he flirted with women too much, particularly the mature sort…"

"Did he flirt with you?" asked Borja.

"No, he didn't," she answered, turning bright red.

"Can you think of anyone who might have a reason to want him dead?"

Cecília hesitated for a moment before she replied.

"Things between him and Sònia were in a bad state," she said. "They had frequent quarrels. Usually work-related. But that's as much as I know."

Cecília explained that after everything that had happened, Sònia had decided to ring the changes at Zen Moments, and that was why she was on holiday. However, she couldn't help us track down Horaci's murderer because she really didn't have a clue. Borja and I politely drank our coffees and said we had to go.

We weren't so lucky with Edith Kaufmann. She lived on the Diagonal, level with Tuset, but according to her maid, she was away from Barcelona for the time being. As she refused to give us further details, once we were back in the street we rang Edith on the mobile number the Inspector had given us. She was in Sant Sebastià and apologized when we said we were ringing on behalf of Horaci's brother and she wouldn't be back until Sunday night. We agreed to drop by her place on Monday morning.

"It's almost eight o'clock," I said, looking at my watch. "I'd like to be home early."

"I'll drive you there," Borja offered. "I'm meeting Merche at nine."

"So you're not seeing so much of Lola these days?"

"She's annoyed with me. But I'll solve that this weekend," he replied.

I got home and found that Joana had set the table, and made a salad and a couple of potato omelettes.

"How come dinner is so early?" I asked.

"They're showing *Titanic* at half past nine," my mother-in-law explained.

"*Titanic*? But didn't you see that the other day?" I asked, remembering how Montse had said she thought she'd watch it while I spiritually exercised at Zen Moments.

"In the end they showed *Cleopatra*, with Elizabeth Taylor. Montse stayed up to see it, but I felt sleepy and went to bed. I hope they don't change it tonight as well!" my mother-in-law muttered.

When we were having supper I asked Montse if she was sure they didn't show *Titanic* on TV the night Horaci was killed.

"Of course I'm sure," she said, not understanding why I was asking the question. "Solé wanted us to go out for dinner, but I preferred to stay at home and be company for my mother who wanted to see the film."

I smiled. I had just caught Sònia Claramunt out lying. She had said she'd stayed at home watching *Titanic* the night of Horaci's murder, and that was clearly untrue.

"Do you know what?" I told her. "I think your mother has just helped me solve the case of the murdered homeopath."

"Really?"

"Shush, will you, the film's starting!" growled my mother-in-law.

"Well, you can tell me all about it later, OK?" said Montse, sitting on the sofa.

I left them glued to the screen and went to my bedroom to read.

20

When I told Borja the following morning what I'd discovered
thanks to my mother-in-law, we both agreed the widow had
gone up several rungs on our list of suspects. Her lie about
the film she'd seen on television the night her husband
was killed at the very least showed she'd not been straight
with the police. All the same, before we told Inspector
Badia, we decided to continue our round of questioning
in case we discovered anything else related to the events
on the night of the murder or to any other motives that
might exist. It was the turn of the married couple, Xavier
and Carme, and we thought we'd speak to Xavier first,
and then to his wife.

As Carme had mentioned during the introductions at Zen
Moments, Xavier was an entrepreneur, if a quite modest
specimen. He ran a small firm that refurbished houses, work
he subcontracted to other firms of self-employed workers
who did the grind, and with the crisis it was experiencing
a lean time of it. Xavier's firm had premises in a basement
on Balmes, down past plaça Molina, and, as on previous
occasions, Borja and I turned up mid-morning without warning. Xavier gave us a warm welcome that seemed genuine
enough and invited us to coffee in the bar next door.

"Luckily we were able to save something when the going
was good and now we can manage until things start to

pick up," he explained. "Even though Carme sometimes has dreams of grandeur that make it difficult to keep any money in the bank!" he added, sighing like a husband resigned to satisfying his wife's extravagant whims. "If she'd had her way, we'd have a yacht in hock and a house in the Ampurdan that the bank would have repossessed by now."

"At times it *is* difficult to make the ladies see sense," agreed Borja, who is fond of these chauvinist clichés. "I expect Carme spent a fortune at Zen Moments?"

"To tell you the truth, it was cheaper if she meditated and did yoga at the centre than if she spent a day in the operating theatre," he continued. "What with getting new lips, firming up her breasts, butt and belly, removing her varicose veins and having operations on her nose and ears, Carme has spent a fortune on plastic surgery. Luckily, at the time we could afford…"

"It's not easy for women at the moment," I suggested. "They're bombarded on all sides with the idea that they're duty-bound to be eternally young. It must be difficult to resist the onslaught."

"Well, you know, it's true that after she'd given birth twice the operations improved her a bit," he said, shrugging his shoulders. "Particularly her tits, which were really drooping for her age… Though I don't like what they did to her nose. I preferred it the way it was."

"The fact is, Carme is a sight for sore eyes," Borja soft-soaped him. "Some people think you were jealous of Horaci!…"

"Jealous of Horaci? Come off it!" Xavier started laughing, as if that was an absurd idea. "I was more concerned about *his* wife," he added.

"Sònia? You mean…" Borja didn't finish his sentence.

Xavier wrinkled his eyebrows, as if he didn't understand

what Borja was hinting at, and then he burst out laughing again.

"No, no way! Come off it! The fact is that when Carme got her monthly ticket to Zen Moments, she stopped going to her plastic surgeon for a time, and that came as a relief because she'd become quite obsessed with him. And it wasn't just the money, you know? I was worried about her health: going in and out of operating theatres so much can't do you any good."

"So what's that got to do with Sònia?" I asked.

"Can't you see? That woman's got nothing natural left on her!" exclaimed Xavier. "The fact is when Carme got to know her, she was crazy about plastic surgery. She even had her small toes amputated so she could wear some shoes or other... Can you imagine?"

"Do you mean Sònia voluntarily lost some toes? Why on earth would she want to do that?" I asked, recalling how I'd noticed that detail quite by chance.

"Apparently, some shoes are the fashion now that you can wear *only* if you have your small toes amputated. But I had to dig my heels in and threaten Carme. I told her if she cut any toes off, I would divorce her."

"Ah, so you mean Carme and Sònia became good friends through Zen Moments..."

"Not likely! Sònia is only interested in people who are loaded. I earn a decent amount (or rather, I used to), but Carme and I aren't rich. Besides, we're both from Sants, and it shows, however much cash you have. Sònia is too much of a snob to forget that."

"You told the police you spent the night Horaci was killed together in Carme's room..."

"Yes," he replied, as if he didn't grasp what we were after. "It would have been the last straw if I couldn't sleep with my wife!"

"But, if I remember correctly, you spent both days arguing," I added.

"It's the way we are," he said, shrugging his shoulders. "If we argue, it doesn't mean we don't love each other. On the contrary, the day Carme and I stop fighting like cat and dog, I'll start to be worried."

"Do you have a theory about who killed Horaci?"

"I hardly knew him, but Carme is convinced it was Sònia. Obviously, Carme isn't entirely impartial, because she envies her. However much she denies it. She'd like to have Sònia's class and savoir-faire."

"We'd like to speak to Carme," said Borja. "Do you think we will find her at home now?"

"No, she's not in Barcelona. She's gone to spend a few days with a friend who has a house in Pals. But she'll be back next week, if not before, if she gets bored." He added with a smile, "In any case, I can tell you that you are wasting your time if you think Carme or I are suspects."

We said goodbye to Xavier and went to see Marta in the belief that Mònica was much more of a suspect because she has a monthly ticket to Zen Moments and had known Horaci for some time. If one of the pair was covering up for the other, it was Marta for Mònica. We phoned her and, as she worked in Gràcia, we agreed to meet her on a café terrace in the plaça del Sol at half past one.

"You are quite wrong if you think I'm covering up for Mònica," she told us after we explained why we were paying her a visit. "I thought Mònica was really worried about me, but she only wanted me to go with her to Zen Moments so she could try to get off with Bernat."

"Did she tell you as much?" asked Borja.

"Yes. She came to my room that night and we talked and talked. I wanted to let it all hang out, because I was going through a really bad patch," she said, looking down.

"So you chatted until two a.m.?"

"It might even have been later. In the end, we quarrelled, because when she told me about her infatuation with Bernat and the real point of our stay at the centre, I asked her to return the two thousand euros I'd paid out. And naturally she couldn't because she didn't have them. No, Mònica didn't kill Horaci." And she suddenly added, as if she'd just remembered she might be a suspect as well, "And nor did I either, obviously!"

Marta had a short lunch break, and Borja and I bade her farewell, assuring her the police didn't think she was a suspect either.

We went home for lunch as we were in Gràcia. At around four we decided to visit Isabel, who seemed quite dotty and had no alibi, though I had heard her snoring at some point in the night. We knew she was off work on sick leave, and turned up at her place on spec though we realized she would probably send us packing when she heard why we'd called. But she didn't. Even though she was surprised to see us and hear that we were detectives, she invited us in for a cup of tea.

"I know who killed Horaci," she declared. "It was the pharmaceutical transnationals."

"What on earth do you mean?" asked Borja ingenuously.

"Well, Horaci taught us to mistrust the prescriptions and diagnoses of conventional medicine. He said – and quite rightly too – that it was big business. That's why I decided to cure my cancer using natural therapies."

"Isabel, cancer isn't an illness you can diagnose light-heartedly. If you are ill, you should go to a proper doctor. It may not be cancer, but anaemia." I couldn't stop myself from saying that when I noticed how underweight she was.

"Yes, I could see at Zen Moments that you were one of *them*," she counter-attacked warily.

"I'm not saying medicines aren't big business or that doctors don't often make a big mess of it and prescribe more medication than is really necessary," I retorted. "But doctors and medications do save people's lives."

"Medicine makes people sick," she declared categorically. "That's why I never take any."

"But if you don't take any, and now have cancer, what does that imply?" My reasoning was ruthless in its logic and Isabel was nonplussed for a few seconds.

"You can say what you like, but you're not going to trap me." Then her expression suddenly changed. "I see it all now... I expect you were the people who killed Horaci." I realized she had just entered a spiral of paranoia.

"No we didn't, we are only —"

Isabel got up and stepped back from her chair, a look of terror spreading across her face.

"So now you have come to kill *me*, haven't you?" That being a statement of fact rather than a question.

"We'd better be going before we get into real trouble," I whispered to Borja.

Borja and I got up and tiptoed quickly out of Isabel's flat, leaving her convinced that my brother and I were a couple of killers hired by a pharmaceutical company to send her to the other side.

"You are quite right: that woman's not all there," was Borja's comment as we beat a retreat from her neighbourhood.

As I'd listened to Isabel, I'd realized to what extent we live in a world still under the sway of superstition, irrational beliefs, misunderstandings and magic. Isabel was sure that scientific research and advances were merely a plot, organized at planetary level by the powers that be, and that the noble profession of doctors was simply evil commerce orchestrated by the pharmaceutical companies. The idea that real knowledge resided in antiquity and that the ancients, by dint of being ancient, were necessarily wiser, more disinterested and purer than present-day mortals was another of the misunderstandings that many so-called alternative therapies used in order to manipulate the ignorance of individuals of good faith, like Isabel now.

"In any case," I told Borja, "one has to recognize that doctors themselves are to blame if there are so many people who think like Isabel. A large section of the scientific community has surrendered to the interests of the pharmaceutical and food conglomerates; too many studies with a 'scientific' label produce results suspiciously favourable to the people who commissioned them. On the other hand, there are issues scientists can't agree on, like, for example, whether transgenic food is good or bad for you. I myself don't know what to think on that subject…"

"So what you are saying, then, is that Isabel is right…"

"No, not at all. At the very least, scientific studies are there to be compared and refuted and, in effect, that is what scientists do all the time. The problem with homeopathy and Bach flower remedies is that their therapies are based on faith rather than scientific method. You have to believe in them if you want to be cured. The advantage of conventional medicine is that you don't have to be a believer for them to take effect. Their abuse is another issue entirely."

"Anyway, I think we can discount Isabel!…" sighed Borja. "Horaci was her hero."

"So what do we do now? It's very early," I asked.

"I think it's time to pay Sebastià a visit."

Sebastià lived in Sant Joan Despí, and, as it was Friday, and he might have decided to go away for the weekend, we decided to ring him to avoid going on a wild goose chase. Borja dialled Sebastià's number and he immediately picked up the phone and seemed pleased to hear Borja's voice. He said he was busy that afternoon, but suggested we should go and have dinner with him. Borja was free, because Merche was going to the Liceo with her husband and some friends, and Lola had a working dinner, while I was looking forward to a quiet evening at home with the family. After I'd sighed and nodded in agreement, my brother accepted his invitation.

"Montse will be furious," I said.

"It won't go on until late, you just see."

The house-cum-workshop Sebastià had in Sant Joan Despí was impressive. The first thing he did when Borja and I arrived was to show us the sculptures he'd made and those made by other artists he collected. He didn't look like a man with financial problems, and Borja asked him some straight questions.

"I've been able to devote myself to sculpture thanks to the fact that my father made a lot of money," he explained. "And I'm doing very well as a sculptor," he said with a wink.

"But I thought Horaci had owed you money for some time for the sculpture he commissioned for the Zen Moments lobby," Borja continued. "The police might think you were angry and split his head open."

"Do you really think so?" he asked, seemingly taken aback.

"Well, they're not discounting any possibility. You know how they work…"

"I don't in fact," he said, as if he genuinely didn't. And then laughed and said, "It would be really idiotic for me to kill Horaci because he owed me for that sculpture! I've had a load of commissions because of the one he displayed in the lobby."

"Bernat claims that's why you go at the weekends: to get customers."

"Yes and no," said Sebastià. "It's true I do a bit of self-promotion, public relations, as the Americans say, but the fact is…" He didn't finish his sentence.

"The fact is what?" Borja asked.

"Well, you know, Zen Moments is a good place to get to know ladies of a certain age and status who haven't let their figures slide. My wife died two years ago and you'll understand I'm not the kind of man to sign up to one of these Internet agencies that help you find a partner. Valèria, for instance, is an interesting woman and we've met a couple of times since that weekend."

"I thought as much," said Borja.

As it was past ten o'clock and the temperature had dropped, Sebastià lit a fire and served us a supper of cold meats, cheeses, pâtés and bread with tomatoes. The bottle of red wine my brother and I had brought was soon dispatched.

A few more bottles bit the dust. I got home at four a.m., after Sebastià persuaded Borja to park the Smart in his garage and call a taxi. According to Sebastià's theories, Sònia was also the chief suspect, since she and Horaci had been more than living separate lives for a time, and divorce was on the cards. Now only Edith Kaufmann remained on our list, the mysterious lover whom only Sònia and Alícia knew. But we'd have to wait until Monday to speak to her.

21

After a quiet weekend when Lola and Borja smoked a pipe of peace or two, we went to see Edith Kaufmann on Monday morning. The painter had forgotten about our appointment and looked surprised to see us.

"Oh, yes… It's true we'd agreed to meet today," she said, swathed in a gauzy turquoise tunic, with an absent-minded expression on her face that struck me as sincere. "You're here on behalf of Horaci's brother, I take it?"

Although she was American with a strong Chicago accent, she spoke Catalan well.

"Yes," nodded Borja. "We are collaborating with the police to try to find the murderer."

"I thought the murderer had been arrested. As that all happened almost a month ago…"

"Well, three weeks, to be exact," I noted.

"So, who do you think they arrested?" asked Borja.

"I don't have a clue. I rarely read the newspapers. I'm not interested in current affairs."

"Don't you want to know who killed the man you were in a relationship with?" I asked, rather shocked.

Edith looked at me in amazement as if she couldn't see why she should be interested in discovering who had killed her lover.

"I spoke to an Inspector," she finally confessed. "Do you

know how long I had known Horaci? Eight months. We got on well and occasionally went out for a drink followed by a fuck. No commitments or *mals rotllos*, as you Catalans put it. I am very sorry he is dead, obviously, but, to be frank, I wasn't that interested in the guy. I don't know if the person who bumped him off had a decent motive or not, but the fact is I find the whole issue quite boring."

"Didn't it bother you that he was a married man? Weren't you jealous of his wife?" asked Borja.

"That was his business, not mine," she replied with a shrug of the shoulders. "And in any case, I'm not after a husband, if that's what you are insinuating. I've had four, and I can assure you there won't be a fifth. Whether Horaci was married and was or wasn't happy with his wife was no concern of mine."

"What kind of paintings do you paint?" I asked, pointing to a big canvas that dominated her lounge.

"Oh, no… That's by Yves Tanguy. Another surrealist painter." And she added with a smile, "I'm not that good yet."

"I think we can wrap this case up," said Borja as we left Edith's house. "It is obvious Horaci was killed by his wife."

"I think 'obvious' is too strong…" I replied. "Edith doesn't have an alibi either."

"I know, but you've seen how almost everyone has plumped for Sònia. And that lie of hers confirms it was her."

"So what do we do now?"

"We'll give the Inspector a call and tell him what we've discovered and what we've concluded."

"But the Inspector will want proof."

"I know. And I've got an angle on that: we'll ring Sònia and blackmail her. And if she falls for it…"

"So, you are definitely discounting Edith?" I asked.

"Well, if you want we can blackmail Edith as well, and see which of the two we catch out... But my money is on the widow," he said.

The Inspector arrived at Harry's punctually, at eight on the dot, and ordered an alcohol-free beer. Borja and I, who'd got there early in order to land a table that was out of the way, were already on our gin and tonics that the Inspector was looking at askance. I'm not sure whether it was disapproval or envy.

"Do you think this place is discreet enough?" he asked, looking suspiciously around at the tables, most of which were still empty.

"Oh, definitely!" Borja hastened to soothe him. "There's never anyone here at this time of night."

"Yes, but the waiters..."

"They're real professionals," responded Borja. "And they prepare great cocktails! You should order one."

The Inspector looked around again and sighed.

"If you say so," he said finally. "I suppose the off-the-record nature of our encounter justifies meeting up in a cocktail bar, though I can tell you for nothing that I don't like bars. So what have you found out?"

"We've spoken to all the suspects and eyewitnesses and boiled the list down to two," said Borja, smirking.

"And?"

The Inspector couldn't hide his impatience, and Borja, who wanted to savour every moment of our little victory sitting opposite the man who'd caused us more than one upset in recent weeks, took his time finishing his sentence.

"The front-runners are Sònia Claramunt, the widow, and Edith Kaufmann, the lover. But we plump for the widow, don't we, Eduard?"

"Yes," I agreed, nodding my head.

The Inspector sighed, raised his eyebrows, and then sprawled backwards. He'd yet to taste his beer.

"Well, Deputy Inspector Alsina-Graells also comes down on the side of the widow," said the Inspector. "Though it is only an intuition, because she has no proof. Might I ask how you reached the same conclusion?"

"Quite simple, really: if we take the list of suspects and put to one side those who don't have an alibi, and, on the other, those who have a strong motive and we think capable of the crime, you'll see that the names that select themselves are Sònia and Edith," said Borja.

"That's not enough," replied the Inspector. "Maria del Mar reached the same conclusion days ago. But judges want proof, not intuitions."

"Oh, but I think we have something the Deputy Inspector failed to find out," said Borja.

"What might that be?" asked the Inspector, raising his eyebrows.

"Sònia Claramunt said she was at home watching *Titanic* the night her husband was killed."

"That's why she has no real alibi," interjected the Inspector.

"Yes, but we've caught her lying. The lady did not see *Titanic*," said Borja, beaming all over. "It would have been quite impossible."

"So what?"

I felt the Inspector was beginning to lose patience.

"Well, it just so happens they didn't show *Titanic* that night on the TV. They showed an Elizabeth Taylor film instead," explained Borja.

The Inspector stared through him as if he didn't understand.

"The fact is they decided to pay homage to Elizabeth Taylor that night, because she'd recently died, and changed the film at the last minute. According to the newspaper they were going to show *Titanic* at ten o'clock, but at the last minute they decided on *Cleopatra*. I know because my wife and mother-in-law adore *Titanic* and organized dinner so they could see it afterwards."

"And that means Sònia Claramunt lied!" added Borja in case the Inspector couldn't see what he was getting at.

"Maybe." The Inspector shook his head. His reaction was less enthusiastic than we'd anticipated. "But I don't think that will convince any judge. She can always say it was a mistake, or that she was watching another programme, like *Big Brother* or a porno film, but was too embarrassed to say so. This is hardly incriminating stuff. Lying about the film or programme she saw on TV is no crime," he said.

"There's another argument in favour of her candidacy for the chief-suspect spot," revealed Borja.

"What might that be?" asked the Inspector, sitting up in his seat.

"All the people we have spoken to think she is the murderer. If they were members of a jury, they would undoubtedly declare her guilty. And so many people can't be wrong, can they?" asserted Borja.

"Even so, this is no proof," I piped up.

"Well, such unanimity is remarkable…" retorted Borja as if the power of his logic couldn't be challenged.

"No, your brother is right," said the Inspector. "The opinions of eyewitnesses must always be treated with a pinch of salt. And, by the way, what about the remaining suspects? I'd like to know why you discounted them so rapidly."

Borja gestured to me and I took out my notebook.

"There are in fact only three people who were in the centre that night who don't have an alibi: the sculptor, the yoga teacher and the woman who says she has cancer."

"You're sure about that?"

"Mònica and Marta, the two who are close friends, were chatting in their room into the early hours. Mònica eventually confessed to her friend that she'd had a fling with Bernat Comes. In fact, she'd persuaded her friend to accompany her on that weekend in Zen Moments with a view to seducing him. Marta, who didn't know Horaci from Adam, swears they were chatting in her room until three a.m. And Marta is currently feeling too resentful towards her friend to lie to the police just to give her an alibi."

"What about that married couple? The husband was jealous of the doctor, wasn't he?"

"They both say they spent the night in the wife's room," I replied.

"They might have agreed that in order to have an alibi," objected the Inspector.

"To be frank, I don't think Carme has it in her to take the pressure such a crime would bring. Besides, Xavier was grateful rather than jealous of Horaci," said Borja. And he added, "That is a long story."

"So what about the sculptor and the yoga teacher?" asked the Inspector.

"In truth, neither had any motive to want to kill Dr Bou, or at least any motive with substance. Sebastià," I said reviewing my notes, "had been chasing Horaci for months for payment for the stone Buddha in the lobby, but he also wanted to take advantage of the contacts Horaci and Bernat had to sell his sculptures to Zen Moments' clientele. As for Cecília, the yoga teacher, gossip has it that she is in love with Bernat. She had no motive to want to kill Horaci."

"And the woman with cancer?" asked the Inspector.

"You mean the woman who *says* she has cancer, because it is all down to self-diagnosis. She is not all there, Inspector," I explained. "Frankly, I can't see her smashing Horaci's head in and then getting rid of all her fingerprints. Nor did she have any motive, as far as we know. In fact, Isabel admired Horaci, and her theory is that the pharmaceutical companies did him in." The Inspector raised his eyebrows and sighed. "Besides, she was in the room next to me and I can vouch I heard her snoring all night."

"That leaves the lover, Edith Kaufmann, who has no alibi, but a possible motive," recalled the Inspector, sighing yet again. "Even if the Deputy Inspector is convinced she is not the kind of woman who would waste time on killing her lover."

"I agree," said Borja. "Edith belongs to another class. She is far too sophisticated a lady to commit such a vulgar crime."

"It's strange, you know," remarked the Inspector. "Maria del Mar, who also questioned her, was very struck by Edith Kaufmann. She said she wished she could be like her."

"I think Horaci was merely a momentary diversion for her and that she couldn't have cared less if he was married or involved in lots of affairs. Inspector, I know my women, and I can't see her tracking him down to the centre to snuff him out," said Borja.

"Even so, she had a motive and can't be discounted," objected the Inspector.

"Well, I wouldn't waste more time on her," said a supremely confident Borja.

The Inspector finished his beer and looked at his watch.

"Thanks for your help," he said as he made a move to get up. "The Deputy Inspector will be pleased you agree with her. I will tell her everything you've just told me…"

"Just a minute, Inspector," said Borja, grabbing his arm to stop him getting up. "Where are you going?"

"Well, I thought we'd finished…" said the Inspector, sitting down again, rather upset by my brother's imperious tone.

"Eduard and I have come up with a plan to catch Horaci's murderer. That *is* what you are after, isn't it?"

"Though I'm not so sure it's a good idea," I muttered.

"I'm all ears," said the Inspector, ignoring what I'd just said.

"Given the circumstances," Borja began, conscious we had to capture the Inspector's attention, "our only option is to trap one of the two women into incriminating herself. Consequently, we thought blackmail would do the trick."

"Blackmail is a crime," retorted the Inspector.

"Yes, but if we do it with your agreement…"

"I don't think I really understand."

"Oh, come on, Inspector! You know perfectly well what I mean. Eduard and I will ring Edith and Sònia and say we are in possession of a videotape that proves they went to Zen Moments on the night in question."

"Well, I presume you mean a diskette," the Inspector corrected him. "People don't use tapes any more."

"All right, whatever," said Borja.

"But the building doesn't have security cameras, and they are both aware of that," objected the Inspector. "Or at least, his widow must be."

"Yes, but what they don't suspect is that the mansion opposite does have hidden cameras that you can't see from the road and that are filming twenty-four hours a day," said Borja with a smile.

"And is that so?"

"No," said Borja calmly. "But they don't know that. And if we sound persuasive enough…"

Inspector Badia stayed silent for a while, deep in thought. He was a strange guy, not quite your usual ignorant, foul-mouthed cop that I'd met in previous eras. With his longish grey hair, intellectual spectacles and Antoni Miró suit, he could well have passed himself off as a lawyer, politician or executive. If you didn't know he was an Inspector in the *mossos d'esquadra* and bumped into him in the street, you'd never have guessed his line of business. Nonetheless, we couldn't forget that the Inspector was a man of the law and that we were fakes with our office fit for operetta and Borja's false identity. Finally, after a long pause that enabled Borja and I to finish our gin and tonics, the Inspector said, "For any confession to be legal, it would have to authorized by a judge and you would have to use a microphone."

"That's fine," said Borja, keen to seem cooperative.

"Naturally, if I talk to the judge and then neither of them gives in to blackmail, or they take out a writ… I will look a complete fool," argued the Inspector.

"So the best way to play this," said Borja with a grin, "would be to call them and test the waters before speaking to the judge, don't you agree?"

Before the Inspector could raise further objections, Borja took his mobile out and called Edith Kaufmann. He threatened her, saying he had a video that showed her going in and out of Zen Moments on the night Horaci was killed and that if she didn't pay him sixty thousand euros he would hand it over to the police. Edith insulted him in English, threw shit at him in Catalan and hung up.

"You see, Inspector?" said Borja. "It's clear Edith knows it is a trick, because she didn't go to the centre on the night in question. I told you it wasn't worth wasting time on her." And, as he dialled another number, he added. "Now let's see how the widow reacts…"

Borja phoned Sònia and told her the same story. Sònia listened to him attentively and, a few seconds later, said she didn't believe him and that he didn't have any such video.

"Very well," we heard Borja tell her, "I'll take the recording to the police."

"No, wait!" she said. "Sixty thousand euros is a lot of money. Thirty thousand is the most I can lay my hands on." Then she added, "But I need time even to get that sum, because my husband only left me a load of debts."

Borja replied he would give her two days to find the thirty thousand and that he and I would go to Zen Moments on Thursday afternoon with the incriminating video. Rather theatrically he cautioned her against trying anything rash.

"Whoopee!" said Borja after hanging up. "That's her in the bag!"

"Now we only need to persuade the judge!" exclaimed the Inspector with a sigh, as he beckoned to the waiter to come over and ordered a whisky straight. And, shaking his head, he added, "To tell you the truth, Mr Masdéu, I don't know how I ever let you implicate me in such madness…"

Borja smiled contentedly. I would like to have told the Inspector that my brother's persuasive talent was one of his virtues or defects, depending how you looked at it, and that he wasn't the first person to succumb to it. But I said nothing. The Inspector downed his shot of whisky and we ordered another round of gin and tonics as the pianist for the evening opened his performance at Harry's with the classic 'The Way You Look Tonight'.

22

Late next morning the Inspector rang Borja and informed
him that the judge had finally given him the green light.
Deputy Inspector Alsina-Graells would lead the operation
and we should come to the station on Les Corts at nine
on Thursday morning to start off. At the time, Borja and
I were window-shopping in jewellers on the Passeig de
Gràcia trying to find a present for Lola, whose birthday it
was on Sunday. Borja couldn't decide between a white-gold
bracelet and some earrings.

"What do you think?" he asked.

"You know an engagement ring is what would really make
Lola's day."

"I think she'd prefer the bracelet," concluded my brother,
acting as if he'd not heard me. "Its fancy design is more
her style."

As soon as we left the shop, Borja's telephone rang again.
My brother answered, sure it would be the Inspector, but
when he heard the voice on the line his expression changed
and he looked surprised. I could only hear what Borja
was saying, but it wasn't difficult to deduce he wasn't in
conversation with Inspector Badia.

"It was that woman," said Borja rather nervously after he'd
hung up. "The one who gave me that mobile."

"The foreign lady with the sensual lips?"

"That's right."

"So how come she phoned your mobile and not the one she gave you?"

"Because its battery has run out…" said Borja. "I've not found a charger that works."

"Does she want to meet up?"

"Yes, she wants to see me tomorrow to collect the package. She says it's the only day possible because she's very busy on Thursday and Friday, and her plane leaves first thing on Saturday."

"Good heavens, how garrulous! This time she really went into detail…" I said, remembering how sparse she'd been in her use of words when she accosted us in the street. And as I'd heard where Borja had suggested they meet, I queried, "Why did you say the zoo? Isn't that rather recherché?"

"I don't think so. It's the first place that came to mind," he replied. "I once saw a spy film in which the secret agents agreed to meet at the zoo to exchange their messages; I suppose that's why I thought of it." When he saw I still looked bemused, he added, "It's a secure place, open-air, with lots of people with children… Nothing remiss can happen to me in a zoo."

"To us, because I'm coming too," I replied.

"No, you're not," he said, shaking his head. "I got involved in this business by myself and you don't have to pick up any of the fall-out. I'll go alone."

"You're my brother. I'm not letting you meet a CIA agent without someone to cover your back. And I'll remind you I'm the elder brother, so don't answer back."

"No, you're not. You popped out first. So, in fact, I'm the first-born," argued Borja.

"Be that as it may, I'm coming tomorrow," I added. "What I can't fathom is why it had to be opposite the lions. Isn't that rather dramatic?"

"So what did you want?" he retorted, shrugging his shoulders. "An encounter opposite the giant turtles or a tapir? At least you can't miss the lions."

"True enough," I had to agree.

We walked as far as the Diagonal, where our ways parted. Borja had arranged to have lunch with Lola and said he was going to take a taxi. I decided to take the bus home.

"Are you sure it's what we really ought to do?" I asked anxiously. "I mean, the information on the memory stick may be vital for the safety of the planet, and tomorrow you're going to hand it over to a complete stranger. Perhaps you should speak to Badia, tell him the whole story and let him take over."

"Hey, Eduard, forget the Inspector. In the unlikely event that he believed us and didn't lock us up there and then, how can we be sure if we hand this information over to the *mossos*, that the CIA won't be furious and put us on a plane to Guantánamo?"

"Hell, don't give me any more frights!"

"I don't want to, but the risk is there. Just think: Brian didn't know me at all and gave *me* this keyring, not the police. I imagine he was thinking that if something happened to him, as it soon did, the keyring would be safe until someone from his side came to collect it. And this person must belong to the CIA, right?" argued Borja. "So, we'll give them back their keyring, and end of saga."

"Sure, but what if the information falls into the wrong hands?" I persisted.

"Please, Eduard, don't tie yourself in knots. Tomorrow we will get rid of the wretched keyring, period. Let the CIA see to it after that, it's what they're paid for!" he exclaimed, ending the argument.

*

We agreed to meet the following morning at half past eleven by the entrance to the zoo. We both arrived punctually, he in a taxi from Lola's, and I by bus, with Arnau, who was on holiday. That same morning, Joana had gone on a trip with some friends and, as Montse was working and I had to look after the kid because we can't rely on the twins, I decided to bring him along. Borja had assured me we were in no danger, and Arnau was delighted with the prospect of a morning at the zoo surrounded by exotic animals.

A group was demonstrating by the entrance with anti-zoo placards. They'd set up a table with pamphlets where they were collecting signatures, but there were few activists and they weren't having much success: the scant visitors around simply walked into the zoo without paying much attention to their harangues against the alleged mistreatment of animals by zoos. It wasn't like the weekends when mile-long queues formed when, at best, only two ticket windows were open. There was hardly any queue at all. Borja, who'd looked surprised to see Arnau, paid for our entrance tickets and we walked in.

It was Holy Thursday and the school holidays had started some days ago, but the zoo was almost empty: the odd tourist couple with their children and a few groups of kids wearing club caps and clutching lunch boxes on a day's outing. It was hot and sunny, though cool in the shade. A gentle breeze wafted our way, bringing with it the stink of animal excrement that triggered nostalgic childhood memories. Borja hadn't been back to the zoo since then, but I knew the place well because I'd been time and again with the twins and then Arnau. I saw my brother getting all emotional because those visits to the zoo, picnic included, were among our rare memories of our parents, who'd tell us stories that thrilled us to bits. In those days, the distance separating visitors from the elephants was much less and you could give them peanuts and carrots, which they – or rather he, because there was only one – quickly snaffled up with his hairy trunk. I was scared of elephants, but a fascinated Borja spent hours contemplating them.

"I don't remember it like this," he said as we walked past the giraffes. "When we came with our parents, it seemed enormous. In fact, it's very small."

"But they *have* modernized it, and some animals now enjoy acres of space!" I said. "The tigers, for example, aren't caged any more."

"You know what? I'll think I'll come back with Lola one of these days. Just to remember the old times."

I noted that my brother had said "Lola" and not "Merche", and smiled to myself. I'm fond of Lola, so I was glad they were getting on well.

We soon reached the area with the lions and my senses signalled red alert. It was early and Borja suggested sitting down on a bench with shade. The lion and lioness were engaged in seasonal, quite shameless erotic acts, in full sight of everyone, something that aroused Arnau's curiosity.

"What are they doing?"

"Playing."

"The lioness seems really happy," muttered Borja, gazing at the tender scene of love that was keeping the king of the jungle busy.

"She certainly does."

When it was five to twelve, we got up and stood by the rail, opposite the lions.

"I find it very strange to be standing here with Arnau watching this couple," I whispered, referring to the lion and lioness roaring with pleasure and licking away.

"Ah, we're not the only ones watching. It's not a spectacle you see every day."

"I feel we're intruding on their intimate moments."

"Eduard, intimacy is a human concept," Borja drawled, breaking into philosophical mode. "I assure you that the lion and lioness couldn't give a toss."

"I expect you are right."

I glanced around to see if I could spot a spy with shades and sensual lips, but could see her nowhere. The only one who seemed rooted to the spot like us, and looking around as if she were looking for someone was a tall, freckled redhead who was far from pretty. She wore a low-cut, sky-blue T-shirt and a miniskirt, but her long white legs looked like two stunted toothpicks that made you feel sorry for her.

Arnau had got bored of the lions and had been grumbling for some time. Finally, when it had gone ten past twelve, I asked Borja, "Is that the woman who rang you yesterday?" discreetly indicating the redhead with my eyes.

"No way!" was Borja's confident reaction. "She doesn't look one bit like the girl who gave me the mobile. She was very pretty, or have you forgotten? This girl is taller and looks English, not American."

We waited on, listening stoically to Arnau's complaints until, at a quarter to one, the redhead came over and asked us in excellent Spanish if either of us was Borja.

"I'm Borja," my brother declared, quite surprised.

The girl smiled and said she'd been put off by the fact there were three of us because she was only expecting one person. Borja asked her what her name was and she said she was Emily. She apologized for her last-minute call, but said Charlie was moody and impulsive like that. Now she was looking forward to seeing him again, though she'd not set foot in London for three years as it brought back such bad memories. She was also happy to do him this favour. She blabbered away and gesticulated a lot, and though Borja and I understood none of her blabber we listened very politely, imagining it must be a technique designed to deter other spies who might be observing us. Finally, Emily looked at her watch and asked Borja if he had the package. Borja said he did and extracted from his pocket a sealed envelope where he'd lodged Brian's gift-wrapped keyring.

"Well, *we* were expecting someone else," said Borja.

"Oh, I'm completely in the dark," replied the redhead, shrugging her shoulders. "Charlie simply asked me to pick up this package before catching my plane."

"But, you do work for the Agency, don't you?" I asked, wanting to be reassured.

"Yes," she said, rather taken aback. "Did Charlie tell you?"

"It's what he hinted," I said.

"And are you familiar with the agency?" she asked.

"Well, I suppose most people know something about the way it works," said Borja.

"Good," she said, stuffing the envelope into her bag. "I'm very sorry, but I must run, or the agency guys will kill me! Luckily I came on my motorbike!" she said with a smile.

And leaving us rooted to the spot, Emily turned around and walked quickly off.

Borja and I took a while to react and started walking.

"That spy has a really peculiar sense of humour," Borja commented, as we headed towards the dolphins.

"Yes, very peculiar and very macabre; how could she say such a thing after what happened to poor Brian…"

It must be her way of living with the pain. Besides, she was English, and we all know the English are masters of black comedy," he declared wryly, sounding very sure of himself.

Montse had insisted on inviting Borja to lunch, and after watching the dolphins perform we caught the metro home. My brother grumbled all the way, because it wasn't direct and we had to make a couple of changes. As it was only

April, the air conditioning wasn't switched on and it was very hot inside the tunnels.

"Are you absolutely sure she was the woman Brian wanted us to hand his keyring to?" I said suddenly, while we were walking down one of the passages. "If I remember correctly, she called him Charlie, not Brian."

"You heard the Inspector," said Borja, throwing a coin at the cap of a girl playing the violin who had flashed a smile in his direction. "Brian used a pseudonym."

"Yes, but it was his surname, not his first name that was fake!" I replied, remembering how we'd known him as Brian Morgan when in fact he was Brian Harris, at least according to the Inspector.

"Oh, that's because these spies have lots of different aliases," chirped Borja, acting as if he was an expert. "Besides, you asked her if she worked for the Agency and she said she did, didn't she?"

"That's true. But she didn't look like a spy."

"I agree. But what did you expect? There must be all kinds of spies. They can't all have sensual lips!" sighed Borja.

"And isn't that a pity?"

"Yes, I guess it is."

23

We spent the whole of Friday morning with Deputy Inspector Alsina-Graells, fine-tuning the details of Operation Buddha, as the Inspector had dubbed it. We'd arranged to meet Sònia in her deceased husband's flat at five, and the plan was for Borja and I to carry hidden microphones so the Deputy Inspector and her men could overhear and record the conversation. As we had no other evidence, we had to try to get a confession out of her, which seemed easy enough on paper, but less so in reality.

"Above all, don't get nervous or forget you've got the microphones on you. Remember, she must confess to killing her husband," the Deputy Inspector pleaded.

"Don't worry, Deputy Inspector!" Borja said soothingly. "It will all turn out fine, you just see. Won't it, Eduard?"

I'm not so good at lying as Borja, and was as agitated as the Deputy Inspector. We left her office at two and went for lunch with her and a couple of sergeants in a bar full of *mossos* and, as soon as we finished, we went back to the station to go over the plan for the nth time. At half past four, after checking that the microphones Borja and I had hidden under our clothes were working properly, we climbed into a taxi driven by a policeman in plain clothes. Behind us came three Ford Escorts incognito, full of police: Deputy Inspector Alsina-Graells was in the first.

When we reached Zen Moments, we saw what Cecília had told us was true: they were refurbishing. The centre was closed to the public and the Eastern-style garden that surrounded it was full of sacks of rubble and building materials. Workers were constantly going in and out and, as the door was open, Borja and I walked in without asking permission from anyone or being stopped by anyone. Once we were inside, we went straight to Horaci's office and knocked on the door. The sign with his name had gone.

Sònia Claramunt opened the door.

"Good afternoon," Borja greeted her.

"You're very punctual," she replied frostily, as she gestured to us to come in.

She looked daggers at us, but that was hardly strange, I reflected, as Borja and I had come – at least in theory – to blackmail her and she was about to hand over thirty thousand euros to buy our silence. Her jeans and tight-fitting white T-shirt emphasized how svelte she was, and her necklaces, bracelets, earrings and paste rings on her fingers added the finishing touches to her informal, if not entirely casual, style of dress. I stared at her shoes, which were flat and dark blue, and the little toes she'd amputated for the sake of fashion came to mind.

"Have you got the video?" she asked.

"That depends," replied my brother with a smile. "Have you got the money?"

"Yes," she rasped.

"The thirty thousand euros we agreed for the tape where you can be seen entering the meditation centre the night they killed your husband?"

I thought Borja was spreading it on too thickly, and that Sònia might sense this was a trap.

"Here's your thirty thousand," she said, pointing to the plastic bag on top of the desk.

"May I?" Borja pointed to the bag. "I don't want to seem rude, but you must understand I can hardly trust a woman who killed her husband in cold blood," he continued, smiling away.

"I didn't kill him in cold blood," retorted a weary-sounding Sònia. "In any case, that's none of your business. Take your money and leave me in peace."

Borja glanced inside the bag and gave her the empty tape.

"By the way, I am intrigued," added Borja. "Was it an attack of jealousy? You did know your hubby was no saint, didn't you?"

"I didn't have a clue," she replied wearily.

"Obviously you must have inherited insurance money. I saw the building workers outside…"

"I thought we'd come to an agreement, Mr Masdéu. I give you the money and you give me the tape. Our professional relationship ends there." She walked over to the door. "And don't try coming back to ask for more, because then we will all end up in the slammer. I'll get put down for a number of years but you'll lose your thirty thousand and will be inside for a time too," she warned threateningly.

"I told you when we spoke on the phone that we are real gentlemen and, if we hold on to anything, it is our word," replied Borja, as if she'd insulted him. "The truth is, my brother and I would find it much easier to forget this business if you told us why you killed your husband," insisted Borja, determined not to leave that office until he'd extracted the confession the Deputy Inspector needed.

"Why do you need to know?"

"Simply out of curiosity."

"Curiosity killed the cat, Mr Masdéu."

"Is that a threat? Are you going to liquidate us as you did your husband?" retorted Borja.

"Hey, I didn't… liquidate him. I told you it wasn't pre-meditated."

"So what did happen then?" insisted Borja.

"Very well…" she started as if she'd not the energy to argue any more. She walked away from the door and sat down on the sofa; we followed suit and sat in the armchairs. "If you *must* know, it was no sudden attack of jealousy. I'd known for some time that Horaci was carrying on with that artist, Edith."

"And it was all the same to you?" I asked.

Sònia Claramunt shrugged her shoulders.

"Horaci and I weren't just a married couple: we were a business," she went on. "When I first met him, he'd just graduated and didn't know what to do with himself. He'd fallen out with his father, didn't get on with his brother, and, after spending eight years studying medicine, had discovered he didn't like the idea of being a doctor. I was working as a highly paid economist at the time. I had some savings and I suggested he should do a crash course in homeopathic medicine and open a consultancy in this part of the city. Homeopathy was starting to become fashionable, and could be highly profitable if it was done properly."

"And how right you were."

"Then Horaci met Bernat and Cecília. She was broke, but was really into yoga and meditation, and she was very knowledgeable; Bernat, on the other hand, comes from a good family and managed to persuade his father to be a backer so he could get a loan to establish Zen Moments. Indeed it was *his* idea to knock down his grandparents' mansion and build the meditation centre. The project was for all four of us – Bernat, Cecília, Horaci and me – to become wealthy by offering alternative therapies to the residents of the Sarrià and Bonanova districts."

"And business *was* booming, wasn't it?" asked Borja, who by this point had probably forgotten he'd a microphone hidden somewhere on his person: he was genuinely intrigued.

"The fact is it could have worked much better if we'd made the changes we are introducing now," continued Sònia, smiling sadly. "By incorporating a spa, beauticians' studios, a restaurant and a decent menu... People don't just want yoga and meditation, or prescriptions for pills to cure their colds. They want to drink juice with their girlfriends on a terrace, and, after their meditation session, they want their body hair shaved off, facial treatments, manicures..."

"So I suppose the issue was getting the necessary capital together..." I commented. "But with the proceeds from the insurance policy your husband must have contracted..."

"Ah, you really don't get it, do you?" exclaimed Sònia even more wearily. "The real issue was that Horaci ended up believing all this tosh about meditation, feng shui, Bach flower remedies and homeopathy. He suddenly lost all interest in money. He was convinced this nonsense really worked and didn't want to change anything. He'd even started giving sessions gratis."

"So was the decision to remove him from the scene yours alone, or was Dr Comes involved?"

"I told you it wasn't premeditated," replied Sònia, shaking her head. Bernat and I, and Cecília for that matter, had often talked about the changes we wanted to introduce at the centre, but we never contemplated a solution of this nature... It never occurred to us."

"So how were you hoping to persuade him?" I asked.

"We wanted Horaci to sell his shares to Bernat and me. Cecília had almost persuaded him that if he wanted to make progress on the path to complete spiritual purification

233

he ought to sell his shares and free himself of all material worries and ties."

"That Cecília is another fine specimen," muttered Borja.

Sònia Claramunt shrugged her shoulders.

"Nobody likes to be poor, Mr Masdéu. Apart from Horaci, who'd evidently gone round the bend."

"So what did happen then?"

"We'd agreed that he'd come home last Saturday after dinner with the residents, and we'd talk it through. But he phoned me at around eleven to say he wasn't coming home to sleep, that he was staying at the centre to meditate because he'd had a vision."

"So you jumped into your car and drove here."

"Yes. I simply wanted to talk to him and bring him to his senses. But when I found him sitting on the floor and he came out with all that nonsense about how we should leave everything and go off to India flat broke, I got so angry I just grabbed the Buddha from his desk and crowned him with it."

"And then were cold-blooded enough to complete the deed and wipe off your fingerprints…" I chipped in.

"Won't you ever understand? Horaci had gone stark raving mad!" she exclaimed. "This is just a business. A business, period. That's why we set it up!"

At that precise moment the *mossos* burst into the office and arrested her. Sònia immediately realized we'd set a trap for her and stared at us with hate-filled eyes. While they were handcuffing her, she started shouting, "Nothing I've said is true! I was making it up! Do you hear? It's not true! I'm not the person you can see on this tape! It's not me!"

Back at the station, Inspector Badia thanked and congratulated us. When we thought that was the end of that and

234

we could go home, he asked us to step into his office for a moment. He said he wanted a word in private.

"I've come up against a snag in the Brian Harris case," he snapped.

"A snag?" asked Borja, instinctively leaning backwards.

"Well, maybe not a snag, more a question of detail," smiled the Inspector.

"So what's it all about?" asked Borja, trying to stay deadpan.

"Well, it's like this, Mr Masdéu, we know who killed Brian Harris because we found him with the pistol that was used to shoot him."

"Oh, really, who was it?" I asked, relieved.

"One of the Russian mafia who died in the shoot-out in Poblenou," declared the Inspector.

Borja didn't react, and let the Inspector continue.

"Somebody cleaned the flat when Brian was already dead," he revealed. "And we think they did so wearing the gloves that were in the laundry room."

"The Russian who killed him, I imagine?" asked Borja.

"That is precisely the snag, Mr Masdéu. We've found fingerprints and traces of DNA in the gloves, that were new according to the scientific chaps, and they don't belong to the assassin or to Mr Harris," said the Inspector, lolling back on his chair and rubbing his hands together.

"Good heavens…" I thought I heard Borja swallow.

"We've checked them against our database, but they don't match anyone on our files," the Inspector went on.

"Perhaps they belong to the cleaning lady," I whined.

"No, Mr Harris didn't have a cleaning lady, according to the concierge."

"In any case, if you've caught the assassin, I don't see what difference it makes…" Borja wasn't able to finish his sentence.

"You know, Mr Masdéu, I've had a sudden intuition. Naturally, I can't compare the prints and DNA with those of all the inhabitants of Barcelona," he said with a cunning smile, "but I could ask the judge to authorize me to compare them with those of the other people living on the staircase."

Borja and the Inspector stared at each other for a few seconds.

"I believe that would be a waste of time and a waste of the taxpayers' money, Inspector," Borja finally said, recovering his usual sangfroid. "Frankly, I thought you had enough real problems to deal with, Inspector."

"Well, that is all I was after. I only wanted your opinion," countered the Inspector.

"Well if I were you, I'd leave things as they are," replied Borja defiantly.

"Now, if we did a check of that nature, we wouldn't find *your* prints on those gloves, would we, Mr Masdéu?"

Borja said nothing for a few moments and looked the Inspector up and down. He finally burst out laughing as if the Inspector had cracked a joke he'd only just understood.

"Inspector, your sense of humour shows how intelligent you are," he said. "Just listen to me and let sleeping dogs lie." He strode towards the door and added, "There's no point pouring oil on waters that are no longer troubled."

24

Teresa Solana returned to Barcelona that same evening, just in time for the Sant Jordi celebrations on the Saturday. That meant we had to arrange to see her at the beginning of the following week to tell her about our foray into the world of alternative therapies, and this time we couldn't make an excuse to avoid seeing her in our office. As our main problem was the smashed fake doors, Borja spoke to a carpenter who was prepared to measure up and install two new mahogany doors in the record time of three days. We'd agreed to meet the carpenter at eleven and, when I got to the office at a quarter to, Borja was already there.

"You're looking very smart," I said, surprised to see him in a new jacket and tie.

"I've arranged to see Mariona. We're going for lunch at the Via Veneto."

"Give her my best regards. And my thanks!"

"I've already done that a thousand times… By the way, what were you thinking of doing today?"

"Well, I thought I'd go home and spend the afternoon in bed reading a novel," I replied with a smile, anticipating my pleasant afternoon at leisure.

"I told you not to bother coming in today!" he said, clicking his tongue. "I can deal with the carpenter by myself."

"You know, it's a nice day. I took my time walking here. Besides, it will soon be summer and I need to lose some weight or Montse will keep grumbling," I replied, stroking my paunch.

The bell rang.

"He's here already!" said Borja, walking towards the door.

However, the man who'd rung the bell didn't look very much like a carpenter. He was wearing a dark suit, an elegant tie and a light-coloured shirt. I'd say he was in his early forties.

"Mr Borja Masdéu?" he asked in very correct Catalan, though with what sounded like an American accent.

"Yes, I am he," answered my brother, unable to hide his surprise.

"I need to discuss an urgent matter with you. Can I come in?" And he strode inside and closed the door behind him, not waiting for Borja's say-so.

"Hey…" said Borja. "Where do you think you are going?"

The stranger didn't reply. He gave me the once-over and stared at Borja questioningly. Curiously, the spectacle of the smashed fake doors didn't seem to worry him.

"And who might *he* be?" he asked, pointing his chin in my direction.

"This is my partner, Mr Martínez," replied Borja. "And you are?…"

"A friend of Brian's. Can we talk in front of him?" he asked, referring to me.

"That's not an issue, my partner is about to leave, aren't you, Eduard?"

"Not likely! I don't intend leaving you all alone with this fellow!" And addressing the stranger, I added, "I know all about this. My partner wants to protect me, but I don't intend on leaving. And watch it, I have a friend in this pocket!"

The man who had introduced himself as Brian's friend looked at me and smiled.

"A friend?" he said, raising his eyebrows.

"A friend that shoots bullets," I added, sticking my hand in a trouser pocket to make the threat seem more palpable.

"I understand. Very well then, why don't you invite me to take a seat?" he said, swaggering his way to the sofa. It was obvious he wasn't impressed by my threat.

Borja and I exchanged worried glances and sat down as well.

"It wasn't easy to track you down, Mr Masdéu, as the individual in whom Brian confided," the fellow kicked off, sprawling back on the settee as if he were in his own front room. "He told us it was a neighbour on the staircase, but never said which."

"Oh, really?" commented Borja, deadpan.

"Mr Masdéu, let's not play any more games. I've come to get what Brian gave you. It's time to give it back to us."

"Give it back to you? To who?" asked Borja, looking put out.

"To Brian's friends," he answered dryly.

"You mean the CIA?"

"So you know…" the stranger tried to conceal an almost imperceptible note of surprise that was translated in a very slight raising of his eyebrows. "Well, I hope you've not done anything foolish, Mr Masdéu, because that object is highly valuable. Now give me the keyring and I won't bother you any more."

"But I've already given it back!" protested Borja, nonplussed.

"Given it back? Given it back to whom? And when and where?"

All of a sudden the man's face transformed into an unpleasant and threatening snarl.

"To a young woman by the name of Emily. She rang me on Tuesday afternoon and we arranged to see her the day after to hand over the packet. She said she worked for the Agency," explained Borja.

"What did this woman look like?" he asked.

"English, redhead, freckled, thin... Young – twenty-seven or -eight. Not what you would call pretty," said Borja.

"A redhead with freckles? Are you sure she wasn't wearing a wig?"

"No. I think it was her own hair, because her eyebrows and lids were the same colour. And I can tell you the freckles were natural. To be candid, she didn't seem like a spy the way she dressed and talked. But, of course, I supposed it was a disguise to put people off her scent."

The man sighed.

"She's not one of ours," he said finally. "She must be working for another agency. I don't understand. How could she know *you* had the keyring?"

"Well, you know, she never exactly used the word 'keyring'," said Borja, smiling nervously. "I told you she rang me and said I had something that... Shit!" Borja suddenly exclaimed, turning to me.

It took me a few seconds to grasp what had just occurred to my brother.

"So we've made a fucking mess of it yet again!" I muttered.

"It looks that way," said Borja despondently.

"What do you mean?" asked the stranger, getting more and more agitated. "What are you two talking about?"

"We gave her the wrong thing... So that was why she mentioned a Charlie and not Brian."

"Charlie? The wrong thing? Would you like to explain yourselves?" the fellow asked, about to hit the roof.

"It's a long story," said Borja, looking at his watch. "And we are expecting a visitor..."

"Well, they can wait. Tell me your story. Now," he rapped imperiously. "Or your partner's friend and mine will get to know each other," he said, putting his hand in his pocket.

I started to sweat. It was clear the nightmare of Brian and his damned keyring wasn't over yet. We thought we'd said goodbye to one of our problems and it now seemed we'd simply created another. Borja kept his cool and explained all the ins and outs of the statue, the kidnapping by Russian mafia who'd then been defeated in a gun battle with the *mossos d'esquadra* in the Poblenou film studio, how we'd discovered by chance the memory stick in Brian's keyring, and the confusion created over the statue and the keyring. The stranger listened without interrupting, and when Borja had finished, he took a notebook from his pocket and asked for the name of the Dutch antiquarian who'd contracted him to bring the statue to Barcelona. Borja tried to resist revealing his name, but in the end he yielded to the aggressive attitude of that fellow who, unlike me, was most definitely carrying a real firearm in his pocket.

"Wait a minute," I interjected. "You also owe us an explanation. After all, Brian was our neighbour and he almost sent us to our grave. We would be interested to know why."

The man said nothing for a few seconds and just ruminated.

"Very well," he said with a sigh. "I suppose there's no harm in telling you. In any case, if you tell anyone else, I don't think they will believe you."

"We don't intend repeating it to anyone. We just want to know what this is all about," Borja assured him.

The fellow lolled back on the sofa and loosened his tie.

"You perhaps don't realize that Barcelona has recently become, let's say, a point of encounter for employees of the different intelligence agencies," he began.

"You mean Barcelona is a den of spies," Borja translated.

The fellow smiled, but didn't deny that was true.

"There's a group of agents who belong to different agencies and have become what we might call 'friends', and they have decided to save the world from corrupt governments and market speculation."

"A praiseworthy aim," I commented.

"Yes, it's what happens when people are idle," he continued scornfully, interpreting my remark as sarcastic, which it wasn't. "People end up making the wrong friends and doing strange things."

"So what happened?" asked Borja.

"Between them, they managed to collect a lot of confidential information that makes WikiLeaks look like child's play. If this information became public knowledge, it could undermine a number of governments, including yours, and even the foundations of the capitalist system. They had information that was far too dangerous."

"And Brian was one of these rebellious agents?"

"No, Brian had infiltrated the group and managed to get hold of the documents they were keeping encrypted on a memory stick."

"But there must be more than one copy…" interjected Borja.

"For security reasons – that is, so no member of the group might be tempted to sell the information to the highest bidder – there was only one copy in a file locked into a very sophisticated program. It is impossible to copy it if you don't know the code. Obviously, over time, computer experts and methods can break all manner of codes… But it takes time."

"And how about the Russians who kidnapped us? What's their role in all this?" asked Borja.

"The group's fears weren't unfounded. One of these dissident agents decided that if, rather than save the world altruistically, he sold on the information, he'd make enough money to outdo the author of *Harry Potter*. He was negotiating with the Russian mafia, and, somehow or other, they discovered you were the person entrusted with the memory stick."

"This dissident agent wouldn't by any chance be a smallish lady with sensual lips?" I asked, remembering the woman who'd accosted Borja in the street and given him that mobile.

"Could be," the stranger replied in a tone that meant "Yes, it was her". "Did she get into contact with you?"

"Yes, she did," confirmed Borja. "She gave me a mobile and asked me to be at the ready, that they'd be in contact with me. I suppose she was referring to the Russians, but, as I knew nothing at that stage about what the keyring contained, I thought she must be referring to my contact in the matter of the statue."

"Didn't they ring you?"

"The mobile's battery went dead, and, as it was such an old model, I couldn't find a charger that worked..." Borja defended himself. "However, I still don't understand why Brian gave me the memory stick using the ruse that I was holding on to a spare copy of the keys to his flat. He and I hardly knew each other."

"That was precisely why. Brian knew they were after him, and, while he awaited instructions, he decided to put the memory stick in a safe place. That's why he hid it in the keyring and gave it to you. What could be more harmless in a Mediterranean country than asking a neighbour to keep a copy of the key to your door?"

"Well, it almost put paid to us," I said resentfully.

"I'm very sorry. I'm sure Brian didn't think you'd be in any danger. Of course, he didn't think he was up for the chop either..." he added, acknowledging the weakness of his argument.

"So then who did kill Brian? The spy with the sensual lips? The Russians? His dissident colleagues?" I asked.

"Not exactly. In fact, it was a mistake," he said uneasily.

"A mistake?" I repeated.

"This goddam crisis has affected all of us. Budgets have been slashed all round, and that sometimes means we aren't as coordinated as we ought to be in my department."

"What *do* you mean?"

"There was another group of our agents working on the case that didn't know Brian was an infiltrator acting as a triple agent. Unfortunately, they decided to neutralize him before he could share the information with them."

"What a fuck-up!" I shouted.

"Well, Brian was no angel, let's be clear about that. None of us is."

"So what are you going to do now?" asked Borja defiantly. "Are you going to take your pistol out and blast us to kingdom come, as they did with Brian?"

The man stared at Borja as if he had a screw loose and sat up.

"Why should I?" he asked after a while. "Where would that get us? Besides, there's no proof of any of what I've been telling you. And who knows, perhaps you will help us identify the English girl to whom you so rashly handed Brian's keyring?" he said, getting up off the sofa and heading towards the door.

"Don't count on us," said Borja. "We have terrible memories."

"We'll see about that."

When he was in the doorway, he turned and said with that perpetual smile of his, "Oh, by the way. I don't know if this statue you told me about is very valuable, but it is extremely likely that someone, in some corner of the planet, is currently furious with you two guys."

25

This year Holy Week fell at the end of April. The lunar calendar that shapes the religious year meant Sant Jordi coincided with Holy Saturday in the Easter holidays, to the despair of publishers, booksellers and purveyors of roses, so everyone was sure, in a year of economic crisis, that Sant Jordi would be a flop. To cap it all, the weather forecasters, those birds of ill omen, had predicted rain; despondency was widespread and nobody knew how the day would end. In actuality it wasn't such a disaster: the sun came out mid-morning and, like every year, the centre of Barcelona was full of its citizenry strolling up and down with books and roses. Pure torture for those who don't like crowds.

Montse and Lola were curious to meet Teresa Solana and, at around eleven, Borja dropped by, waving five red roses: one for Lola, and the others for Montse, Joana, Laia and Aina, who, along with Arnau, had signed up for the excursion to the centre and the lunch we'd booked at the Set Portes. The idea was that we'd all walk down the Rambla de Catalunya to the stalls on the Passeig de Gràcia, where Teresa Solana had said she'd be signing books.

"Good heavens!" chirped Joana, after thanking Borja for the rose and looking him up and down. "Why on earth are you wearing a winter jacket on such a hot day?"

"My summer jacket's at the cleaners," said Borja.

"Come on, take it off and leave it at home, or you'll sweat to death!" Joana exclaimed in her best sergeant major's voice.

"Yes, it is hot," Borja agreed with a smile.

"Yes, and today is the day of Sant Jordi and we are all family. No need to dress posh!" Montse chimed in. "What's more, with so many people in the street, they'll rough up your jacket."

"All right, if you insist…"

Borja obediently took his jacket off and gave it to Joana.

"You could also take your tie off, while you're at it," suggested Joana.

In his short-sleeved shirt and tie, Borja now looked like a Jehovah's Witness, so he had no choice but to follow my mother-in-law's suggestion.

"Give that to me." Joana folded his tie and put it on one of his jacket pockets. Then all of a sudden she exclaimed, "What the hell is this lump? What have you got here that's so heavy?" she cried, extracting an object wrapped in a handkerchief.

"Careful! It's very fragile!" erupted Borja when he saw my mother-in-law unwrapping the small stone statue.

"Oh, how lovely!" exclaimed Joana, gazing at the tiny object.

"Yes, it's very nice. Now give it back to me before it gets broken," said Borja, taking the piece and wrapping it up again.

"Is that a present for Lola?" whispered Joana. "She adores antiques. She will be delighted."

"Not really… In fact, it belongs to a friend who…"

"And where did you get this copy from? It's an expensive imitation," said Joana. And she then added, "Obviously I've only ever seen it in photos, but you know, it looks like the genuine article!"

Borja and I glanced at each other in amazement.

"In what photos?" I asked her. "You mean you recognize the statue?"

"Of course, it is very famous. They told us about it in the short art course I went on at La Caixa last year. We pensioners get a special rate. I don't know if you remember, but I went with a friend, Roser, who couldn't go to all the lectures because she had an attack of sciatica and —"

"So, according to you," I cut her off before she recounted her friend's entire medical history, "what is this exactly?" Borja had unwrapped the statue again to show it to my mother-in-law.

"You really don't know?" Joana asked, looking very surprised. "It's the Baghdad Lioness. I don't remember exactly how old it is, but it is a museum piece. Archaeologists found it in Baghdad, and that's how it got that name."

"So the original must be really valuable…" said Borja matter-of-factly.

"Oh, absolutely! It is quite unique," said Joana, as if she were an expert. "There's not another one like it."

"You wouldn't remember by any chance in which museum the original could – can – be found?" my brother asked.

"It's not in any museum, my dear. Unfortunately, it belongs to a private collector who has only allowed it to be exhibited a couple of times. And that was only because the Queen of England used her influence!"

"Do you know the owner's name?" I asked.

"What do you think I am? A walking encyclopedia?" she grumbled, not understanding why she was being interrogated. "If you're that interested, you're sure to find it on the Internet!" And, still muttering, she went into the lobby with Borja's jacket.

My brother and I were devastated. The fact that Joana had recognized the sculpture meant it was a famous piece, and, though there had been no reports of the theft in the papers, everything pointed to the statue being a very valuable, antique item that had been stolen.

"How come you had it on you?" I whispered to Borja. "Didn't you hide it among all that stuff you bought at the Chinese bazaar?"

"I'm not happy leaving it at home. The other day Merche saw what was in that drawer and said we were hoarding lots of junk and it was time to have a clear-out. And as she has keys to the flat and sometimes turns up without prior warning…"

"Good God!" I mumbled.

"But I don't understand what Joana was saying about the Internet. What did she mean when she said it could help us find out who the owner was?"

"You only have to key in the item's name on Google," said Aina, who was stretched out on the sofa waiting for her mother and aunt to finish getting ready. "Twenty euros and I'll take a look for you right now."

"Right now?" repeated Borja.

"Yes, while Mum gets ready," said Aina, getting up off the sofa and looking at Borja as if he'd just come from planet Mars. "It will only take a few seconds."

"Ten euros," haggled Borja.

"Fifteen," my daughter countered defiantly. Borja nodded.

"Grandma! What was the name of that statue?" shouted Aina.

"The Baghdad Lioness!" Joana shouted back from her bedroom. Her window must have been open, because their shouts echoed round the patio.

"I'll be with you in a minute!" said Aina, smiling as she went into her bedroom.

Borja and I waited for Aina in the dining room. My daughter reappeared a few minutes later clutching a sheaf of printouts. Lola and Montse were still in the bathroom.

"Here you are: all you ever wanted to know about this lion," she said, handing us the sheets of paper. "Fifteen euros please."

Borja took the money from his pocket and Aina handed them over. Joana was quite right. To judge by the photos, the statue Borja was holding was a sculpture known as the Baghdad Lioness, an item that was thought to be unique and contemporary with cuneiform writing and the invention of the wheel. According to Wikipedia, it belonged to the Elamite empire, a civilization that had occupied the area to the west of ancient Sumeria and north-west of present-day Iran, in the territory of Kurdistan, five thousand years ago, and it was carved from limestone. When it was discovered in the 1920s during an excavation near Baghdad, it was already missing its hind legs that, according to experts, were originally made of silver or gold. Its present owner was an English collector by the name of Thomas Marlowe, a distant relative of the much-lamented poet, Christopher. What's more, the little item Borja was fingering in his pocket was worth a fortune, at least fifty million dollars.

"Not exactly small change," whistled Borja. "Now I see why they are paying me twenty thousand."

"So Brian's friend was right. If this little statue is worth what these papers say, then we've got embroiled in one hell of a mess!"

"*I* have, you mean," whined Borja sorrowfully. "Whatever happens, you are well out of it. From now on, I promise I won't involve you."

"Kid brother," I whispered so the girls couldn't hear, "I may have many defects, but acting like a rat that jumps ship when it's about to go under is not one of them."

Teresa Solana was sitting behind a stall with other writers, looking bored out of her mind. Neither she nor her colleagues had queues of readers waiting to sign their books. A few metres away, an individual by the name of Risto Mejide who was always acting the fool on TV, swearing and creating a furore, could hardly cope with his thronging fans.

Borja went over to the novelist, pecked her twice on the cheeks and did the introductions. Joana, Montse and Lola also kissed her and said they'd been so much looking forward to meeting her.

"He's the guy who's always on TV!" said Borja smiling, nodding towards that ghastly fellow who kept endlessly signing copies and letting his fans snap him on their mobiles. "People like to have books by the famous, but they don't read them."

"Oh, don't suffer on my behalf," said Teresa Solana, returning Borja's smile. "Sant Jordi is the day of the book, not the day of literature. No need to wear sackcloth and ashes!"

"But aren't you annoyed when the people who are not real writers get all the attention?" I asked. "It's encroaching on your professional territory."

"It's inevitable," she said, shrugging her shoulders. "Luckily this isn't a profession where you need a membership card – or at least not yet. It has its drawbacks, but lots of advantages as well."

"Yes, but people are made to think the real writers are those that sell the most."

"No way! People aren't that stupid!" she replied.

Teresa Solana seemed resigned to sitting there doing nothing and being observed as if she was an animal in the zoo. Very occasionally someone approached her with a copy of a novel of hers and asked for a signature. Once again, I observed that there were no half measures on the day of Sant Jordi: writers behind the stalls either signed a pile of books or signed next to none.

Montse and Lola felt sorry for her and both bought a book. Montse's was called *A Not So Perfect Crime* and Lola chose *A Shortcut to Paradise*, in the hope that the title was a good omen. Lola asked her to dedicate the book to Borja and then gave it to him.

"I can't wait to hear how it all went," said Teresa Solana, referring to the assignment she'd given us. "I hope you've got some interesting anecdotes I can use in my novel…"

"Oh, lots! I think you'll have no reason to complain," said Borja, smiling. "Why don't you drop by the office on Wednesday and we will give you a full report. I am sure you won't be disappointed."

"When the book comes out, I'll send you a couple of copies. I've already got my title: *The Sound of One Hand Killing*. And thanks again for your help. I don't know what I'd have done to finish it on time without your help!"

Just then, some women friends came over to say hello to the novelist and we took our leave. We walked down in the direction of La Rambla, prepared to continue our pilgrimage as far as the statue of Christopher Columbus. However, when we saw crowds surpassing our worst expectations, we decided to turn tail and head straight to the Set Portes for our paella.

"This afternoon we'll go and see Pilar Rahola, and I'll ask her to sign her last book for me," said Joana, as we strolled down Via Laietana. And then she added: "Now *she* is what I call a famous writer!"

I winced at her awe before the raucous star of Catalan chat shows.

EPILOGUE

When the thunderclap resounded, Lord Winston Ashtray, weighing in at over two hundred and forty pounds, was comfortably seated by the side of the splendid fireplace that heated the library in his mansion on the Lifestyle Ends estate, in the county of Oxfordshire. Lord Ashtray was smoking one of his cigars and reading the memoirs of the first Lord Ashtray, who made his fortune in India and suffered the Sepoy Mutiny in his own flesh, in the shape of the loss of a limb, before returning to England and receiving from the hands of Queen Victoria the title that allowed his descendants to warm a seat in the House of Lords for the next one hundred and fifty years. A large slice of the wealth of Lord Ashtray's extensive family originated from that stout, moustachioed forebear, whose portrait dominated the library, and the fifth lord considered it his duty not to depart this world before he had finished the seven volumes of memoirs the first Lord Ashtray had bequeathed to posterity in general and his heirs in particular. Sadly, the first Lord Ashtray wasn't as deft with the pen as he was with the sabre or his investments, and his great-great-grandson had sat in the same wing armchair every afternoon for almost five decades and still hadn't reached the end of volume one.

Three months ago the present Lord Ashtray had celebrated his sixty-fifth birthday. He was no spring chicken any more. If he didn't get a move on, he pondered, the Grim Reaper would take him before he'd had time to finish the diaries. As the fifth lord, in his idiosyncratic way, was a God-fearing man, he was afraid that if he met his Maker before he got to the end, his lack of respect for the man responsible for his good fortune would sentence him to spend eternity meandering around Lifestyle Ends like a soul in limbo with the literary ghost of his one-armed great-great-grandfather as his sole companion. This thought pinned him to that armchair in the library every afternoon in the vain hope that, with each new paragraph, the stale prose of the first Lord Ashtray might come to life.

When he heard the thunderclap, Lord Ashtray sighed, looked out of the window and tried to concentrate on his reading, between yawns. How could it be, he wondered, that his forebear who had lived in the glorious era of Queen Victoria, at the height of the British Empire, on which the sun had never set, never had anything interesting to relate? Why the devil should he be interested in the dresses Lady Stouter wore at the official receptions held by the Resident in Delhi or the opinions of Count Dumbderly on the hazards of playing cricket during the monsoon season? Why should he have to dwell on Lady Reeker's bunions or Lord Pile's problems with the spicy local cuisine, problems that derived from his rash abuse of the same because he enjoyed it the hotter the better? Lord Ashtray glanced at the time on the grandfather clock that was buried under two centuries of accumulated dust, stared at the empty glass of cognac next to the Venetian-glass ashtray that contained the ash from his cigar and sighed yet again.

Just like his father, grandfather, great-grandfather and great-great-grandfather, the fifth Lord Ashtray had inherited the first lord's fondness for banquets, a propensity to develop gout, and the habit of ignoring his doctor's advice. So much so that when his faithful butler, George, entered the library, Lord Ashtray had just poured himself a second cognac that was so generous poor George had to strive to stop raising an eyebrow in an imperceptible sign of disapproval. Even though it was almost the merry month of May, the English countryside was still cold, and Lord Ashtray, like almost all of his forebears, preferred to have recourse to cognac for a little heat rather than to those simply dreadful jerseys that winter after winter his wife knitted him from the wool of the sheep that grazed in his meadows.

"Milord, your secretary has arrived. He's just parking the car," his butler announced, rescuing him from his flow of thoughts.

"Thank you, George. Tell him to report here immediately."

Lord Ashtray put the book down on the small table, sipped his cognac and smiled. The big moment had come at last. Thirty-five years after his father had lost it in a poker game, the Baghdad Lioness would be back with the family. The fourth Lord Ashtray, now deceased, had always cursed and sworn he'd lost the Lioness because Lord Marlowe had cheated, whereas Lord Marlowe, for his part, had been telling anyone who wanted to listen for the past thirty years that the night when Lord Ashtray lost the Lioness he was so drunk he'd have bet anything in order to carry on gambling. In fact, the fourth Lord Ashtray had gone so far as to stake his wife, but as Lady Ashtray's beauty was wholly internal and not even the gamekeeper wanted a piece, Lord Marlowe had refused to accept her and had challenged Lord Ashtray by saying he hadn't the spunk to bet the Baghdad Lioness. Lord Ashtray wasn't short of spunk after the pints he'd sunk; what he didn't have, however, was an ounce of nous.

The lioness with the rippling muscles was a unique item, and when the first Lord Ashtray had purchased it from a tinker for a few shillings it was already missing its hind legs. When he returned to England, the small statue had continued to gather dust in the attics of Lifestyle Ends for years, relegated to the bottom of the trunk where the first Lord Ashtray kept his military kit and souvenirs from his time in Iraq. The first Lord Ashtray only discovered the real value of the sculpture many years later, when a young archaeologist from the British Museum was naive enough to tell him it was unique rather than offer to buy it from him for the few pounds he would readily have accepted. The archaeologist's *naïveté* and the first Lord Ashtray's greed prevented the British Museum from exhibiting that wonder in its display cases, and from that day onwards the statue became part of the collection of oriental junk – as the first Lady Ashtray called it – initiated by the first lord and continued by his descendants.

Mr Charles Slothman, Lord Ashtray's secretary, knocked timidly on the door and walked into the library. He had only been in his service for eight months, after the sudden death of his predecessor in circumstances that, given his age and fondness for a little S&M, weren't as strange as some tried to make out. Charles was still scared of putting a foot wrong.

"Come over here, Slothman. Don't stand there like an Aunt Sally!" roared Lord Ashtray from his armchair. "You've got the package, I trust?"

"Yes, sir," answered Slothman, coming over and placing a poorly gift-wrapped package next to the ashtray and balloon of brandy.

"No mishaps?"

"None whatsoever, sir. All concluded most satisfactorily."

"Thank you, Slothman. Go and ask them to make you a cup of tea in the kitchen. Oh, and do tell George I don't want anyone bothering me."

"Yes, sir."

Lord Ashtray's private secretary silently left the library, his cheeks flushing a deep red. Fancy sending him off to the kitchen like the errand boy! He was a man with two degrees, a doctorate and a master's from Cambridge! And all because his brilliant future had been suddenly curtailed by a clutch of unfortunate incidents sparked by his students at Eton, who'd continuously teased him with their adolescent bodies and bulging Calvin Klein crotches. His devastating dismissal had forced him to enter the service of an ignorant, despotic millionaire who took advantage of that shameful stain on his CV to treat him like soiled linen, but one day his luck would change. The downcast Mr Slothman sloped off to the kitchen, swearing that one day he would wreak revenge on Lord Ashtray for the humiliations he had inflicted on him from his lofty position as a fat, self-satisfied aristocrat.

In the meantime, Lord Ashtray had picked up the package and started to unwrap it. As he trusted no one (especially after he'd discovered his own sister had walked through the countryside emulating Lady Godiva in protest against fox-hunting), Lord Ashtray had personally organized the theft. The fifth Lord Ashtray considered the recovery of the Baghdad Lioness a matter of honour, and, as Lord Marlowe wasn't prepared to relinquish it, not even for a sum that had been calculated it would fetch at a Sotheby's auction, Lord Ashtray had decided to take action and hire an experienced gang of crooks to steal the statue. That gambit had cost him the earth, but money was no problem for the lord. Unlike other tawdry, blue-blooded aristocrats with empty coffers who'd been forced to marry off their daughters to foreign magnates or open their mansions to the public in exchange for paltry tax relief, Lord Ashtray was proud that he didn't have to sell off his title or change his Lifestyle Ends estate into a Victorian theme park for Japanese and superannuated tourists. As long as he lived, foreigners or middle-class snobs wouldn't be poking their noses into his house and photographing it with their digital cameras. And if Lord Ashtray had one thing, apart from two useless sons and the gout that also gave him pain day in, day out, it was money. And if one had money, they had taught him at the select boarding school where he had studied, there was nothing in this world one could not do.

Twenty years ago Lord Marlowe, who was now in his nineties, had moved to Provence in search of bluer skies, less primitive cooking and, above all, proximity to the casino in Monte Carlo. Lord Marlowe had left his wife in England and brought with him his butler, his collection of pornographic magazines and his antiques. The Baghdad Lioness was, needless to say, the apple of his eye, not for its monetary or archaeological value, which he didn't care a fig about, but for what it symbolized: his victory over his eternal rival.

As neighbours, the respective families of Lord Ashtray and Lord Marlowe had been enemies for more than a century, despite the fact that at this point in history neither of the two lineages could recall what had sparked the original quarrel. The house Lord Marlowe owned near Arles was a fortress, but the eight million euros Lord Ashtray had offered a band of crooks to get him the Lioness meant the brains of that gang of thieves had worked overtime until they'd thought of a way to steal the statue without killing anyone, let alone Lord

Marlowe, a requisite Lord Ashtray had laid down as non-negotiable, because he wanted to see the foolish look on his old neighbour's face when he realized his sculpture had been stolen. In the event, Lord Marlowe's ancient butler, James, took two days to realize that the Lioness had fled its case, since he always refused to have an operation on his cataracts and was as blind as a bat. By the time the police came to the Marlowe estate, the statue was already out of the country.

The plan was perfect and its execution superb. The mercenaries stole the statue and gave it to the man who spoke French, though one thief thought he might be Spanish. The man, who'd been recommended to Lord Ashtray by a Dutch antiquarian fond of high jinks, transported it to Barcelona in an Audi driven by a woman. In Barcelona the man was to hold on to the antique until things calmed down and Lord Ashtray's secretary contacted him.

In principle, Mr Charles Slothman was personally going to travel to Barcelona to pick up the statue. Mr Slothman and the man acting as postman didn't know each other and neither knew what the package contained. "That is confidential information" was all Lord Ashtray would let on. Mr Slothman, whose alternative job offers had included home deliverer of pizzas or call-centre operator in India, had decided to ask no questions and obediently do as he was told.

However, a few hours before boarding his flight, an untimely attack of gastroenteritis had left Mr Slothman a prisoner of his toilet bowl. Even so, Mr Slothman was nothing if not resourceful, and, when he saw he couldn't go to Barcelona in person to pick up the package, he grabbed his mobile, and, without budging from that bowl, rang Emily, an old girlfriend who'd yet to hear about the miserable episode in Eton, and invited her to spend the weekend with him in London. The girl worked for a translation and English-teaching agency in Barcelona and earned a pittance giving classes to executives with no gift for languages, and as she had discovered it wasn't as easy as she had imagined to get off with the city's footballers or famous architects, she accepted his invitation straightaway. And she would also be very happy to transport a small package that, according to Mr Slothman, was a present for his mother. The butler's mother had passed away a year ago: the young woman wasn't to know that.

Mr Slothman went to Gatwick to welcome Emily and drove her back to a hotel in Bloomsbury with the promise of an unforgettable weekend. As soon as they reached the hotel, he pretended to get a call on his mobile and apologized, saying that Lord Ashtray needed to see him urgently. Emily in fact felt relieved to see him disappear because Charlie wasn't what he used to be and she happily bid farewell to her ex-boyfriend as he grabbed the package, got into the car and disappeared down the streets of London on his way back to Lifestyle Ends.

While Mr Slothman was eating an egg sandwich and drinking a cup of tea in the kitchen, listening absent-mindedly to the cook's interminable complaints about the ridiculous diets Lady Ashtray forced her to prepare on behalf of her quest for weight loss, Lord Ashtray was in the library opening the sealed envelope and smiling contentedly. However, his smile soon changed to a grimace of disbelief and then rage: all there was inside the envelope was a chrome-metal keyring that had been poorly gift-wrapped. Lord Ashtray's face went as red as the velvet curtains that draped the library's picture windows, and Lady Ashtray, who at that precise moment had come into the room to complain of the way the gardener had fiddled with her roses, reacted with extreme alarm.

"What's this? We're back on the brandy, are we?" she snapped. "For Christ's sake, one of these days you'll have a stroke that will reduce you to a gibbering idiot!" She turned round and went off to the kitchen to prepare him an infusion of chestnut buds. The fourth Lady Ashtray's grandmother, who was Welsh, had learnt from Dr Bach in person how to prepare his floral cures and had spent half her life pouring these infusions into her husband.

While his wife stirred in the kitchen, Lord Ashtray's brain slowly flickered back to life. That pathetic Slothman couldn't possibly have betrayed him, he decided: in the first place, because he thought he was a fool, and, in the second, because Lord Ashtray knew his secretary was a coward and wouldn't have dared disobey his instructions. As Lord Ashtray was unaware of Emily's existence because Mr Slothman had failed to mention the fact he personally hadn't gone to Barcelona to collect the package, Lord Ashtray's thoughts turned to the gang of mercenaries he'd contracted to carry out the theft. Those men, nevertheless, were professionals and must be aware that it would be impossible to place such a valuable statue on the black market without him finding out sooner or later. Besides, they knew who they were dealing with, and eight million euros was too much money to risk being chased by another gang of hit men hired by a furious English aristocrat. No, he could swear they weren't behind this. There could be only one other possibility: the man who had transported the statue from Arles to Barcelona and had had it in his possession for three weeks. What was his name now? No matter, he would ask his antiquarian friend in Amsterdam and would have him dealt with.

While he pondered his plan to wreak revenge and recover the Lioness, Lord Ashtray started playing with the keyring and found the small spring. He was intrigued, pressed it and the ring opened halfway down. Lord Ashtray found a tiny metal object inside he was hard-put to identify. Finally, after taking a long look, he realized it was a memory stick and went straight to his computer. Perhaps it wasn't a theft, but a case of kidnapping, Lord Ashtray ruminated, and he would find instructions in the stick on how to salvage his lioness.

Lord Ashtray opened the only document it held and understood nothing. No rescue message showed on the screen, only a series of numbers and peculiar letters that made no sense at all. In a fury, Lord Ashtray extracted the memory stick and threw it furiously at the waste-paper basket along with the keyring, letting out blood-curdling curses and profanities that must have made the cheeks of Lord Ashtray in the portrait blush. The fifth lord didn't like computers or mobiles, or the Internet for that matter; he reckoned all that technology made life far too complicated. Computers also left traces on the net that it was best to avoid in his line of business. Grim-faced, he selected another cigar, poured himself a third balloon of brandy, lolled back in his wing armchair and fumed.

His wife walked into the library with his chestnut-bud tisane, but, when she saw the murderous look her husband gave her, she opted to make a discreet exit and retrace her steps without saying a word. Lord Ashtray didn't budge. An imbecile had enjoyed a laugh at his expense and now possessed a small stone statue that was five thousand years old and didn't belong to him. Under the severe gaze of his great-great-grandfather, Lord Ashtray took another swig of brandy and swore he would not rest until the item was restored to his family. Yes, Lord Ashtray speculated with an evil grin, he would recover the Baghdad Lioness, and, as soon as it was back in his grasp, he would ensure that the fool who had dared to steal what was rightfully his suffered a death as slow as it was painful.

All the situations and characters in this novel are fictitious.

The "Baghdad Lioness" is inspired by the small sculpture known as the "Guennol Lioness" that was discovered in the 1920s by the British archaeologist Sir Leonard Woolley while excavating near Baghdad. It bears that name after the name of the mansion, Guennol, the property of its last owner, the American collector Alastair Bradley Martin. "Guennol" is Welsh for "martin" in English. Sotheby's auctioned it at the end of 2007 and the statue was purchased by an English collector, who remains anonymous, for the sum of $57.16 million, a figure that was, at the time, the highest sum ever paid for a sculpture at auction.

A NOT SO PERFECT CRIME

Teresa Solana

Murder and Mayhem in Barcelona

Another day in Barcelona, another politician's wife is
suspected of infidelity. A portrait of his wife in an exhibition
leads Lluís Font to conclude he is being cuckolded by the artist.
Concerned only about the potential political fallout, he hires
twins Eduard and Borja, private detectives with a knack for
helping the wealthy with their "dirty laundry". Their office is
adorned with false doors leading to non-existent private rooms
and a mysterious secretary who is always away. The case turns
ugly when Font's wife is found poisoned by a marron glacé
from a box of sweets delivered anonymously.

PRAISE FOR *A NOT SO PERFECT CRIME*

"The Catalan novelist Teresa Solana has come up
with a delightful mystery set in Barcelona…
Clever, funny and utterly unpretentious." *Sunday Times*

"Solana's stylish and witty debut makes entertaining reading, and
her two characters, the suave, quick-thinking Borja and anxious,
law-abiding Eduard, make a good contrast as they weave their
way through an increasingly murky mystery." *The Telegraph*

"She paints a glorious picture of an urbane and lubricious
Hispanic lifestyle as the brothers gumshoe their way through
cocktail bars and tapas joints." *Times Literary Supplement*

This deftly plotted, bitingly funny mystery novel and satire
of Catalan politics won the 2007 Brigada 21 Prize.

£8.99/$14.95
Crime Paperback Original
ISBN 978-1904738-343

eBook
ISBN 978-1904738-787

www.bitterlemonpress.com

A SHORTCUT TO PARADISE

Teresa Solana

**The shady, accident-prone private detective twins
Eduard Martínez and Borja "Pep" Masdéu are back.
Another murder beckons, and this time the victim
is one of Barcelona's literary glitterati.**

Marina Dolç, media figure and writer of bestsellers, is murdered
in the Ritz Hotel in Barcelona on the night she wins an important literary prize. The killer has battered her to death with the
trophy she has just won, an end identical to that of the heroine
in her prize-winning novel.

The same night the Catalan police arrest their chief suspect,
Amadeu Cabestany, runner-up for the prize. Borja and Eduard
are hired to prove his innocence. The unlikely duo is plunged
into the murky waters of the Barcelona publishing scene and
need all their wit and skills of improvisation to solve this case of
truncated literary lives.

PRAISE FOR *A SHORTCUT TO PARADISE*

"Solana's second novel made me laugh so much
the tears soon rolled. She shoots from the hip
at the guardians of culture..." *El Pais*

"Solana's Barcelona is exciting, sexy and louche, the city's
literary scene and the people who inhabit it portrayed with
satirical gusto. Charming and great fun." *The Times*

"A delightfully droll double-barreled denouement
provides a perfect ending to this romp, which should
earn its author consideration for the kind of award
she so cleverly lampoons." *Publishers Weekly*

£8.99/$14.95
Crime Paperback Original
ISBN 978-1904738-558

eBook
ISBN 978-1904738-794

www.bitterlemonpress.com